MW01534771

To Catch a Cradle

Howard Glass

ISBN : 1-4196-1005-8
Library of Congress Control Number : 2005905409

To order additional copies, please contact us.
BookSurge, LLC
www.booksurge.com
1-866-308-6235
orders@booksurge.com

To Catch a Cradle

ACKNOWLEDGMENTS AND THANKS TO:

Kristin Walters. Her editing made a huge difference in the quality of this work.

Chris Ithen, for creating the cover art.

Bob Hostetler, for his advice.

Dorothy Smithtro, for her endless encouragement.

My family and friends, for believing I could do this.

Most of all to my best friend and beloved spouse Julie. You convinced me this was worth seeing through.

PROLOGUE

They were a sleeper team, the man and his wife. Independent contractors who drove an 18-wheeler hauling produce from the southwest to the east coast. They weren't crazy about fast food, but they had been eating it to save time since the failure of their truck's water pump in Flagstaff. Though the shop that had replaced it for them was first rate and they had been fortunate enough to break down close to that shop, they had still lost nearly 10 hours.

They were fortunate to be a team. One of them could always be resting, if not sleeping. Keeping the schedule meant they would receive the kind of healthy revenue they needed to maintain their cash-gobbling equipment and give them something more than bags under their eyes for their three days of nonstop travel.

Neither of them could have articulated it, or even cared to try, but they thrived on the pressure. Keeping the schedule was a challenge they were meeting together, the way they had met all the other challenges through 30 years of marriage, three sons and a dairy farm on the windswept plains of western Minnesota.

Trucking, even hauling produce, was easy compared to delivering a calf at 3 a.m., when January brought temperatures averaging well below zero and the only sign of warmth was the steam rising like smoke from the fresh manure. But the farming was behind them. The property and the herd were leased to the kind of factory-farm operation that could still squeeze a profit out of teats.

With a few more months of hard work they would be set.

They would retire and enjoy the carefree life they had always dreamed of. That is, if they could adjust to the ease it promised. He swore he could handle it, but she could see how fidgety he got after four or five hours of sleep. She could read or type letters to their grandchildren on the laptop when she wasn't driving or sleeping, but not him. He had never relaxed enough to know how it was done.

She bought them subs at the truck stop in Girard, Ohio, while he was fueling the rig for the last time before they would finish the run. They should be at Hunt's Point Terminal Market in New York City by 5 a.m.

He wolfed down half of his sub between the fuel pumps and the on-ramp. He steered deftly with the sides of either hand, manipulated the gear-shifter with the right and the sandwich with the left, taking hearty bites of ham and cheese between the gears. A tractor-trailer was child's play to a man who had spent 30 years handling a variety of farm equipment.

When he had finished the sandwich, he spent a few minutes chatting on the CB with another hauler who was heading for the east coast. He would have liked to keep it up, but that would make it hard for his wife to sleep, and she needed the rest.

"I hope the next thing I feel is the bumps across the George Washington Bridge," she said. She unbuckled her seat belt and moved to the sleeper. "This trip's been one mess after another. I'll be glad to get this one over with."

"It's all downhill from here, honey," he said. "I can almost smell the city now." His eyes left the road just long enough to meet hers. "You want me to wake you when we get to that rest area in Jersey, so you can go to the bathroom, don't you?"

"Whatever," she replied. She was too tired to care.

He was tired too—she could see that—but working with fatigue was nothing new to him. She had seen him fight off sleep for hours on the seat of a combine, working through the night like they had to sometimes, to get in the harvest. He was a confident, capable man, and she didn't worry, even if the roads got icy. She straightened up a few things in the cab and slipped out of her jeans and sweatshirt for some shuteye.

As she pulled down the blankets and prepared to get into the bunk, she imagined a more relaxed place. Tomorrow night they would be in a motel in New Jersey. The place had a good restaurant with a big salad bar, and she would have time to indulge herself with a long soak in the tub. She kissed her old man through the thin hair on the side of his head and pulled the curtain behind her. Maybe 20 more loads, she figured, 25 at most if the rates held up, and they would have the amount of money their financial planner said they needed.

Interstate 80 was getting smoother all the time across Pennsylvania, and anyway she was tired enough to sleep across a washboard. That is just about what the rumble strip would have felt like if she had awakened enough to feel it, but there wasn't time.

He did feel it and jerked his head up and shook it, just as he had done so many other times when running at night. But this time was different. Instead of the usual field of headlight glow, he saw a wall of concrete that filled his entire side of the windshield.

Even as he drew the wheel to the right, he was conscious of the fact that it wouldn't be soon enough. The already small spots his headlights made got smaller and brighter as the hood of the truck closed on the bridge pier.

He remembered where the Bible said that a thousand years with God was like one day and that one day was like a thousand years. In his last sliver of mortal existence he knew how that was; in the fraction of an instant it took for their custom-painted semi-tractor to go from shiny wholeness to a pile of wretched, steaming junk, his consciousness rebounded back over the threshold of eternity to catch up with what his fleshly senses could never comprehend. He felt the truck crumble like the crust of an apple dumpling being hit with a baseball bat. He saw the fiberglass hood filling with an endless multitude of cracks, as if a broad streak of lightning were passing through it.

The full weight of what was happening reached his mind, but the fear and adrenalin never actually made it. He had a brief moment of clarity to regret wrestling the sandman. His wife would never believe he had fallen asleep. He hoped she had.

PART ONE

"Blessed are the pure in heart, for they will see God."
Jesus Christ, "The Sermon on the Mount"

"It is safe to tell the pure in heart that they shall see God,
for only the pure in heart want to."
C.S. Lewis, *The Problem of Pain*

CHAPTER ONE

The tension in Ross Martin's guts got stronger with each white line passing under the hood of his truck. Like stout hands wringing a soggy rag, the wretched memory pressed against his thoughts until only sheer will kept the voice away.

It always started here. Here where the westbound lanes of Interstate 80 crested the eastern ridge of the Allegheny River valley. It was just beginning to sprinkle rain, and, as if taking a cue from the tiny spots of water on the windshield, the gradual twisting sensation in his stomach began. It was gentle at first, like always, but it swelled until it seemed to consume his whole being. Not as sharp as it once was, it still forced a ragged sigh from his breast and shrouded his glad sense of expectation from being homeward-bound in a familiar layer of misery.

Home was another 40 miles, and he was glad there were no more rivers to cross, once he got over this one. All rivers did it to him, but the ones close to home were the worst.

No matter how determined he was to keep his mind distracted, he was going to hear the voice again and along with the voice that dull pain in his guts. The pain that never went away completely, the agony that stole the taste from his food and nearly all of the pleasure from the things he once enjoyed. The pain that turned him into the sober, sullen, inwardly desperate man that he was. The pain that even his wife Shelley with her boundless adoration and gratitude could only spread a thin film over. Like butter melting into hot bread, her love soaked in and left him yearning for more.

The hunger in his soul could never be satisfied completely; he had learned to accept that hard truth. The reality carried with it a callous lethargy of doom. It was like his soul was covertly making friends with death and its casually intimate offer of comfort and release. Never mind what they said about suicide being the "coward's way out," Ross knew that the people who followed through with it did so because they craved, in fact needed, relief.

The frantic, bubbling cries for help were every bit as sharp and horrible as they had been years ago. "Ross! Don't leave me, please! Please!"

But Ross had left him. He'd had no choice.

"Keep telling yourself that," the other voice in his head whispered, with just a hint of mockery.

Sometimes he would hear the voice just before dozing off at night, and it would leave him tossing fitfully in a state that was not really sleep. When he awakened from it, always early, the day would stretch endlessly before him. The lack of sleep would mean a dull headache in the afternoon, followed by drowsiness even before the sun went down—nagging reminders that his existence was, at best, one of slow, tormented recovery.

But he would recover. They all said that. He could outlive it. People had outlived worse things. Besides, he had Shelley and little Randall to brighten up his otherwise dreary life.

As Ross's tractor-trailer rig closed the distance between him and the river, he felt somewhat better to see the thickening mist. It meant that the river hollow might be holding a cloud of fog. A person would have to peer past the fog to see the surface of the water, and Ross did not want to see it. In fact, he would take whatever barriers he could get between him and the vistas that tormented him. And although every traveler thought it was a lovely valley, with the historic houses of the little village nestled on the eastern hillside poking their steeply angled rows of shingles through the dense treetops, Ross could not enjoy any view that contained a watercourse.

The rainfall was increasing now, the gray, lowering sky making good on its promise of a bone-chilling, steady precipitation, as if dreariness were a requirement for November, meant to steel the inhabitants of the earth for the months of unforgiving winter.

As the weight of his load pushed the truck faster down the hill, Ross switched on the engine brake and scanned the road ahead, along with the surrounding countryside, in an effort to distract his mind. He observed that the leaves were nearly all gone now. Even the tenacious white oaks that seemed to have clumps of brown deadness hanging on until spring were thinner than usual this year. Ross wondered if that meant anything in the encyclopedia of folklore his friend Leeroy Foust had written on his brain.

Leeroy was somewhere near 70 years old and still drove a truck for a living. He had trained Ross to drive an 18-wheeler. In the process they had developed a relationship much like father and son, though neither of them would have felt comfortable acknowledging it.

Leeroy defied the stereotype about truckers being mostly burly and unlearned. The older man was a fountain of information, being somewhat self-educated from reading the kind of thick books one did not find for sale in a truck stop, listening to the better radio talk shows and taking every opportunity to learn whatever he could if and when his deliveries took him to historic places.

Leeroy was something of an enigma in the trucking trade, and conversation with most drivers bored him. Ross, having tacitly assumed the role of receptive pupil, had learned some practical knowledge from him during the long drives when the two of them could converse on the CB radio.

So much of the conversation between truckers on the CB was shallow and useless, often profane and banal, the product of restless tongues, idle minds and souls who could not abide alone for extended periods of time.

As Ross cleared the end of the bridge and started up the grade, he realized he hadn't reset the cruise control soon enough. His speed had dropped below 65. Concentrating too much on keeping the demons at bay had cost him precious momentum.

A faster truck went around him, as if there were no reason to moderate speed for such a trifling thing as rain.

Now the weight of the load impinged itself upon his consciousness again as he started up the western grade. He dropped a gear, and the engine pitch increased with the additional RPM. He found himself sitting up in the seat a little higher now, an old habit he had developed. With every shift, check your gauges, speed, mirrors, and sit up straighter in the seat. Taking care of the old back was important, and who wanted another trip to the chiropractor? That might mean taking a day off work. "Life's too short to waste time in a doctor's office," Leeroy always said, and spending 50 hours a week driving an 18-wheeler was not known to be good for one's lumbar region.

It took a conscious effort to keep in good condition when so much of a trucker's lifestyle worked against it. Posture mattered a lot when you had to spend so much time in one position.

As Ross approached the Emlenton exit, he saw a welcome sight coming up the on ramp before him. It was Leeroy's distinctive tractor, the only one in the fleet with twin exhaust stacks and extra chrome accessories. It was the flagship of the fleet, meant for use in parades and photo-ops for company advertising.

Ross turned on his CB, keyed the mike and tried to mask his delight with a layer of jesting. "Old man, don't be bringing that beat up, old, slow truck out here to get in my way. Can't you see I'm almost home? Don't want to have to push your sorry butt the whole way to Heritage."

"You just hush that smart mouth, now boy. Or I'll have to stop long enough to teach you some manners. You should have been there by now anyway," Leeroy said.

"Cool down now, I wouldn't want to give an old grandpa a cardiac arrest or nothing," Ross said, chuckling into the CB. "I'll just fall in behind you here and see to it that you get home safe. It's the least I can do for a senior citizen. Boy scouts taught me to treat you old-timers with kindness."

"You haven't been listening to the radio, have you." Now Leeroy's voice didn't match Ross's bantering tone.

"Just turned it on now," Ross said.

"Turn your squelch down, there's some problem down here," Leeroy said. "I just heard something about it as I turned in the ramp, too late to go across 208. Some kind of wreck, I guess. There it is already."

Way off in the hazy distance Ross saw the brake lights of another truck come on. The lights lingered as if the driver were slowing gradually. Ross could see the distance between them closing. Obviously there was something wrong. Now he could see that the traffic had stopped completely, a long line of cars and trucks sitting idle. Like a clogged drain, it offered untold dismay and probably had something nasty at the end of it.

Then it hit him. The spare time he had worked and sacrificed his sleep for all week could be piddled away now. If the reason for this stoppage was anything major, he could lose it all. Ross was not a cursing man, but he bit his teeth together now to stifle one. He told himself to wait and see; it might not be all that bad.

The CB chatter broke the silence then, as if the radio had been asleep somehow in the dreary forenoon and had just wakened with a start. Though he usually avoided the CB chatter, he welcomed it now. Maybe there would be good news.

If he'd had the foresight to check with the eastbound truckers he might have been able to avoid whatever it was by using some bypass route on a state highway. That's what Leeroy meant about going across 208, if he had found out about the trouble sooner. It was too late for that now. "Screwed myself again," muttered Ross, under his breath. As much as he disliked monitoring the CB talk, there was often a price to pay for not doing so. "Why the slowdown?" asked Ross, into the mike, to anyone who might want to answer.

The annoyed voice of some delayed trucker came on the air then, "You guys should leave your radios turned on so you'd know what's goin' on. An eastbound produce hauler put it into that bridge pier there at the 28 sometime last night. They're pulling the tractor out now. They already got the trailer. The traffic's getting through, but it's slow. They're both dead."

"Must have fallen asleep," was the general speculation among the stuck and restless travelers who chatted to each other on the crowded and rude CB. Ross had seen this sort of thing before.

The conversation between Ross and Leeroy dried up then, both of them content to listen to the chatter for a while. Ross wondered what it all looked like. Would he get a glimpse of the shattered truck before it got taken out of sight to some remote scrap yard? Would it be recognizable or so badly damaged that no one could even tell what make it was? Did anyone witness the crash? Would there be tire marks to indicate that the last moments of the driver's life were spent in hopeless terror, or did he just fail to follow the turn and instead go drifting off into eternity with nothing but the shudder of the rumble strip to rouse him before the lights went out for good? Did the man in the sleeper know his partner well? Had they been a team long? Did the drivers have a family?

Ross ventured a question over the air. "Anybody know anything about the drivers?" There was a torrent of information sent his way then by several different voices, a more domineering one finally winning out in a competition to relay the information.

"The drivers were a husband and wife team from Minnesota," the brusque-sounding trucker said. "They hadn't been in contact with anyone over the radio since changing drivers at the state line. The wife must have been in the bunk. The husband signed off the air so it'd be quiet for his wife to sleep. Apparently it was a little too quiet. Looks like he fell asleep."

Ross knew the curve where it happened. He keyed the mike again. "I guess they didn't make that turn under the bridge, huh Leeroy?"

"Sounds like it to me. Not the first time that's happened," Leeroy said.

Ross had heard enough. There was no way to know if any of the scuttlebutt was true or not. Most of it had been handed down through many drivers in the intervening hours since the wreck. Probably it had changed dramatically. Ross would probably never know for sure. To find out would require getting the local paper here, and Ross wasn't planning on coming through again until the following Monday. By then the story and any photographs would be part of history, the local publishers seeing no reason for any follow-up on the deaths of two out-of-state truckers.

"There's too much chatter here," Ross remarked to Leeroy. "You want to switch to another channel?" It was what they usually did when they ran together.

"No. Let's just stay down here so we know what's going on." Leeroy's voice was sober now. Ross guessed the idea of a couple truckers getting killed along with the callous comments of that one driver had soured the cheerful mood they had before they came upon the wreck.

His thoughts shifted to home. He wondered what Shelley might be up to, and the thought of her made him smile. She was always excited about something. Even in the latter days of her pregnancy, with the extra weight putting a strain on her back and a grimace on her face when she got up from her chair, she was cheerful, ready to laugh. There was plenty for her to laugh about, too, with a 4-year-old son and another child on the way.

Ross remembered the moment when Shelley had told him he'd be having another son.

"How did your visit to the doctor go?" Ross had asked over dinner one night two months earlier.

"He says I'm right on schedule, doing good," Shelley said, spooning applesauce onto little Randall's plate.

"What about the ultrasound? Can they see if it's a boy or girl?" Ross asked.

"I thought we agreed not to ask," Shelley said, keeping busy with Randall's plate, not looking him in the eye.

"Did you tell him we didn't want to know?" Ross said.

Shelley was silent. Ross turned his head and saw she was doing her best to hide a smile.

"Shelley, you didn't tell him that, did you? He told you what it is, didn't he?" Ross said. "I knew it. I knew you wouldn't be able to wait and see."

"You're right. I admit it," Shelley said, dropping her hands to her belly. "I couldn't go through with it. You disappointed with me?"

"Why would I be? I never thought you'd be able to wait and see," Ross said, cackling. He leaned back in his chair and shook with glee. Randall laughed along with his dad, not really knowing why they were laughing. Shelley, her face red, joined in, but then she sat upright, waiting for her husband to settle down. A look of delighted superiority grew on her face, and Ross knew where the conversation was going next. He pretended to be aloof.

"And of course, you don't want to know, do you, Mr. Smarty Pants?" Shelley said.

"Nope. I can wait," Ross said. "I'm not like some people I know."

"Liar, liar, pants on fire! You can't wait to know. But see if I tell you, Mr. Smarty Pants," Shelley said.

"I don't need you to tell me. I'll bet I can figure it out with one trip upstairs," Ross said, grinning.

"You're bad," Shelley said.

"Now, if I know you, there is already either a pink or a blue set of pajamas in this house. Right?" Ross said.

Shelley reached over and cuffed him on the shoulder. The kind of playful blow Ross loved to get. It meant his guess was dead on.

"You may as well tell me now. You won't be able to keep it from me. I bet your mom already knows," Ross said.

"We're going to have to have a third child if you're sure you want a daughter," Shelley said, in an effort to be cryptic.

"A baby brother, Randy," Ross said, ruffling the child's hair and grinning at his son and wife. "You hear that? You're gonna have a little brother."

Shelley was born to be a mother, and she loved every frustrating and glorious minute of it.

The notion of being involved in some career was lost on Shelley. She gave it no thought. To Shelley's way of thinking, women would be happier if the liberation movement had stopped short of demanding they all treat home and family like a burden. "Most women secretly wished to be under some man's protection anyway," she liked to say. She said the problem was that the feminists had muddied the waters so much with their disdain for the traditional woman as homemaker that most people didn't know what their roles were anymore.

Shelley was certain that eventually the culture would turn back and her philosophy would be vindicated. That's the way she talked anyway. Ross couldn't tell how much of her conservative philosophy was genuine and how much of it came from her fear of having to face the world outside of the comfortable cocoon she kept herself in.

It wasn't that Ross minded Shelley being so devoted to home and family; he was certainly the beneficiary of her effort, and he knew it was her intent to protect him as much as anyone. He did wonder, though, if the limits of exposure she kept would mean their children would grow up too sheltered.

What was the big deal anyway? He got used to her face. Others could, too. He knew that attitude was flippant, though easy for him to have. It wasn't he who must endure the double-takes and deliberate turning away that people did when they first saw the purple and reddish splotch that took up most of Shelley's left cheek. Port Wine Stain was the medical term for it.

You couldn't blame people for their reaction. Shelley's condition was uncommon and curious. In all his life Ross had only seen one other person who was afflicted the way Shelley was.

Children were the worst, according to Shelley. They didn't know it was impolite to stare or point or ask questions loud enough for her to hear. She had learned to smile and behave as if the attention didn't bother her, but it did. She had learned to cope, but it wasn't something she could ever be expected to do well, Ross supposed.

Shelley's unique complexion had its good side too. Ross believed she worked harder than most women to make sure that everything else was above par. Except for the left side of her face, she was a stunning woman. She was blond-haired and blue-eyed with a body shapely enough for a swimsuit model. Like her perfect apple pies and neatly folded stacks of fresh-smelling laundry, Ross knew the majestic figure was no accident. She availed herself of every workout program and exercise video she could get her hands on. She left no stone unturned in her effort to be the consummate homemaker, wife and mother. If Ross even hinted wanting some change or improvement, she would pursue it doggedly. He had learned to be careful with what he said, lest he put some undue pressure on her.

Her efforts to please him knew no bounds. Ross smiled. He was no fool in learning to overlook the imperfection so visible in his wife. When Ross compared Shelley to other women, she surpassed them all in everything that mattered. He considered himself very shrewd to have married someone whose only drawback was something superficial. "Who else would have you?" the small voice in his head said. Ross ignored it.

The traffic was moving now, though slowly. Ross could see in his mirrors that the vehicles were backed up behind him as far as the eastern horizon. If the reported position were true, he was still three miles from the scene. Maybe 40 minutes before he reached the open road, unless of course the wreckers were finished and the whole width of both lanes could be returned to the travelers.

The pace of the flowing traffic undulated. Ross went up and down through the gearbox time and again, not allowing any gap to build between him and the truck he was following. He was too anxious to finish this week's work and get home to Shelley and little Randall.

Randall was nearly 4 years old and cute as a whole basket full of puppies. That was how Ross described him to his family and friends, to the strangers he met in his travels, to anyone who would listen.

He knew that Randall would be waiting at the door when he got in. The thought of the happy reunion of father and son left him almost oblivious to every other sensation for a moment. He would wrap the tiny boy in his arms and squeeze him gently for a moment. Shelley would be close behind, giving them a moment, drinking in the glow of it with misty eyes. Then he would open one arm and gather her into the hug with him and Randall. The loneliness of the highway would melt away as Ross plunged into the quiet glory of house and home and loving family.

The left lane was beginning to get ahead of the right as the traffic approaching the accident scene was forced into one lane.

"Odd how the lane that's open always seems to move slower than the one that's closed," Ross heard a voice on the radio say. He agreed with the observation.

The scene was coming into view now, what there was left to see. The remains of a semi-tractor were being winched onto the bed of another truck. The trailer it had been pulling was already gone. Ross only knew it was a truck because that was what he expected to see. It looked more like one of those cubed junk cars he had seen from time to time, only bigger.

The rig must have hit the pier at full throttle, the irresistible force hitting the immovable object. This wreck would likely be the substance of conversation in truck stops for a day or two, until a fresher or more bizarre tale came along to take its place. Ross shuddered. It could have been him.

"Better to hit that than to try breathing water," the quiet voice in his mind said. Ross shook his head.

"Man, that would be quick," said a real voice on the radio. "Like somebody pushed the delete button on two lives."

Being sleepy at the wheel was a failing truckers rarely admitted to. It was the kind of thing that labeled one unfit for the trade. Most drivers being men, their masculine pride scorned such weakness, at least in the superficial conversations that were a part of their daily lives. None of the observers of this tragedy voiced any contempt for the dead man's weakness, though—mute testimony to the fact that sleep was something they all battled from time to time. Not even a thought of shame for the hapless driver who fell asleep at the wheel; any criticism would seem cruel in light of the grave consequences.

Ross and the traffic moved slowly by the scene now, each driver pretending to be concerned about the safety of the workmen. Actually, they wanted to gape at the scene, "rubbernecking," the metropolitan traffic reporters would call it.

The bridge pier stood mute and ambivalent to the grisly work it had done. Ross would remember to take a close look at the pier when he came east again. He knew he would see some fresh scratches or gouges on the concrete face of the massive structure, like the infamous notches on the grip of some long-ago gunfighter's pistol. Even the smaller vehicles left some impression.

"Who was saying this ain't the first one?" said the dominant trucker's voice, with a trace of echo in it.

"That was me," replied Leeroy.

"Other trucks run into that before?" the unknown trucker asked.

"I've lost count, to be honest with you," Leeroy said.

Ross had heard stories about it. He was surprised that it had never been given a name. Some handle of notoriety was fitting for such a deadly landmark. He remembered seeing a large rock on a sharp turn, on a meandering state highway somewhere in his travels. The locals had painted "R-U-Prepared?" on the rock. Ross speculated that it had ended the lives of many motorists.

The crew of men working on the cleanup wore bright yellow rain suits, some of them streaked with mud, doubtless because it had been necessary to get down in the dirt to hook up the chains and the winch cables for the recovery job. Ross saw the blank look in the faces of the men and made eye contact with a few. They stared back at him with a look of hunger or wanting, he thought, as if they could sense their lack of tenderness toward the victims and would gather, wherever they could, the sympathy that somehow eluded them in the misery and weariness of their soggy, grim task.

"Not much fun, working out in that slop, I guess," Leeroy said.

"I guess not," replied Ross.

Like restless dogs released from a kennel, the westbound traffic surged now against the persistent fall of rain. Ross urged his own rig forward with a renewed deliberation. It seemed more important to get to the house now. He struggled with whether or not to stop and phone Shelley about the delay. He decided to wait until he got to the terminal and phone from there. He would be late enough then, but at least he could tell her a certain time for his arrival home.

He would have to make up some excuse for his tardiness. He was so punctual in his schedule, so good at predicting his arrival time at home that Shelley would know something had stalled him. She would ask, but he would never tell her what had slowed him. He could see no reason to burden her with stories of dead truck drivers and unyielding concrete structures. He preferred her smiles undimmed by needless reference to tragedy.

He heard a couple of voices, older-sounding truckers he thought. Men who ran together but who talked little, seasoned men whose souls contained enough substance that they needed little conversation to be comfortable with each other. "How many does that make, Red, hit that bridge?"

Ross supposed the earlier exchange between Leeroy and the unknown trucker had triggered some memories for the voices on the CB.

"Let's see, there was that one in'79, then that lime truck that powdered everything." He paused, the mild drone of the CB's carrier wave holding his place on the air. "Then, I'm not sure, but I think two flatbeds in a row that bad winter we had in the '80s. Hasn't been one since that, not that I can recall. Course, how many we didn't see or hear about?"

The man that asked the question did not reply again; somehow Ross did not expect him to. It was as if they were observing a moment of silence to honor the dead.

Ross's exit sign came at last, the large green sign that might have said "Welcome Home," for the warming effect it had on him, State Route 81, Heritage, Pa. It was only a few more miles to the terminal, and Ross soon forgot about the wreck he had just seen.

Leeroy and Ross pulled their rigs into the warehouse yard of the H.A. Murphy Industrial Service Company, affectionately called "HAM" by the locals and employees.

The chilly rain gave Ross an excuse to run to his pickup, which would have seemed strange to most people during nice weather. He usually was in such a hurry to get home that he had to force his feet into a dignified walk to keep from tearing across the parking lot.

He drove to the semi and unloaded his things into the back, which was covered with a cap. He picked up Leeroy and his things to save the older man from having to walk very far in the rain.

"Yes, it's nice to be old and frail," Leeroy said, grinning. "Fine young men like you give me a ride. Keep me from catching chill. Yes sir, you're a good boy, Ross."

Ross parked close to the building, and the two men went into to the terminal office. Ross knew Leeroy would not leave immediately; he never did. Taking the time to talk to the office people seemed like something Leeroy was required to do. He put his things just inside the building so Ross would be free to go as soon as he turned in his paper. Ross had no reason to hang around. He dropped his paperwork off, got his assignment for the next week and called Shelley from a telephone in the driver's lounge. The conversation was brief. Both of them wanted him to get home as soon as he could.

He lost no time driving the 15 minutes across town. He found himself being almost careless now that he was driving a pickup truck instead of an 18-wheeler, and his haste did not help the problem. The relative ease of maneuvering, quick acceleration and ease of braking made him think he could almost do it in his sleep. He told himself not to be so cocky about driving. He would feel doubly foolish if he had a fender-bender in something as small as this after running so many miles in the big truck and not hitting anything. He shook his head somberly then, recalling the tragedy he had passed only an hour before. "Be careful, Rossy," he told himself.

Shelley and Randall met him at the door as he had daydreamed they would. "Daddy!" exclaimed the shrill voices, Shelley parroting Randall to the delight of all three. Ross forgot the cold rain and everything that had to do with the road and work.

CHAPTER TWO

Ross made his way to the shower as Shelley finished getting their dinner on the table. He was just turning off the water when she stuck her head through the curtain and gave him one of those cute, mischievous smiles. She let her eyes wander around and giggled a little at his nakedness. He wrapped one wet forearm around her neck and pulled her face close to his.

"What's so funny, little lady?"

She replied with a soft pinch of his flesh, just below his hip.

"Later, dude," she said. Her voice was husky, and Ross felt the rush of desire, but knew there was no point now. It was Shelley's way of teasing him, letting him know that she was as eager as he was for their conjugal reunion, made clumsy but no less delightful by her enormous midriff.

"Have to do it while we can," Shelley said, with twinkling eye.

Dinner was Yankee Pot Roast with fruit salad and biscuits—made from scratch, not the pop-open store-bought dough that was the rule in most kitchens—and pumpkin pie for dessert. Ross helped Shelley get everything on the table.

He put Randall up on his high wooden stool so he was almost eye-level with the adults. The stool was something Ross had made from a kit when he was first getting into woodworking, a hobby he was getting better at all the time. Shelley waited until Ross had his pie cleaned up and then reached over to the counter, holding a ladies' magazine folded open.

"You think you can make this?" she asked. It was a rocking cradle, Early American style, with a handle cut out in the headboard and footboard. "I know you want to make something for the baby," she said.

"It looks small. Will this be something he grows out of soon?" Ross asked. He wanted to make something that would be treasured for a long time.

"Can't you make one bigger than the one in the picture?" Shelley said. "Anyway he will eventually grow out of it, but then we can use it for a magazine rack or something."

Ross looked at the picture, surveying the lines of the cradle, the wood. " I can make that," he decided. "It's gonna take a few weekends, but it won't take much material."

"No problem, you've got a few weekends," Shelley said. She beamed at him, feeling good about helping him find something that was sure to become a family treasure. Something that would make her feel as if Ross were right there with her and the baby on the many evenings he would be away. She imagined rocking their child to sleep in the little cradle that Daddy had made, singing a lullaby as she watched the sun go down.

After dinner Ross took Randall into the living room to read a story to him. When she had the kitchen in order, Shelley slipped quietly into the dining room and leaned against the wall beside the window so she could listen to Ross's voice without them being aware of her. She could see the rain outside continuing to fall. Inside their house they were cozy, and Shelley felt blessed. They were an idyllic family growing and glowing in the warmth of each other and the promise of tomorrow's joy.

The wind shifted now, bringing a more northerly tack to the breeze. The storm door rattled a little, and an alien draft of air found a tiny breach in the front door. The cozy home chilled a bit, making Shelley wrap her sweater a little tighter around her shoulders and check the setting on the thermostat. Outside, the rain began to take on a ghostly haze as the northern air crystallized the drops of water into snow.

❦

Ross slipped out of bed when the sun was just bright enough to see well outside and surveyed the ground around his house. The bad weather had moved on. The front that brought it had probably worked its way to the northeast. That was the prevailing weather pattern in Pennsylvania. The clouds, still thick with moisture, might give the first serious snowfall to Vermont and upstate New York, he supposed.

The streets were wet and still held scattered patches of snow, but it was thin and of no consequence. No snowplows or salt trucks would be mustered out to condition the roads. The heavy onslaught of winter was yet to be felt. This was a foretaste, a token really.

Ross slipped back into bed and eased one of his now-chilled feet against Shelley's calf. She started mildly, only half awake. He pulled his body close to hers and stroked the bulge of her belly until she stirred.

"If he wakes up and kicks me, I'm gonna kick you," Shelley murmured pleasantly.

"Go ahead, kick me. Hit me. Beat me. Take me to the mall and make me write bad checks. I love you so much you can abuse me," Ross chanted.

"You better watch it. One of these days I might take you up on that mall thing," Shelley said, more awake now. "What's it like out there?"

"Not bad. The tail end of some lake effect snow, I guess," Ross said.

"Lake effect snow?"

"Sure. When the wind blows over Lake Erie, it picks up moisture and spreads it downwind in the form of snow. We're far enough downwind that we don't usually get it bad. Go toward Cleveland or Erie and see how much heavier it gets," Ross said.

"Has my travel-wise husband become an amateur meteorologist?" Shelley asked.

"Your husband has lots of time to listen to the radio, that's all," he said. "You can pick up a lot. For example, if the winter is cold enough and the lake freezes over completely, then there is nothing for the air to pick up, and the snowfall returns to normal. That's why people in the Great Lakes region prefer cold winters.

"Professor Ross Martin, from the trucker's institute of applied miscellaneous knowledge, at your service my dear," Ross intoned in the academic drone of a British scholar as he threw the blankets away from his wife and clambered over to cover her body with his own, his toes extended to keep his weight from her swollen abdomen. "No, don't try to pull the covers back on, my dear. It is my express intention to keep you warm with my manly physique until you decide to get up and fix my breakfast." He nuzzled her cheek and breathed lightly in her ear. She responded by rolling under him, pulling him closer.

He wrapped her up in his arms and kissed her lightly on the lips. Her breath was sweet, even in the morning. It was something he had always marveled at. It was as if their body chemistry was matched to each other. His morning breath never seemed to bother her either.

She joined him then in affecting the British accent. It was something they had begun long ago, after watching an old movie on TV, some story set in the Victorian era.

"Professor Martin needs to study the fine art of being kind to a drowsy wife on a Saturday morning," Shelley said. "No doubt you'll expect me to be pleasant all day after such a rude awakening? And it's tea you'll want for breakfast, I suppose?"

"With lots of sugar!" he said, kissing her again.

Ross and Shelley dressed and went downstairs. Ross paused in the living room to switch on the TV. He found the weather channel, got the day's forecast and the extended forecast, then joined Shelley in the kitchen.

"Is it going to snow some more?" she asked.

"Not today. There's a possibility of enough snow to make slippery roads next week, but I could be back before it gets here," Ross said.

Sooner or later, he would have to face miles of snow-covered and possibly icy roads, with no option but to drive slower across the slippery surface, his senses on edge for any sign of lost traction. A few hours of such stress would leave him with a headache and an arc of dull pain from one shoulder blade to the other. It would be that way until he once again adjusted to the season, which might take a couple of good snowfalls. Then he would begin to take the whole thing in stride.

"I don't know how you can drive on those icy roads. I pray for you every time it snows," Shelley said.

"No more talk about icy roads. I'll deal with them when they happen but not until. It's Saturday, and I'm home with the woman I love. I'm going to make the most of it. You know dear, working for H.A. Murphy has its advantages compared to a lot of trucking companies. The automotive business keeps the fleet busy. A lot of guys that drive truck have little or no idea when they will get a load back to their home terminal. We get back nearly every load. That's why everybody works hard to keep the business."

"Yes dear, I'm glad you work for the people you do. Your job could be much worse," Shelley said. "But it doesn't help to know that when I need you here."

Something about her voice suggested that she'd heard the spiel before and knew it by heart. It was true that Ross had a better job than many guys who drove for a living, but he'd heard how high the divorce rate was among drivers. He'd heard stories of wives who gave ultimatums to their trucker husbands: Change jobs or I'm leaving you. He wondered if the appearance of Shelley's face meant he would never receive such a notice.

Their eyes met. In that instant Ross was sure she could read his thoughts. He dropped his eyes and turned his head away, searching desperately for some way to change the subject gracefully.

"Well, I guess that's what they mean when they say, 'mixed feelings.' I'm sorry you miss me, but I'm glad you do," Ross said. "Now, how about some French toast?"

"French toast to go with English tea? How positively gauche!" Shelley spouted, switching back to the British accent.

"Not gauche my dear, merely tacky," Ross said, thankful to have recovered so easily.

Ross would have been embarrassed if some of his friends

and fellow workers could see how lighthearted and playful he was with his family. Shelley made him feel like both a grown man and a little boy at the same time. The contrast confused and mystified him somewhat, but he didn't want anything about his life to change. He secretly wondered if other men had such a relationship with their wives. "Just the lucky ones," he told himself.

With a few more years of Shelley's love, he thought he could put the drowning of Donny Ritts behind him at last, or at least keep the guilt he felt in a proper perspective.

Ross went to the front door for the morning paper and looked it over while Shelley got the breakfast ready.

"So, are you gonna get the wood you need to start the cradle today?" Shelley asked.

"That's a good plan. I'm glad it's a small project because the wood won't be cheap. I want to use oak or maple," Ross said.

"Does that mean you have to go across the river?" Shelley asked as she set their plates of food on the table.

Ross waited until he had a forkful of breakfast in his mouth and then nodded. Again their eyes met in a level of communication deeper than words. Now it was Shelley's turn to look away. She did her best not to bring it up.

"It's okay, Shell," Ross said, seeing her discomfort.

"It still bothers you some, huh?" she said.

"Probably always will. A little less every time, though."

Shelley leaned around the corner of the table and wrapped her arms around him again. "As long as it takes, babe. I'm here for you."

After they had finished eating, Ross got his jacket and hat and left the house. The lumberyard was across town, through the valley and across the river, the Sugar River. There was nothing sweet about the Sugar River in Ross's mind. He could not cross it without getting that old tightness in his chest.

A river gave a town character, he thought. It was an abundant source of water and a place of recreation for those who were not intimidated by it. Ross no longer fit into that category. The surface of any river triggered the memories, but the Sugar was the worst.

At the southern end of Heritage was a gravel road leading downstream. There was a low dam on the river that kept the water through town deep enough for navigation. In the old days there had been barge traffic that serviced the mills along the Sugar. That part of the river was languid, with muddy banks and brush growing out over the water.

Below the dam the river was more picturesque and inviting. The rapid flow of water kept mud and litter washed downstream. People had been going there to escape the summer heat for generations. There were deep pools beside rocks broad enough to serve as little beaches. It was an ideal place for swimming, and the younger population of Heritage practically owned it in the summer.

Ross and his friends used to spend lots of time there, but Ross had not gone back since the day of Donny's death. He might never go back.

Ross could still hear the sympathetic words of Pastor Sawyer, "Hard things happen sometimes, son, and a man can't go blaming himself for that. It was an accident, that's all. There was no intent to do harm. Donny wanted to have fun, too. If it had been the other way around and you were the one that died, would you hold it against Donny? Of course, you wouldn't. The best thing you can do, son, is to make the most out of your life as a way of honoring Donny."

Ross remembered feeling even worse then. The truth was that Donny had every reason to hold it against Ross. Donny had not wanted to be in that part of the river. He was a good swimmer, but he didn't like fast water. Ross should have confessed the thing then, but he didn't have the courage. He let the well-meaning pastor go on with his false assumption.

"Donny would want you to be happy, not to waste your life feeling sorry for yourself and reliving the past every day. Folks that do that are dead, in a sense, when it was God's will that they go on living. Don't try to second-guess the Almighty or His ways, Ross. Just live every day grateful that you had such a good friend, for a while at least. Lots of folks never have a truly fine friend like you had in Donny. Don't grieve that he's gone. Rejoice that he was. That's what I want folks to do when I pass on."

Ross agreed with the pastor's words because it helped him bury the truth even deeper. Everyone encouraged him to go on without grief, so he had acted as if he was okay. He had been acting that way ever since. He lived in his own little purgatory, conveniently hidden from the view of his loved ones.

Ross had never told anyone, not even Shelley, all the details about how Donny came to be in that particular part of the river or about how he had left him to die alone. The full story was so bizarre, so hard to explain, so full of frustration for Ross that he had just let people think Donny had been the victim of fast water, which was true, but not the whole truth.

Ross tossed his head to shake it off again. The memories would carry him away like that sometimes. Once he'd allowed himself to dwell on the memory of that day while he was driving across Interstate 70, and his mind had been trapped in it. He came to his senses after missing his exit by 30 miles. After that he had determined not to let it take him away again. It was no good—he might have caused another tragedy with the distraction, and that was the last thing he wanted.

Distraction from the memories was his only salvation. When he wasn't totally busy, he had to keep them balanced between his conscious and subconscious minds. They lay rocking, like a seesaw in the back of his head, ready to tip heavily in the direction of any contentment he might find, as if spoiling his peace were their sole purpose for existing. It was as if joy had weight and gladness were an illegal substance. If Ross partook of them, the universe would be thrown out of kilter, so it required another measure of remorse to balance things again.

Someone once told Ross, "Some things you never get over, you just learn to live with." Ross had learned to live with it, but he hoped it would keep fading until maybe he could go even one whole day without feeling guilty. He had a wife to think about, a son. And now a baby on the way. "Buck up." That's what Leeroy would say. "Buck up, Laddybuck." Ross guessed that he would "buck up" one more time.

Ross pulled into the parking lot at the lumberyard and remembered Steve Neff worked there. Steve had been the first person Ross met up with after leaving Donny in the river, the first person he had lied to. After that, it became easier.

Ross usually avoided him, but he had to face the memories again when Steve came out from behind the shelves with a clipboard in hand, apparently taking inventory.

Putting on the mask again, Ross smiled at Steve. "Hey Steve, whatta you know, partner?" he said with forced energy.

"Hello, Ross, long time, no see. You still chasing the white lines for HAM?" His voice was friendly enough, but his eyes met Ross's only for a moment before they flickered away.

"You betcha. Gonna be a daddy again, too."

"Oh yeah, somebody said Shelley was pregnant. That's nice, buddy, how many you guys want to have?" He doesn't really care about us, Ross thought.

"Maybe one more. Maybe not," Ross said. He wanted to keep the conversation brief.

"Hope you do. Tell Shelley I said hello, will ya?" Steve said.

"I'll do it," Ross said. An observer might have guessed that there was something unpleasant between them, Ross supposed. And he would not bother to tell Shelley that Steve had said hello.

Ross remembered the days of junior high school when Steve had been cruel to Shelley, referring to her when she wasn't around with that stupid nickname someone had given her.

Shelley had been an enigma in school—every ounce of her desirable and glamorous, except for the spot. That was what they had nicknamed her in junior high, when the heartlessness and insecurity of early adolescence seeks its victims: Spot. No one intended for her to learn about the name. But, of course, she did.

Like all young girls, Shelley craved a relationship with a boy. For her it was not so easy. She would never dare to flirt or even hope to be noticed. "I settled for not being picked on," Shelley once told Ross.

"I won't let anyone be cruel to you, Shelley. Not anymore," he had responded. He had heard the full story of her struggle in bits and pieces over the years. He had some hard feelings for a few people in Heritage.

"You have to understand, Ross, most of that happened when we were kids. You can't hold kids responsible for being ignorant," Shelley told him.

"Just when does a person stop being a kid and start being responsible for his words?" he said. But he found his judgmental attitude mocking him. He had not used words responsibly after Donny drowned.

When the school year started that fall after Donny's drowning, Ross had a stigma surrounding him that kept most of his classmates distant. Much of it was of his own making. He'd developed a hard edge in his personality that his friends didn't know how to handle. He felt alone and vulnerable. Shelley helped him work through it.

She never showed him any concern about what had happened. She let him be the one to bring it up when he was ready. He had done so in due time. It seemed like Shelley could act instinctively to comfort and reassure him. It was something that came naturally to her, the same way mothering had. Ross knew he still needed the support Shelley gave him. But what was wrong with that? Weren't married people supposed to support one another?

Ross suspected she felt some guilt for luring him into their romance during his depressed state. There had been a hint of it now and then. But their relationship had been good for both of them. It was hard for Ross to reassure her about that without coming right out and saying he knew the way she felt.

They were as happy as any two people could be, weren't they? If God chose to give Shelley her unique burden to bear, couldn't he also act graciously toward her by giving her a great marriage? Would that marriage have happened if Ross had not suffered his own kind of affliction? Maybe she and Ross were meant to be together. Who understood the wounded better than someone with a scar?

The subject came up once when they were planning their wedding. Shelley was sitting on the sofa, surrounded with samples of announcements, napkins and all the paraphernalia that went into the affair, doing the things that men take little interest in but that women enjoy. Ross was beginning to tire of it all, and his annoyance triggered her guilty feelings.

"Are you sure you want to marry me?" she said. The tears had come so instantly it unsettled Ross.

"Of course I'm sure," Ross said.

"No. No, don't answer me because I'm crying. I need you to tell me why a good-looking guy like you wants me and my face?" Shelley said. "We have never talked about it. We should talk about it. You could get a nice-looking girl."

"You are a nice-looking girl," he said.

"There's nothing nice about this," she said, pointing to her Port Wine Stain.

"Okay, I admit you would be even more attractive without it. But you wouldn't be the person you are without it." Ross curved his hand under her jaw and caressed her face with his thumb. "Shelley, I don't love you for the way you look. Or for the way you don't look. If you didn't have the mark, I might never have gotten the chance to be your boyfriend, let alone marry you. You'd have so many guys chasing you that a shy fellow like me wouldn't have a chance. Look at your figure. Look at your hair. Look at the rest of your complexion. The stain is the only part of you that isn't perfect."

"The rest of me isn't perfect," Shelley demurred.

"Yes it is," Ross said. "Without the stain you'd probably be a movie star. And you'd be lonely, too, because there wouldn't be anyone good enough for you. The way it is I get to marry a real babe, and all I gotta do is remind you every once in a while how silly it is for you to feel bad about your cheek."

"You're a liar, Ross. A sweet liar, a poor liar, but a liar no less."

"Maybe I'm a little bit glad you have the stain on your face.

I do know that I'm awful glad you're mine," he said. "Tell you what, give me 50 years of marriage. If you aren't convinced then that I'm happy as your husband, I'll let you go. No hard feelings. Okay?"

Her tears were drying now. "Okay," she said. After that she had allowed herself to believe that he really loved her, despite the spot.

Ross supposed that the anguish he'd endured in the weeks after Donny's funeral had made him old before his time. He became determined to live cautiously so that nothing else bad could happen. He was ready to settle down, and something about dating Shelley Clark seemed safe. She was warm, homey and totally non-judgmental. She had not yet had a boyfriend or even a first date. She welcomed his affections and returned them doubly.

They dated steadily from that fall until graduation and became engaged as soon as Ross found a job he could count on.

Ross started out working on the loading docks at H.A. Murphy. He handled freight and did inventories, prepared orders and did janitorial work until his supervisor slowly became aware that he was a hard worker and trustworthy enough to be given more responsibility. They offered him a position as a salesman, but Ross had his eye on the trucks. He would see them come and go, their shiny paint and polished aluminum wheels gleaming in the sun.

The whole business revolved around the trucks; Ross and the others were merely a support group for them. Everything they handled came in on a truck and went out on one. The drivers seemed to be in another world entirely. They worked completely on their own and never had anyone looking over their shoulder. The work they did was either good or bad because of the man in the driver's seat.

A truck driver was a little higher on the pecking order, Ross could see, at least among the blue-collar staff at H.A. Murphy. The warehouse-bound employees treated them with a special deference that suggested there was some envy for them. Ross knew how much he looked up to them. They had cockiness, a swagger of sorts, especially when they came back from their trips with some story about a wreck or a bad storm they had come through. The rest of the staff would repeat the stories for a day or two, until everyone had heard them or until some new tale came along.

☙

When the lumber for the cradle was stacked neatly in the bed of his truck, Ross headed for home, dreading the drive back across the Sugar River Bridge. Ross had shaken off the flashback on his way to get the lumber, only to have it resurrected by the appearance of Steve Neff. He reran all the pleasant memories he could muster through his mind in an effort to recover.

He was better by the time he reached his driveway, and the chill air of the morning was enough to help him shake it off again. When he got to the front door, he was putting on a good mood. He would give Shelley a big hug and smother her in noisy kisses until she begged him to stop. It was an emotional bath he had learned to take, and it was good for their marriage because Shelley liked his clowning that way. How many times had her laughter been his medicine? Yet he wanted another dose. He smiled inwardly, confidant that he would never become immune to its smallest tincture.

CHAPTER THREE

"I better hurry and get these things put away," Shelley muttered to herself as she struggled with a heavy basket of laundry. Ross would be beside himself if he knew that she routinely carried the basket all the way from the basement to the upstairs. They had agreed that she would leave most of the laundry for Ross to carry up when he was home.

She smiled to herself at what he would say: "Shell, you shouldn't be lifting this in your condition; it's too heavy." Three trips or more when one would do was ridiculous—she was perfectly healthy. Ross's attempts to be protective weren't practical, but humoring your spouse was part of being married.

As her foot landed on the top step, she felt a rush of water down her legs. Not realizing what it was at first, she dropped the laundry and bolted for the bathroom. By then it was too late. Her baggy jeans, socks and shoes were soaked. She leaned over against the vanity, trying to collect her thoughts. Though she wanted to deny it, the wetness had to be her amniotic fluid; her water had broken.

She felt a stinging in her eyes that was the precursor to tears, and she thought for a moment that she might faint. Though she had run to the bathroom, she banished any thought of sitting on the commode. The idea of letting any part of the precious life inside her mix with the inside of the toilet repulsed her, and she opted to let it dribble slowly onto the floor. Besides that, she had heard tales about women who'd had miscarriages where the baby had fallen into the toilet when the woman sat down, and those thoughts and fears played through her mind, though by now her baby was too large for that sort of thing to happen, even if the stories were true. She imagined herself sopping the water up with a clean washcloth, "and doing what with it, do you suppose?" she asked herself out loud.

Randall would be getting up any minute now, she knew. It was just past 10, and he was usually as punctual as his father was. She wished she could somehow avoid him and wondered whether it would be okay to close the bathroom door and speak softly to him through it. She knew that the sight of her dripping water would scare the boy, and it wouldn't do to tell him that she had simply peed herself.

Shelley had spent considerable time trying to pique Randall's interest in the advent of his sibling, without much success. She supposed it would be confusing to him if she should lose the baby now. She didn't want to think about that possibility.

She stood motionless for several minutes, half-afraid that any movement might cause a greater crisis than she already had. At last she heard the slam of Ross's pickup truck door and she brightened, knowing that he would be at her side in moments.

It struck her then that the telltale laundry basket was still sitting where she put it upon reaching the top of the steps. She knew there was no time to put the clothes away now before Ross saw it and realized that she had been toting the whole thing. Well, maybe he would not put two and two together. She decided not to mention it. No sense meeting trouble halfway.

Ross was surprised that Shelley did not come near the door to greet him as he expected. He usually heard the shuffle of her feet as she moved toward him whenever he entered the house after being away. He supposed she was in the basement doing laundry or some other task. He put away his coat and hat and went in search of her, calling, "Honey, I'm home."

He heard a reply from the upstairs, somewhat muffled or distressed, as if she were busily engaged doing some chore and wasn't free to speak clearly. He wondered if something might be wrong. He bounded up the steps two at a time and rounded the corner into the bathroom, sensing that was her location.

Shelley stood there unsteadily, a look of shocked wonder

on her face. She was leaning against the sink at an odd angle, standing in a puddle of water that soaked her shoes and stretched the whole way up to her crotch. They stared at each other for a silent moment. Shelley assumed that Ross would know what it was, but he didn't.

"What happened, honey?" he queried with wide eyes.

"Ross, my water broke."

It still did not register with Ross.

"Ross, the baby…is coming," she said a little more firmly.

"But it's not time yet." The absurdity of the statement brought a hint of impatience to Shelley's face. Ross realized then that all was not well, not at all.

"Should we go to the hospital? Should we call the doctor? He's not in on Saturdays, is he?" His voice was calm, but he was struggling to control it.

"Yes dear, we need to call the hospital. They will call Doctor Zilafro if it's necessary." It was all an act. She had checked her visage in the mirror and prepared herself for his arrival. She was afraid Ross would overreact. "Why don't you get Randy up and dress him?" Shelley said in a confident tone she didn't feel. "I'll call the hospital after I put on some other pants. It's gonna be okay, Ross." But the fear was already leaking into her voice. "Don't let on to Randy that there is anything wrong, okay?"

"No, of course not."

Ross went across the hall and opened his son's bedroom door slowly. He had no sooner stepped in before the lad was throwing his blankets back and reaching up to give his dad a hug.

"Hey, buddy, did you sleep good?" asked Ross.

"Hi Daddy. Was Mommy crying?" A concerned wrinkle crossed his little forehead.

"Oh, you know how girls are," Ross said. "They cry over every little thing. You'll understand some day." He made a conscious effort to sound upbeat then. "Think you might like to go to Grandma's?"

"Can I really go again so soon?" The boy's eyes were bright from sleep and now excitement.

"Sure can. It turns out your mom and I got something important to do today. Big people stuff, ya' know. You may as well go see Grandma."

"Can I take my backpack?"

"You gotta take your backpack."

The boy knew then that it might turn into an overnight stay, and he got even more excited.

"All right!" The two of them loaded Randall's little pack with an extra change of clothes and a few toys.

Shelley came then and stood in the middle of the hall just outside the room.

"I'll bet if you ask your mom real nice, she might let you stay a couple days," Ross ventured with a wink at the boy.

Randall ran to his mother and pleaded, "Can I, Momma, please?"

"All right Randall, but when I get lonesome, you'll have to come home."

"Yeah!" Randall responded. "Thanks, Mom."

Shelley meant to be as strong as possible, knowing that Ross's calmness was a thin veneer indeed.

"I called Mom and told her what was going on. We can drop Randall at her house," Shelley said.

"What did they say?" Ross quietly asked Shelley.

"They wanted to know if I'd had a contraction or not," she said.

"Have you?" Ross asked.

"Maybe a teensy little one," she responded. "They said they would call the doctor."

Ross put Randall in the middle of the front seat between him and Shelley. The lad liked riding there, and Shelley could get in and out of the pickup easier than she could their car. With the pickup she could just step up a little and slide in. She knew then, to her dismay, that the labor was starting. There was no mistaking the second contraction. But she said nothing to Ross. The hospital was only minutes away.

They dropped Randall off. Ross exchanged an apprehensive

look with his mother-in-law at the door and returned quickly to the pickup.

"I feel bad about leaving him there again so soon," Ross said. "Do you think he can tell something's wrong?"

"I feel bad, too. But kids live in the moment, thank God. He probably won't think anything about it," Shelley said.

"Good thing he's so little. Then again, if he were bigger, we could tell him what's going on," Ross said. Relieved by the absence of Randall, they dropped their pretense and quickly joined hands, the tightness of their grip conveying mutual fear.

"It'll be okay, honey," Shelley whispered through tight lips with a false conviction she was trying hard to feel.

Ross felt strange driving right up to the emergency entrance of the hospital. He had always thought that only someone who was bleeding to death had the right to do that. But his desire to get Shelley into the relative safety of the hospital overwhelmed his inhibitions.

He beat a hasty retreat back to the pickup after he had her inside, moving his vehicle to a proper parking spot before trotting back in. He knew he was trying to do everything just right out of fear of something bad happening again.

The nurses were calm and professional. It brought a wave of frustration to him. Couldn't they see she needed to be examined and treated immediately?

"Her water broke. Did she tell you?" he blurted out as if he thought Shelley had been mute since he was out parking the pickup. Immediately he felt embarrassed, and the nurse sitting calmly at the computer turned to him and studied his face for a moment. He realized that she was observing him to see if he might be near hysteria.

"Okay, I'll calm down. I'm sorry," he said with a controlled voice.

"That's okay, Mr. Martin. We get excited husbands every now and then. We'll take good care of your wife, I promise." She smiled at Ross—a little too sweetly, he thought. He hoped Shelley would not see it and be jealous. Even as distracted as Shelley was, she would catch any exchange between him and the nurse that could be taken as flirtation. Shelley sensed Ross's distress and gave him a reassuring look.

"I love you," she mouthed and Ross returned her silent communication.

After the usual misery over insurance coverage and medical history, Shelley was taken away to be examined. Ross found himself tagging along, feeling that his presence was only tolerated because he was family. He could contribute nothing and would probably be in the way if any treatment were to be given.

He made it to the room with her but was left sitting in a chair as the long silky curtains were pulled around the bed. The metal slides the curtains hung on protested with a sort of growling sound, like some sterile monster that would swallow Shelley rather than encircle her in their opaque streams of linen. Ross thought the sound was out of place here, where the emphasis should be on comfort. Sounds like that usually made Shelley cringe. Like fingernails being dragged across a chalkboard.

Shelley's obstetrician was a broad-faced, balding man who looked at first glance like some wax figure you might see in a museum. There was almost no expression in his facial features or in his voice.

The man could have excelled at playing poker, thought Ross, since his face would never reveal how good or bad his hand might be.

Two other doctors arrived now and entered the sacred interior of the curtain without so much as a nod to Ross. His feeling of insignificance increased even more. He could hear the doctors talking to the nurse in low, esoteric terms that allowed these professionals to keep Ross and Shelley ignorant of her real condition if they chose. He knew that was not their purpose, but he wondered if doctors didn't overdo the big words sometimes just to show off in front of ignorant truck drivers like himself. He caught enough fragments of everyday terms to realize they were going to try to stop Shelley's labor with drugs, though he knew they preferred the more innocuous term "medication."

He finally heard Shelley's voice, though he couldn't make out her words.

"Bring the husband in now," one of them said. Ross was chagrinned at the generic reference to himself, "the husband." The curtain parted and Dr. Zilafro's stone face beckoned Ross out of the chair with a slight sideways toss of his head that Ross took for a statement in itself. He held the curtain aside, and the new doctors nodded and smiled at each other. Ross felt he should offer a handshake, but they were on the other side of Shelley, and the intervening bed made that impractical.

"Dr. Cleland and Dr. Morrison here," Dr. Zilafro said. "They both agree. Your wife is in excellent health, and we see no reason to be overly concerned. However, your baby is in a bit of a rush to be born. We think it would be best if we delay your wife's delivery for as long as we can—probably a few days, maybe a week. The child needs to be as close to full term as possible before delivery. We trust the baby can survive if it was born now, but it's far better if the lungs are fully developed. This isn't extremely premature, you see, but the closer to full term the better. You understand, don't you? After another two weeks, if she should go into labor again, we can let things progress without interference."

Dr. Zilafro, it seemed, was doing his best not to sound as if he were condescending to Ross's ignorance. But the way he said, "you understand, don't you," annoyed Ross. He wondered why Shelley was so fond of this doctor. It was something Ross would ask her when all of this was over.

"You do that with drugs, don't you?" Ross asked with tight lips, deliberately using the word "drugs." He wanted to ask some intelligent, even provocative questions to console his pride a little. The doctors all nodded, and Zilafro rattled off several multi-syllabled names of drugs, which only served to trump Ross's efforts to look intelligent. Nevertheless, he tried again.

"Will there be any side effects on Shelley or the baby?"

The doctor's eyebrows came up a little now, as if surprised Ross knew about side effects. "Of course there can be side effects, but we know what to watch for. None of them is life threatening. There is the outside chance of an allergic reaction with any drug, mind you, but I've never seen it with any of these." With that he looked at the other doctors and said "gentlemen?" as if deferring to their collective experience for further support.

"No unusual risks," Cleland said.

Ross and Shelley hesitated for a moment, absorbing everything. "So, you give her the drugs, the labor stops and I take her home?" Ross said.

"Well...no." The tone of Dr. Zilafro's voice indicated that now it was time for the bad news. "She will have to stay here in the hospital until the baby comes." His face was still deadpan.

"Stay here!" Ross said. He and Shelley had been holding hands, and now her grip tightened. Then he caught himself. Of course, whatever the doctors thought was best would be okay. Ross had not been prepared for anything like this, though. The casual way the doctors had been acting about Shelley seemed to Ross to be just that, an act. He sensed that this was serious and that there was danger. But he decided to keep himself as calm as he could, for Shelley's sake. He looked into her eyes and saw the fear.

The authority of the doctors gave both Ross and Shelley mixed feelings. On one hand they trusted them because of the knowledge they commanded. On the other hand they felt helpless, as if they were arrayed against something they did not understand.

They felt like victims, quite helpless and at the mercy of men who may or may not truly care about their baby's health. They could only trust, and the cold, calculating face of Dr. Zilafro was no comfort. The other doctors seemed to follow his lead in being devoid of emotion, as if it were his call whether to show the couple any sympathy or hope. It was as if they were detached from Ross and Shelley, maybe for the sake of their safety. Ross wondered, was the situation really as bright as they said?

The three doctors excused themselves then, and a team of nurses or technicians came into the room. Ross was kindly moved aside so they could rig up an intravenous drip for Shelley's left arm. They took blood from her other arm and attached a variety of monitors to her. There was a display on the screen above the bed, and the baby's heartbeat was shown and pointed out to them. The drugs were administered through the IV, and Shelley seemed to become only a small part of something large and mysterious, swallowed by the impersonal technology of medicine.

An hour went by as the medicine took effect. The timing of Shelley's contractions tapered off, and their intensity diminished. She was no longer in labor. The various members of the nursing team drifted away, and Ross and Shelley were left with a thin, mousy woman who told them her name was Michelle. She chatted with them in a friendly sort of way Ross appreciated. The doctors had seemed a little too distant, and he wondered why.

"That's a cheerful crew, those three doctors," Ross commented wryly.

"Don't mind them—they're really very nice," the nurse said. "It's just that they've had a hard morning. You're really fortunate that the three of them were here. If it weren't for the other emergency they had this morning, neither Cleland nor Morrison would have been here at all. You're actually fortunate that Dr. Zilafro was free to come in so soon. People sometimes wait hours for him." Ross wondered what made the morning so hard for the trio of physicians but thought it would be better not to ask, since the answer to the question might add further weight to Shelley's apprehensions.

"I thought the insurance companies didn't let people stay long in a hospital," Ross queried Michelle. "Dr. Zilafro said she might need to stay until the baby comes, which could be weeks. What gives?"

"That's true. Hospitals costs are so high. It's just that the water she lost is pretty important," Michelle replied. She didn't seem comfortable answering his questions.

"It's hard to imagine you being in here for two weeks," Ross said. Shelley forced a smile.

"I know. I don't like the idea of leaning on Mom for that long. I don't guess they'd let you take off work, huh?" Shelley said.

"We couldn't really afford it if they did," Ross said.

Perhaps sensing that the Martins needed some time alone, the mousy Michelle made her way reluctantly to the door. "Now you just ring if you need me, honey. I'll be just down the hall. I need to check you every 10 minutes so you know I can't get too far away." She smiled as she pulled the heavy door shut behind her. Shelley looked like she would burst into tears. Ross moved close and knelt by the bed.

"I'm sorry, Ross," Shelley wailed.

"Oh, baby, no, don't be that way. You can't help this," Ross reassured his wife. He stroked the side of her head and pushed the blonde tresses away from her face.

"I understand how important it is for you that everything happen right," Ross told her. "What is it about women that makes them think they are responsible for things that are beyond their control? I know you're doing your best." He was doing his best to sound understanding.

He knew that part of Shelley's fear was that his regard for her would be diminished if she did not produce a healthy child. The unfairness of it bothered Ross. He knew it would be pointless to protest the presence of guilt in Shelley's mind. It was something women seemed to expect from each other as well as themselves. The sorority of childbearing was something women had exclusively to themselves, Ross thought. Men couldn't be expected to understand it.

He leaned in, and her lips pursed to receive his. They kissed in a desperate lunge for the elusive feeling of security. It helped a little.

"Gotta call the folks," Ross said suddenly. He stood up, knowing it would be good for Shelley to talk with her mother.

"I think you have to dial nine first to get an outside line," Shelley advised.

Ross knew how to dial out but nodded to Shelley anyway as if he appreciated her assistance. The phone was answered on the second ring, and Ross could hear Randall's voice in the background. He strained to hear what the little guy was saying, so he hesitated a second until Shelley's mom said again, "Hello."

"Hi, Momma Clark, how's the boy doing?"

"Oh, he's fine, Ross. What's up with Shelley?" Virginia Clark's voice was strained and carried the hint of a sob.

"She's right here, I'll let her tell you herself." Ross handed the phone to Shelley.

"Hi, Mom."

"How are you, dear?" Virginia said.

"I wish I knew, Mom. The doctors say that my water breaking isn't that big a deal, but I have to stay in the hospital until the baby comes. They don't want it to happen for the next two weeks, though, and they've given me something to stop the labor. At least two weeks in this bed, maybe longer. I'm gonna go nuts."

"Nonsense, dear. You'll be fine for two weeks or two months. There's nothing you need to worry about that Dad and I can't help you with. Ross can go right on working as if nothing has happened, and we'll see you get taken care of. Randy can stay right here with me. You just do what the doctors say and try not to fret. Do you need anything, dear?" Shelley got the distinct impression that her mother had rehearsed the speech she had just delivered.

"Thanks, Mom, I knew I could count on you."

"That's what family is for, Shelley. Now when can we come see you?"

"We'll have to check with the staff here, but I don't see why you can't come today if you want." Shelley paused then and took a deep breath.

Her mother noticed that Shelley was doing her best to sound as if she were not in distress, but the deep, almost frantic way she was breathing betrayed her.

"Are you sure you are okay, dear?" she asked.

"I'm as good as I can be under the circumstances, Mom. Don't worry."

Again she drew in a deep breath but tried to do it in a controlled way, so she would not sound desperate for air. She was starting to realize that things were not at all comfortable for her. She was getting numb and did not like it.

It was not so much a sensation of impending pain that she was aware of now but rather a lack of sensation, a feeling of no feeling. Like silence, which can be even louder than the noise it replaces, the numbness roared in her body. A presence in her flesh even more unwelcome than the pain, for it was unnatural and threatening. She was supposed to be in pain, and as miserable as that was she preferred it to this numbness.

The labor was diminishing. The medicine was making her body obey its demands. She found herself preoccupied with her breathing. Michelle reentered the room just then.

"It's really getting hard to breathe," Shelley said.

"Don't worry, that's just one of the side effects of the medicine. I know it's sort of uncomfortable, but you'll get used to it. If you just try to relax, it will help some," Michelle reassured her.

It was indeed uncomfortable. Shelley would lie there and deliberately draw a deep breath. Ross watched her chest heaving and felt afraid. He couldn't get comfortable with her having to struggle. He knew he should just trust the professionals, but there was something about Shelley's deliberate drawing of breath that bothered him.

Ross suspected the truth then, but it seemed incredible to him. He dismissed it for a moment. Then, partly as an attempt to show her his concern, he asked, "Shelley, what happens if you don't try to take a breath?"

"Why wouldn't I try to breath?" she asked.

"Just try not to think about it. Don't do it deliberately. See if you breathe without thinking about it," Ross said.

"Oh, I see what you mean. That isn't easy to do, though," Shelley said.

Shelley relaxed and did her best to put all thoughts of respiration out of her mind. She had to concentrate to be able to tell. It shook her then, as she realized that she had to breathe deliberately or she would not breathe at all. She was scared now.

"Ross, I don't breathe if I don't think about it. It's not just hard Ross, it's not happening. This is weird!" She gulped a large measure of precious air then and tried to fill her lungs more completely as she suddenly felt in danger.

Ross turned to Michelle then with desperation and anger in his eyes. "Get the doctor back in here, quick!" He knew he should be calm about it, but he could hardly accept what was happening. It seemed like the nurse could not understand what Shelley's lack of breath meant to them. Was she so detached emotionally, so conditioned to follow procedure without question that she could let her patient stop breathing and call it a side effect?

Dr. Zilafro entered then and took charge of things. "Not breathing well?" he asked in his trademark deadpan.

Ross spoke in a tone that he deliberately measured, afraid of seeming to be out of control. "She's not breathing at all unless she thinks about it. What happens if she should pass out now? I think you'd better take her off this medicine."

The doctor was silent now, studying the situation and trying to gauge whether to do what Ross said. After a long pause, punctuated by Shelley's exaggerated breathing, he acquiesced. He reached up and closed the valve that metered the flow of drug into Shelley's I.V.

"I'm sorry, Shelley, it seems that you are a little too sensitive to this medicine. A dose strong enough to stop the labor can also slow your autonomic functions. Any shortness of breath usually passes quickly. In your case, it is not quick enough."

"You said there wouldn't be any dangerous side effects. You all agreed." Ross spoke in a measured, disappointed tone that caused the doctor to grudgingly acknowledge his presence in the room, or so it seemed to Ross.

The doctor was cornered now, and he knew it. He would have to talk honestly and openly to Ross about what was happening. "I know you're upset, Ross. May I call you Ross?" His tone was almost plaintive.

"Sure, call me Ross."

"I don't blame you really. We try to minimize any talk about risks for the sake of the patient, your wife's, peace of mind. Sometimes it does backfire on us. I know it sounds cliché, but we meant well. I hope you two understand."

"It's okay, Doc. It just seems like we're helpless in all this. It's frustrating, you know?"

"I know. I know. Well, we shall try to do better from now on. The plain truth is, you're going to be parents again before long. There won't be any stopping the labor now. Let's hope your child is as ready for the world as he seems to be."

Ross felt a sudden tightness in his stomach, like someone had just reached in and squeezed it. This baby was coming, ready or not. Ross gulped. "What are the chances that the baby will be healthy, normal I mean?" he asked.

"The chances for normality are no different than they would be with any baby. The difference is in the development. At this stage the child can develop outside the womb. Some do so with no apparent problems. Most critical are the lungs. We will put the child on life support at once. Then we wait to see how well he develops and matures. He has a good chance of being as healthy as any baby, once he matures. It's sort of like he has to catch up on his own, you might say. We do all we can to protect him while that happens. I can give you a better idea once he is delivered and we've had a chance to watch him awhile. The thing is, he is very vulnerable outside of the womb, especially to infection. That's why we wanted him to stay in the womb. We can't protect him the way Shelley can." The doctor turned and looked at Shelley now, who had been listening without comment. He smiled reassuringly.

"He'll be in one of those incubators, won't he?" she asked.

"Yes, probably for two to three weeks."

Ross was starting to see why Shelley liked this doctor so much. He was actually very personable once you got behind his façade of professionalism or whatever it was that gave him that irritating poker face.

Ross supposed that even accomplished people like doctors

had their insecurities, reasons for remaining on guard and distant from people. Lord knew Ross had more than enough of them. He mused that Shelley's warm manner had long ago drawn the doctor's friendliness out for her. That was probably why she had liked him from the start.

CHAPTER FOUR

"I feel a lot better now that no one is playing games with us," Ross said.

"Don't be too hard on them, Ross," Shelley said. "They do this sort of thing all the time. They know what works most often. Don't you think?" They were alone in the room again, for a few minutes anyway.

"You're actually defending them?" Ross could not believe it. He knew Shelley was trusting, but he thought even she would have reached her limit after what just happened. "You could have died."

"They have me on a monitor, you know." She pointed to the panel above the bed. "It has an alarm. They would have been here instantly if my breathing had stopped.

"Besides, you were here. They knew you'd keep an eye on me." Shelley was doing what she could to keep Ross from overreacting to the breathing incident. The last thing she wanted was a doctor who felt like he was in danger of some charge or lawsuit coming against him.

"So, you don't think we have a right to be upset?" asked Ross.

"I think this is the worst possible time for us to get upset," Shelley said. "Both Dr. Zilafro and Michelle expect us to think bad of them. If we choose to give them the benefit of the doubt, then they will see us as generous and reasonable people. They're used to people expecting them to be perfect and then jumping all over them if something isn't. That's why Michelle is nervous. Let's give them a break. You'll see. They'll treat us like gold if they see we're going to forget about what happened."

Ross looked into the eyes of his wife. He had always known she was more sensitive to other people's feelings than he was, more sensitive than most people he knew. But he was seeing how inordinately generous she could be, too. There was something in what she said, though, about how people were always looking for the chance to find fault, especially in those who were supposed to be experts or authority figures. It struck a chord in his soul, and he didn't like it. He knew she was right, but he felt like she was trying to teach him something.

"You did fine talking to him a minute ago," Shelley went on. "Even though I could see you wanted to be mad. I'll bet he appreciates it more than you know."

"You're probably right, I guess. I just wish I could do more to help you. Here the best thing I can do is keep my mouth shut and stay out of the way. I never liked that much," Ross said.

"You don't like frustration, I know. That's one thing I love about you—you take care of everything you can. You want to fix this for me. I appreciate that."

"I guess being scared makes it hard to trust people," Ross reflected.

Shelley began to arch her back now as the labor contractions gradually returned. Michelle came back in and observed Shelley's intensity as if gauging something. She seemed more self-conscious as she moved now, evidently having some fear of the situation. Ross could see how right Shelley was, and he gave Michelle the warmest smile he could muster while Shelley was in the midst of a labor pain.

Michelle stretched a latex glove onto her hand and smoothly reached under the sheets to check Shelley's dilation. She held up the fingers for Dr. Zilafro as he came through the door and reported calmly, "seven centimeters."

The doctor's eyebrows came up noticeably, though he corrected that and assumed his deliberate calmness. "Well, she is moving along quickly, isn't she? We better get her to the delivery room.

At 8:37 p.m., Shelley delivered their second boy, 4 pounds 7 ounces. Ross was in the delivery room, but the nurses or technicians or whatever these people all were, worked as if he were not there. He felt like he was in the way.

Ross knew most people disliked hospitals, and now he knew why. There was a kind of detached coolness about all the trappings and equipment that made him feel like his family was at the mercy of some machine instead of in the hands of caring professionals.

Shelley made eye contact with him just before each pain began. When she was in the midst of the pain, though, it seemed she made contact with nothing. It was as if Shelley went off by herself when the pain struck, to struggle alone against it. Ross could only hold her hand. It probably gave him more comfort than her.

The contraction would come upon her with just enough warning for her to draw a deep breath before it dominated her whole being. With each new spasm her face drew up in a tight grimace that Ross thought might change her facial appearance permanently if it did not end soon.

Ross had been with her when Randall was delivered and remembered how little difference his presence seemed to make to her. Her labor then had seemed endless, lasting from early afternoon until the wee hours of the morning. This time the rapid pace of Shelley's dilation offered him hope that her delivery would be short. But it was still long enough to drain him of his energy and make him feel completely useless.

With Randall it had all been forgotten when he arrived. The long hours of waiting swallowed up in the joy of hearing his firstborn cry with that strangest of wails—the noise only a newborn makes, sounding like a creature from another world, which in a way, it was.

This time though, there was no release from the foreboding, no sudden cry announcing the start of life. The presence of the extra medical staff, the quick transfer to neonatal care and the cautious way Michelle and the doctor behaved all worked together to deny Ross and Shelley any end to fear just because the child was born. Ross knew it could be weeks before the dread would be lifted from their shoulders. Even then the relief would be metered to them in little doses, providing everything went well.

The little baby was so fragile and small that Ross would not have wanted to hold him anyway. He looked as if he would fit inside one of Ross's shoes. There was no crying or noise of any kind except what the green-coated medical types made as they hovered over mother and child, working in a state of quiet urgency, doing whatever it was to transition the baby from the womb of flesh to one of plastic and linen, glass and stainless steel.

Ross imagined the child's sensory perceptions. A world filled with glare and echo and the smell of medicine and disinfectant, tubes, wires and electronic monitors with LED displays looking like video games. But none of Ross's imaginings would mean anything to the baby, who could relate to none of it. It would all be shockingly different from what he was used to. Where was the liquid warmth, the muffled sounds and the reassuring rhythm of his mother's pulse? Could this newborn creature sense how fragile was his existence?

He wished he could somehow speak to the little guy again, the way he had done so many nights in bed with Shelley. Ross would lay with his cheek against Shelley's tummy and talk to the baby, just as if there were no wall of flesh between them.

He wanted to let him know how welcome he was, to give him a reason to hold onto life and to grow. His mouth moved as if he was talking to himself, and he didn't care if anyone saw him or thought him strange. Little pleas for the baby's health came out of Ross, and he whispered and whimpered and pleaded with God for the little life. Much in the way he had pleaded for the life of Donny Ritts that day among the rocks in the Sugar River. The sense of having done this before came over him, but mercifully the full weight of the memories did not show up this time to haunt him.

A mild sense of shame began to creep over him now as he realized Shelley would be suffering more than he was. He caught her eye and gazed at her face, but she was too exhausted, it seemed, for any communication. Just as well, thought Ross.

While all the post-delivery work was being done on Shelley, Ross sat alone in a chair in the corner of the room. It had all happened so quickly. From the time he had come home this morning until their baby was born, only nine hours had passed.

He slipped up close to Shelley's bed and took her hand. "How you doing, Shell?" he murmured. "Say, I thought I'd go out and find a phone. I'll call the boss and see if I can get off the first of the week." Ross went down the hall until he came to a phone by the elevator and dialed John Murphy's home number.

"Hello, Murphy here." He was a second-generation businessman, wealthy and a little too confident in his inherited position for most of the people who worked for him. But Ross and John Murphy had a good relationship. Murphy knew that the continued success of his company depended largely on the quality of his people, and he worked at treating them as equals. Many of his underlings did not see it that way, though. Ross Martin did, however, and Murphy took notice.

"Hi, Mr. Murphy. It's Ross Martin. Sorry to call you this late on a weekend."

"It must be important, Ross. What's up?"

"You knew that Shelley and I were expecting in January. Well, we're not anymore. The baby was born today. Tonight actually, just a little while ago."

"Great, Ross, good for you. Or wait a minute, isn't this too early?"

"Yeah, about six weeks premature. He's okay, though—at least they think he will be. The doctors won't really know till they have some time to watch him." There was obvious strain in Ross's voice, and the other man responded with appropriate kindness.

"How's Shelley?" Murphy asked.

"Tired...and worried, I think," Ross said.

"No doubt. I guess you need to talk about work, huh?"

"That's right. I was hoping to get a few days off now if I could."

"You know how things are, but I can't expect a man to go out on a run with something like this on his mind. Tell you what—

just forget about your load. We can put someone else on it or work out something. But, if you would, call me Monday morning and tell me what's happened. I will need to use you a little if I can. Nothing long for sure, and if you don't want to that's okay, too. But if your wife and baby are okay and you feel like it, we could sure put you on something. Things like this always seem to happen on holidays. Only three days to deliver, and some of those customers don't understand our limitations."

"I appreciate this, Mr. Murphy," Ross said.

"A boy, huh? What are you going to call him?" John asked.

"We were gonna talk about that this weekend. We haven't decided yet."

"Better come up with something pretty quick. I've heard that if you don't name a baby within 72 hours, the hospital picks one for you," he said with a chuckle.

Ross knew his boss was trying to lighten his mood.

"Oh, we'll come up with something," Ross said, putting a little pep in his voice. "Maybe Ross Jr., I don't know. Well, thanks, Mr. Murphy. I'd better go. I have several calls to make to our family."

With Monday through Wednesday, along with the four days for Thanksgiving, he had a full week off work.

❧

"You just go right to sleep," Michelle told Shelley. "You're exhausted. I'm sure your husband will understand."

But Shelley was not sleepy. She was remembering the laundry basket and how she had carried the heavy thing up two flights of steps so many times. She was remembering in particular how she had carried it that morning and how certain she was that Ross had seen it sitting at the top of the steps where she had left it.

He would be coming back before long, and she didn't really want to face him now that she was thinking about it. He might see what was in her mind. Or was it that she might see what was in his? Did Ross know how little regard she had given to his orders not to carry the basket? Did he realize how few were the times he had carried the laundry up the stairs for her? While Ross was sitting in the corner of the room waiting, had he been putting two and two together? Would he accuse her of putting the child in jeopardy?

The idea that the lifting had had something to do with the early labor and the water breaking had been haunting her mind since it happened. She told herself that it was silly. She had been convinced that her reproductive machinery wouldn't feel the physical strain. Now she was not so sure. She wanted to ask the doctor about it but could not do so without admitting how much she had done. She was not one to meet trouble half way. Besides that, it would be easier to deny that it had had any effect as long as she didn't talk about the possibility. She could ask those questions later if need be. She pushed the thoughts off stage in her mind again, but they would not disappear. They lingered and whispered to her of the possibility of loss. They reminded her how thin Ross's affections might actually be if he ever reached the point where he fully forgave himself for the death of Donny Ritts. If the baby died and Ross thought she was responsible for it, would he stop looking past her face?

❧

After talking to Murphy, Ross made two more calls, the first to his parents and the second to Shelley's. Both sides were surprised at the news, and both promised to come visit Shelley and the baby the next day. Shelley's mom assured him again that Randall was fine and welcome to stay as long as was needed.

Ross made his way back to the room where Dr. Zilafro was just finishing up with Shelley. She did look tired, but it was plain she was not interested in rest. "When can I go see the baby?" she asked. The physician looked like he'd had enough time on his feet for the day.

"You should just rest now, dear. But I'm too tired to argue with you. Just be sure you're in a wheelchair if you go out of this room." He turned to Ross. "She's amazing, isn't she?"

"She's ornery, if you want to know the truth," teased Ross. "But that makes her tough, I guess. She gets a notion in her head, you best get out of her way. She's liable to cuff us both if we don't let her go see him." He laughed and tweaked the back of Shelley's hand. Then he switched to a more serious tone. "How did the baby seem to you anyway, Doc?"

"Not ornery, I can tell you that. Infants that small are fragile. All of them are. But he was as strong as any I've seen. That's the straight story, too. I'm not saying what you want to hear, so you'll feel good," Dr. Zilafro said.

"Good enough for me. Thanks, Doc," Ross said, as he offered him his hand.

They got a wheel chair, eased down the hall to the elevator and descended to the basement where the neo-natal ward was located. Ross didn't like the way the doctor had used the word "fragile," but he determined that he would not show any apprehensions to Shelley. Now imitating the poker-faced physician, Ross masked his thoughts and forced a smile to his lips.

"They say labor pain is the easiest pain to forget. Anyone needing evidence of that could find it on your face, Shelley," Ross observed as he pushed her chair down the hall. The bouncy manner she was displaying now practically answered any questions about her condition. Ross asked anyway.

"I guess you feel pretty good, honey?"

"I feel like I just had a baby and that is way better than feeling like I'm gonna have a baby," she said, grinning up at him. She was as buoyant as he had ever seen her, maybe too buoyant. There was a healthy glow on her face. But Ross thought he saw a shadow in her eyes, too. Maybe only Ross could see it because he knew the eyes so well.

Like always, Ross picked up her hopeful mood, even though he suspected it was fabricated. "So do you have a short list of names yet?" Ross asked.

"Actually, honey, I've been sort of busy lately. I haven't had much time to think about the subject," replied Shelley in a playful voice. "The short list wasn't supposed to be needed just yet."

Ross and Shelley were positioned now in front of the neo-natal room. There was no broad expanse of glass like they had seen in other newborn wards. There were only three windows, counting the two in the double door. Ross wondered if the idea was to create the illusion of security for the fragile lives of the premature babies. Not for the babies, of course, but for the families who came to get a look at them.

The place seemed more like a vault to Ross, as if the contents of the room were not yet presentable to the eyes of the world. It reinforced in the couple the persistent notion that the life of their child was tenuous. Another fear, that the child could prove to be substandard in some way, seemed even more probable, here in the cold sterile confines of this isolated, almost-hidden place.

Shelley began to stand up from the wheelchair, and Ross rushed to prop her up with a firm hand under her elbow. They both peered in one of the high windows and saw him there, their little nameless baby, naked except for a diaper under the heat lamp. Hooked to a machine to help him breathe, tubes snaking into his tiny body.

The positive outlook they were trying to maintain was beginning to show signs of strain. There was an uncomfortable silence between them that got worse the longer it dragged on. Both of them wished the other would break it, knowing that whatever words came out first would be smitten with the contrast of the silence and come out awkward at best.

Shelley was still wondering if her disobedience to Ross's wishes about carrying laundry had been a factor in the premature birth. Even more, she wanted to know if he was aware of it, if he had noticed the laundry basket where she had left it and how full it was.

Shelley knew that her desire to have the matter settled was something she needed to drop. Other times in her life she had ventured thoughts better left hidden, and it had been disastrous. "Why can't I just forget it?" she puzzled. It was almost as if some abstract sense of guilt or justice within her demanded confession. She decided to try distracting herself with an almost equally tricky subject, one that carried no weight of personal guilt. "Ross, what do you think of calling him Donny?"

His response was so instant that Shelley guessed he had anticipated the suggestion. Yet he was hesitant. "Shelley, well...I don't know," Ross said.

The thought that the child may not even live to hear the name was something Ross did not wish to think about. He had been toying with the idea of using the name of his childhood buddy for some time. He did not know if it was correct to do something like that or not. Hearing Shelley propose it gave the idea some validation.

"Why don't we wait and see what the doctors say later today." The implication would be plain enough to Shelley, Ross knew.

"I'm not sure I like the way you're thinking."

"I know, I'm sorry," he said.

"Please try to hope for the best, okay Ross? I don't think we should give any thought to the negative possibilities." She was using the strong attitude to stave off her feelings of guilt. She knew she would have to deal with them one way or another, but that must wait. For now she would believe and hope and pray for complete wholeness for little Donny Martin. She would use that name for now, to herself at least.

"I should be close to him; I want to cuddle him." Shelley was speaking softly, staring through the glass at the baby's fragile body, and Ross knew there would be tears slipping out.

"You should be sleeping," he said. He let the idea of sleep have a chance to grow on her.

"I know you're right, Ross," she said after a moment and allowed him to help her sink back into the wheelchair. "I need to get myself in good shape so I'll be ready to take care of him when they let me take him home. Whenever that is."

Ross wheeled her back to the elevator, and soon they were back in the room. Before long a thin young man came in and introduced himself as Dr. Riley. He looked too much like a teenager to inspire much confidence in the Martins, but he clearly knew his medicine. He explained how they would monitor the baby's progress.

"Once we have a good steady heartbeat for awhile, then we see if he can breathe on his own. Once he's breathing okay, we try to feed him. If he does everything like he's supposed to, he could be out of here in a week. We just can't take anything for granted with someone this small." The young doctor smiled at the Martins. "You have every reason to be hopeful."

CHAPTER FIVE

Ross kissed Shelley goodnight and made his way home in the wee hours of the morning. The town was empty; even the late night cruisers did not stay out this late in November. The streets seemed lonely and desolate to Ross. His home was dark and quiet as he unlocked the front door and stumbled in. The quietness and emptiness of the house roared in his ears, and he wished he had just spent the night in Shelley's room. At least he would not have had to sleep alone in the death-like quiet.

He climbed the steps in a sort of stupor until at the top an image filled his mind and jerked him wide-awake. The laundry basket. That morning when he had come home it was sitting right there on the second floor landing. He had picked it up and put it in their bedroom after Shelley had explained about her water breaking and they had decided what their course of action would be. He had handled it without thinking. It simply had not registered in his brain. He had been distracted by Shelley's troubled voice and had not caught the meaning of it until now. Shelley had been carrying the wash up the two flights of stairs when her water broke. She had to have been doing it on a regular basis. He had made her promise not to lift anything that heavy, but to leave the basket in the basement until he was home and could do it for her. She had only asked him to bring it up on one occasion that he could think of, though she clearly took care of the laundry much more often than that. There was no shortage of clean socks, or anything else, for that matter.

Ross had a sick feeling now as he realized that Shelley would have to be conscious of the fact that she had ignored his advice and that now he was painfully aware of it, too. Whether or not her unnecessary physical exertion had anything to do with the premature birth of their son was a question neither one of them would wish to ask.

Ross loved Shelley deeply. He did not want to say anything to her that might make her feel bad. Surely she was chastising herself enough for it already, he thought. Or was she? There hadn't been any mention of the subject throughout the day. She had acted a little strange a time or two, but who knew how a woman was supposed to act when she was delivering a child? It wasn't like he could expect her behavior to be completely normal or predictable. He couldn't remember having any similar feelings when Randall was born.

Ross undressed and got into the shower. He wished he could wash away all the uncertainty he was feeling. He was plenty tired, but he did not hurry to bed. It seemed spacious now as he got under the blankets. He lay awake in the darkness asking himself if he should say anything to his wife about the matter. There was no point now, really. If little Donny were going to be okay, it wouldn't matter. If he were not okay, there would be enough remorse in Shelley's mind without his adding to it. Better to let it rest, he decided. But he could not rest.

As he tossed in the darkness, Ross's mind conjured up a bulwark of rationale against his disappointment with Shelley. She was really healthy. She was strong and athletic. The stairs were not especially steep. He didn't really think that being pregnant meant that a woman was fragile. Didn't women in the old days do hard work right up until delivery? He wondered about the women in third-world countries. Surely they could not afford the luxury of inactivity in the third trimester.

"Anyway, Ross," he told himself. "You only said all that about being cautious because Shelley loved it when you were concerned and worried about her well being." Men were always being accused of insensitivity and callousness. He figured he had probably been doing what he could to distance himself from that image when he showed all that anxiety about her doing heavy lifting while pregnant.

No, that was nonsense, Ross knew. He knew the reason he

had warned her about not carrying the clothes was because of the danger of a fall. Carrying a heavy basket of laundry made an already top-heavy woman even more unstable. It was just like when he had a high load on his trailer—he went around turns slower, kept off sloping shoulders and didn't do anything jerky with the wheel.

The biggest reason for his concern about her lifting had come from a neighbor Ross and Shelley had when they were first married, when they lived in a small apartment. Her name was Connie something or other, one of those long Italian names that people tend to shorten in frustration. The poor woman had been forced to spend the last two or three months of her pregnancy completely immobile. She was in bed, flat on her back as much as she could stand. She couldn't do anything that might shake her baby. It was something about how well her womb carried the baby; any shock could mean miscarriage. She had lost her first two before the seventh month, if Ross remembered right.

Ross knew that Connie was an exception. Who could tell how well any fetus might be positioned or how prepared the mother's uterus might be? Ross thought it was better to be careful, especially when Shelley had a husband that was so willing to help her. On the other hand, since he was usually away four nights a week, his demand seemed stupid.

Anyway, what right did he have to expect Shelley to do everything right? He was the one who led his best friend into the slippery rocks of the devil's gate and let him get stuck, then let everyone think Donny was a poor swimmer.

The thoughts went through his head in a steady cycle, as if they had arranged themselves in time with some dreadfully solemn drumbeat, like a dirge. Each took its turn presenting its case, some for Shelley, some against her. The Plexiglas cube that sheltered the tenuous life of his son filled in the background, its tubes and monitors and medicines looking like some scene from a late night, third-rate movie.

Shelley wasn't sleeping well. The sounds of the hospital filtered through the half-closed door. The noise wasn't loud enough to keep her awake — the soft footsteps of the nurses and the faraway ringing of telephones and alarms — yet more than enough to tell her that she was not alone.

Yet, she was alone, more alone now than ever, now that she was separated from her beloved Ross. This time not separated by something as insignificant as distance the way they were when Ross drove away each week in his truck. This separation would be something real, something that would be felt keenest when they were together. The silly idea Ross held so strongly, that her carrying laundry baskets was dangerous, was going to become an issue after all. Ross was going to go home and see the basket. She never got the clothes put away, and even though he was thick headed sometimes, Ross would realize who had carried it up from the basement. He would conclude that she had caused the premature labor with her strenuous effort. He would become convinced that his fears had been well founded. Men just loved being right.

Ross would realize how little she had obeyed his admonitions. She had asked for trouble, and now she was going to get it. Every day since she first made a play for Ross's affection after Donny Ritts drowned, she had feared a situation like this. She had been desperately careful to do everything right. Deep down, where she wasn't supposed to go in thought, was the reality of her decorated face. "Decorated" — that was the word her Daddy used when she was small. She had learned to say the right things, to behave as if she could cope with the spot, to pretend it wasn't that big of a deal. But there was no way to pretend that her courtship with Ross could ever have happened if he had not been so wounded by his friend's death.

She had moved in, like some predator. She had sensed the weakness and insecurity of Ross Martin, and like a lioness choosing the gazelle most isolated and vulnerable, had struck without mercy.

Ross had been a boy with a solemn demeanor even before the drowning occurred. She had always recognized in him the same longing for acceptance that she craved herself. His need resonated with hers, and she had seen his personal tragedy as a golden opportunity. She moved in and attacked his wounded heart with every warm fuzzy affection she could muster. But she had been subtle, oh, so subtle. Like a devious imp she had measured his every reaction to her positive projections. She had learned to cater to his moods and pander to his frustrations until he was dependent on her for the daily courage to face life. She had steered him into marriage, never once letting on that she would take anyone she could get.

But justice didn't sleep forever. She would ultimately have to pay the price for her opportunistic behavior. Ross would see the discoloration now. He would no longer be able to look past it. She would be forced to endure his scorn. Even if he never said it directly or even implied it, they would both know how guilty she was. She might even lose him. It wouldn't matter how well she performed as homemaker and wife, her learning to enjoy the same things he did, even pretending to like the same foods, watch the same sort of violent movies he liked, none of it would matter now if their child died or was abnormal. Even her unabashed willingness to cater to his every sexual fantasy could not balance this weight of sin.

She made a feeble effort to muster the positive thinking she had learned as she was growing up. She reminded herself how committed she was to selflessness and virtue, all the good Christian characteristics they talked about in Sunday School. How God could use the painful events in her life to shape her into someone He could use and approve of. But, truth be known, every good thing in her was not her own but was in fact a fee she had paid in an effort to buy some normalcy in life.

She knew she was wallowing in self-pity, but what of it? Hadn't she had enough misery in her life, growing up with a disfigured face in a world where glamour was everything? Was she supposed to just sit back and watch her marriage fall apart? Hadn't she done more than anyone should have to do to have a good life?

In spite of her anger and self-pity, Shelley knew that

tomorrow she would be her usual sweet self. The baths of self-pity were something she allowed herself. Never able to avoid that particular sin completely, she had come to believe that if she indulged in it at times and places where no one could know she was doing it, it actually helped her. Like a great steam boiler bleeding off pressure to keep from exploding, she would vent her rage at the unfairness where only her and God could know about it. She wasn't so sure this time, though. The usual feelings of ease that followed her inward wrath seemed elusive now. Perhaps the stakes were too high this time.

Or maybe she could no longer lie to herself. Weren't the private pity-parties just a masochistic exercise she did, hoping that private suffering and self-loathing would somehow stand in for the kind of merciless teasing she got when she was in grade school?

"Spot," they had called her. "Spot." They would use the word in a sentence as if they were reciting the first-grade reader, "See Spot run. Run, Spot, run!" At least the covert abuse allowed her to pretend sometimes that they weren't really talking about her. Except when the kinder children chastised the ones who talked that way. Then it was obvious to everyone that they were referring to her cheek. People just didn't know when to keep quiet, especially kids.

She felt as if there were a wedge inside her chest, slowly driven by the twisting sensation of her emotions. Things got tighter and fuller, until she feared the pressure would cause her torso to fracture in a fit of desperate release, like a gigantic stone being split by the pressure of a tree root.

She wanted to cry, thought crying was fitting and proper. She was able to cry, but the outward manifestations of her emotions had become disconnected by years of deliberate restraint, until she was never sure if what came out of her was genuine or rather some façade her fears had dreamed up to protect her.

She believed she had a great strength inside her, but it was that curious strength found only in people of guarded sensitivity. The quantity of joy allowed to cross her drawbridge was carefully measured to insure no Trojan horse of disappointment got within the fortress of her heart.

CHAPTER SIX

Ross was still in bed at 8 o'clock, feeling like trying to sleep had been a waste of time. His slumber had been shallow and sporadic. He got up and made the bed haphazardly. He was stumbling to the bathroom when the doorbell rang. He grabbed his jeans and went to answer the door. His sister Robin stood there clutching a small white sack. "Got a couple bagels here; you can have one if you give me some coffee," she said.

"You can have all the coffee you want, if you go make it while I get dressed. I won't be long." Ross's face was unshaven, his hair disheveled and his eyes underlined with dark circles. Robin could tell he'd had a rough night and a rough day before it.

"Mom told me what happened," Robin said. "I figured you'd be alone this morning. You're in for a hard day, I'll bet. I figured I'd help you get it started right."

When Ross got back downstairs, Robin had toasted the bagels and spread each with a thick layer of cream cheese. The strong smell of coffee hit his nostrils and woke him up more than anything yet had.

"Thanks, Robin," he said and sat across from her at the kitchen table.

"I wouldn't worry too much," Robin said. "They do wonders with preemies these days. I expect Shelley's family will make a big production of it, though." Her opinion of Shelley's family was no secret to Ross. She considered them shallow and prone to melodrama.

"You talk like there's nothing to worry about. I'm worried," Ross said.

"I didn't mean that. But you know as well as I do how the Clarks will treat it like the biggest tragedy ever to hit mankind. As if they're the only bunch that ever had anything hard happen to them. They'll be crying with each other and supporting one another and telling everyone who'll listen every detail. When the baby comes home, they'll have a party and act like a miracle has occurred. Admit it Ross, you get sick of the attention that family gives itself."

"Well, today they will give it to me," he cheerfully replied.

"You mean to Shelley, don't you?" Robin said. "The only attention you'll get is what drips off her.

"You're just jealous 'cause the Clarks are a close family and we're not," Ross said

"We're a close family, too. Not as big as them, but we're close," Robin said. "It's not just that."

"Just what is it then?" Ross countered.

"The Clark family has never had any problems. None of them have been in jail or gone to a mental hospital. They always get preference in town. Every one of them was treated like something special in high school. They all go to college and get married to someone else who has their nose just as high in the air as they do. They all get good jobs because of who they are." Robin paused to get a breath. "And they think they deserve it; they think they're special. You know what I mean. The worst thing that's ever happened to them is what happened to Shelley."

"You mean Shelley's face?" Ross said.

"Yes, that's what I mean, little brother. Don't get me wrong. You know I love Shelley to death. She's the one member of the Clark family that isn't stuck up. I'm glad you got her. I wouldn't trade her for anything. But without the stain, she'd probably be worse than the rest."

"I suppose you think the only reason they let her marry me was because she wasn't perfect?" Ross said.

"Don't tell me it hasn't crossed your mind," Robin said. She was known for her direct manner, and Ross knew she worked hard to maintain the reputation. He usually enjoyed her total lack of pretense, but this was blunt, even for her.

"Sure it has," Ross said.

"But you've done your part for the Clarks, too, you know," Robin said.

"How's that?" Ross said.

"Look around here, little brother. What do you see?" She swept her head from side to side for emphasis.

Ross scanned the kitchen with his eyes, pretending that she meant tangible things. "Let's see, range, refrigerator, toaster, coffee pot…"

"Not that stuff. I mean look at you and Shelley. The traditional American family unit, high school sweethearts, engagement announcements properly published in the newspaper and that in a day when most couples live together first," Robin said.

"No, most couples don't live together first!" Ross interjected. "That's just more of your liberal propaganda."

Robin went on, never missing a breath, "You honeymooned in Niagara Falls. House with a white picket fence, sedan and pickup truck—not new, but nice—swing set in the back yard, regulars at church and Sunday school. You guys are a poster couple for family values. You two just drip with hominess and tradition. You're the personification of the American dream. All the protocols of family establishment honored completely. You guys belong in the 1950s. Yuck."

Ross was laughing now. "Yeah, you're right, Shelley even enters apple pies in the county fair," Ross said.

"See what I mean? You've become a Clark, Ross. The name on the mailbox might be Martin, but the house and the people inside say Clark. And you, the son of a drunk."

Ross ignored that last comment. "Funny you should mention that swing set," he said. "When I put it together, I drilled two holes in the wrong spot. I measured from the wrong end, so these two holes look like a mistake. It doesn't hurt a thing, you see. But, Shelley's dad sees these holes, and you would not believe how important it was to him to point them out to everyone in the family, first chance he got. After a while, I think her mother made him stop. It was like he had found a way to put me down and get away with it. I couldn't believe the guy."

"It hurt, though, didn't it?" Robin probed. "You wanted to drill some holes in his face, didn't you?" She gave Ross a knowing look.

"Oh, I guess it did, some," Ross admitted.

Robin was sitting there smiling as if she had cornered her little brother and wanted to gloat over the triumph. Ross reached out and patted her on the shoulder

"There, there, it's all right Robin. I get it now. You really are jealous." He knew there was no truth in it, but it made him feel better to make the accusation.

"We'll see who's jealous of who after you spend all day telling the story of the baby over and over again to every Clark son, daughter, aunt, uncle, in-law and outlaw in three surrounding counties. They're gonna descend on Heritage Community Hospital like a swarm of bees. By the end of the day, you'll be so sick of Clarks, you'll want a divorce. Of course, Shelley will be happy to give each and every one the same full and flowery account of what happened."

"Let's talk about something else," Ross said. "I'm gonna see a lot of Clarks today, and I don't want to be carrying any of your contempt for them on my shoulders. They've been nice to me for the most part." He was surprised at how well Robin understood what it was like being married into the Clark family.

"How's Beany Boy doing?" Robin said. "Beany Boy" was her pet name for Randall. "Does he like the idea of a baby brother?"

"He's been pretty quiet about it. Shelley thinks he knows he won't be the center of attention any more. She's probably right. We've spent a lot of time talking about the new baby. Never mind how much her mother and sisters have fussed about it where he could hear them."

"Yeah, and since the new baby was premature, he'll get treated like he's even more precious. Beany Boy's gonna need his Aunt Robin to balance things out for him. But don't you worry, brother, Aunt Robin can handle it. By the way, what did you name him?"

"Shelley wants to call him Donny," he said, hesitating and avoiding Robin's eyes.

"That's Shelley's idea?" she said.

"I've considered it too, on my own," Ross said.

"So does that mean what I think it does?" Robin said.

"What do you think it means?" Ross said.

"That you're finally getting over what happened?" Robin said. She wished she had let it be. The scared-rabbit look on her brother's face revealed more than his words ever would. She usually liked being direct and the way she was able to unnerve people with her candor. But this time she felt bad.

"I'm sorry. That isn't any of my business maybe?" she said.

"It's okay. Who knows what 'getting over it' means anyway?" Ross said.

"Hey, it might help you in the long run," Robin said. "A cute little dude running around with your buddy's name. Gotta be a plus."

As much as Ross wanted to think otherwise, it was painfully evident that Robin was right about the Clarks and their behavior at the hospital. Shelley acted precisely as she had described, treating each relative who came in to the full story of her baby's premature birth.

They seemed to have a heightened interest in the baby, and Ross felt that it was linked to the name they had chosen for him. There was no way they could miss it, but it was uncomfortable to dwell on. He wondered how much had been said when the relatives first heard the name from other sources than him and Shelley. There were a few who got the name directly from Ross and Shelley, and there was no mistaking the hesitation, the mild surprise, maybe even shock that people felt. They raised their eyebrows, betraying what was passing through their minds upon recognition of the name. Each time Ross saw it, he got more uncomfortable.

The young Dr. Riley came in and looked at Shelley. "You can go home tomorrow. There's no reason for you to stay here.

You two parents can get in to see him any time you want. I'd like to see you stay with him, but the insurance company won't pay after tomorrow. So unless you want to sleep in a chair..." He shrugged.

"No thanks. We only live a few minutes away," Shelley said.

When the doctor left, Ross turned to his wife. "So, what do you think I should do this week, Shell?" he asked.

"You mean besides take me home tomorrow?"

"I mean maybe I should try to get a couple days work while he's still in here. I can't take a couple weeks, although he might be here that long. If I work now maybe I can get a few days when we bring him home."

"Worried about another mouth to feed, honey?" Shelley asked.

"Not exactly, I just don't know how long they will put up with me wanting to stay close to home," Ross said. "If I act as if I'm eager to work, maybe they'll stretch it a little farther. I'm just afraid that if I don't stay in touch with John about this, he'll put me on some 1,500-mile route and not give me any notice. Then I'll have to go out, and that will be the end of staying close to home. He'll figure I got what I asked for. There are some guys that milk stuff like this for all it's worth, and I think he sees through it. If I see the boss every day, I can keep him up to date about how the baby's doing and grab some good local stuff as it comes up. Maybe I can show him I'm not trying to take advantage like some do."

"Kiss up, you mean?" asked Shelley with a wry smile.

"Kiss up, I mean," replied Ross matter-of-factly. They both smiled.

CHAPTER SEVEN

"As far as the doctor can tell, there is nothing out of the ordinary about Donny," Shelley told Ross when he showed up to get her around 9 o'clock the following morning.

"Yes, there is," Ross said. "He's got an extraordinarily beautiful mother. Any fool can see that." He slung his arm around her shoulders and gave her a quick squeeze.

"I'll go along with the extraordinary part," Shelley demurred.

They drove home and took inventory of groceries. Ross made a quick trip to get what Shelley lacked so that she could spend the rest of the day relaxing and not have to go out.

Ross called work, and they said they would call him back when they found an assignment for him. It wasn't 10 minutes before they called him. They told him they wanted him to pick up a load in Altoona, a town in central Pennsylvania. He would be able to go out and return in about eight hours. It was ideal as far as Ross was concerned.

"You have to go so soon," Shelley moaned.

"But this is a good one, Shell. I'll be back before midnight, Lord willing and the creek don't rise," Ross spouted cheerily. "Just like a real working man, eight hours and then home again."

"I've heard words like that before," she said, with a crooked purse of her lips.

"I guess maybe you have," he said apologetically. "Traveling is an unpredictable thing, even for someone who does it all the time. I wish I could make you a promise." Ross remembered the accident that had delayed him on his way home Friday. Soon he would see wrecks with increasing frequency as the advent of winter impinged rudely on the trucking industry, bringing with it roads that could be slippery and treacherous. He decided he should say something upbeat.

"You're gonna call Mom and have her bring Randy back, aren't you?" Ross asked.

"I said he had to come back when I got lonesome. I guess I'm gonna be lonesome," Shelley said. "You want some sandwiches and a thermos, I suppose."

"Why don't you let me get it," he said. "When you get both babies here at home it'll be harder to do that stuff for me. I might as well get used to it. You need to rest anyway. Randy is going to be enough for you today."

He put on a clean uniform with a bright white patch over the left pocket that said "H.A.M." in bold blue embroidery and "Ross" in a somewhat smaller script over the right pocket. Wearing the uniform was part of his job, so the company said. Since the drivers met the customers more frequently than any other employees, it was important that they make a good impression. Ross considered it a perk, since only drivers were provided with the uniforms free of charge. Another symbol of success or significance, something he took some pride in.

He gave Shelley a warm hug and kissed her with all the tenderness he could manage. He felt the start of a tear himself as he picked up his things and reached for the door. It was always a drag leaving the house. It was worse now, with the uncertainty about their newborn. Although he expected to be gone only about eight hours, he was going on the road and nobody could say for sure when he would return.

The look in Shelley's eyes as he turned around and went through the door was something he could not quite fathom. He thought he saw a look of relief in her eyes. That was something he had never seen before. It was disconcerting to him, and he pondered the strangeness of it as he drove across town to the terminal.

He was used to seeing a wistful look from Shelley as he departed for his runs. It always made him feel partly bad, because he knew she would miss him, and partly good for exactly the same reason. Why she might be happy to see him go after all the drama of the weekend was a mystery.

He decided to pay particular attention to the way she acted when he slipped into bed beside her around midnight. Normally she would get up to greet him if he came in late. She seemed to think it was her duty to give him a hug and kiss, although it was usually accompanied by a deep yawn. He always chuckled to himself when she yawned that way. He believed it was never genuine, but an affectation she used to dissuade him from any notions of sex. The yawn meant, "Don't bother asking, I'm too sleepy to make love."

Ross arrived at the terminal and found it strangely quiet. He rarely went out at an odd time like this. He had never left for a trip in the middle of the day before that he could recall. The only unit sitting in the lot was his, and it looked alone and forlorn out there, with all the space surrounding it, a harbinger of the loneliness he would soon have to deal with as he worked his way eastward across the rolling hills. He went into the dispatch office to get his papers and found himself face to face with John Murphy, who asked him a lot of questions about Shelley and the baby.

It was nice of the boss to act so concerned about him, but Ross believed the man's concern was just that, an act. Murphy was expected to express appropriate compassion toward his people. Ross thanked him for his concern and promised to keep him up to date.

Ross was just getting ready to roll out when Leeroy Foust came rolling through the gate in his truck.

The older man tooled his rig up beside Ross's with deftness only a true master could possess. He stopped the truck by setting the parking brakes. The heavy machine eased to an abrupt stop with the running boards on both vehicles parallel to one another and just enough space between the mirrors so that the doors could be opened without one striking the other. Leeroy shut the engine off while the rig was still rolling and was striking a match to light the cigarette in his mouth just as the window came down on his door. Ross was wondering how the older man could seemingly do the work of three hands with only two when the quick gray eyes came up to meet his and through a thick cloud of smoke, Leeroy grinned in his usual way.

"What's your hurry, Laddybuck?"

Ross knew it was a joke, as did all the people who worked with Leeroy. It was Leeroy who always seemed to be in a hurry. He was a thin, wiry man with outsized hands. His finger joints were knobby from arthritis, and the first two fingers were stained by tobacco. He wore a red cap with the brim curled tightly down on the sides. The downward sweep of the brim was met by the upward sweep of the ends of his mouth, almost forming a circle. It made his long face seem almost round and gave the man a distinctiveness that people never forgot.

From the diners in southern New Jersey to the big truck stops in Illinois, Leeroy Foust was greeted by his first name more often than Ross was in his hometown. He had been an over-the-road driver since before there were interstate highways and could retire whenever he wished. He kept going, though. "Don't like fishing," was all he ever said if anyone suggested he take his pension.

"Do I look like I'm in hurry?" Ross said. "You're the one with the jealous husbands chasing you up and down the road."

The older man grinned. He had a reputation of being a ladies' man in his younger days, and Ross knew he liked to be teased about it.

"You're only partly right there, Laddybuck. There are jealous husbands all right, but it's not them doing the chasing. It's their wives."

Ross guffawed, "You wish!"

"What are you doing still here so late?" Leeroy asked.

"Well," Ross said slowly and with measured matter-of-factness, "when you're the top hand you get to start whenever you want." He looked at Leeroy with one eye winking slyly.

"Hu, hu, huuh!" Leeroy almost choked as his laughter disrupted the flow of smoke and irritated his throat. "That's a good one, Laddybuck!" Then with all seriousness, "Everybody okay?" Ross realized then from the look in his friend's eyes that he cared deeply.

"Yeah, Leeroy, at least we think so. I guess you heard our baby came early?"

"They were talking about it this morning when I left. I didn't expect to see you out so soon."

"Well, he's gonna be in the hospital for a few days at least. I can't do anything except sit around and worry, pester Momma when she doesn't need to be pestered. I figure I might as well try to make a buck while I can. I'll take a few days when we bring him home from the hospital, I guess."

Leeroy nodded. "Where you heading out to now? Or do top hands get to sit in the lot all day and listen to rock and roll on the FM?"

"No, even us favorites have to hammer. I'm going to Altoona. Supposed to drop and hook and come straight back. They're trying to keep me close to home, best they can."

"If you'll wait till an old man swaps trailers, I'll chase you that way. That is unless you're too good to run with an old timer."

"No, I'd appreciate the company. I'll even help you swap out," Ross said. The loneliness Ross had dreaded would not materialize, at least for a while yet. He would be running with a man everyone in the company admired. Ross was accustomed to loneliness, but the events of the weekend and the uncertainty surrounding them gave him a need for reassurance. He knew he could gradually unload all his fears on Leeroy in the space of a few hours.

The older man's seasoning and confidence would help Ross gain a perspective from which he could face whatever happened in the next few weeks, whether good or bad. Ross did not realize and would not have articulated this to anyone had he been asked; yet the overall sense of well being that Leeroy's company brought gave him a vigor he could almost touch.

"You want to lead this time?" Leeroy queried into the CB.

"Nope, I get tired of having to slow down and wait for you. It's easier to stay behind and just match your pace."

"I guess you're not so concerned about your boy that you could leave off teasing an old man for a day, huh?" Leeroy said. "I declare. You're a cold one, Ross."

The two men took to the highway with Leeroy in the lead, the only position Ross felt comfortable with. Leeroy knew Ross didn't want him on his tail where he could scrutinize his every action. Not that Leeroy would have been critical of him, but Ross did feel subordinate to the old man and preferred a deferential position. They put their CB radios on an empty channel to converse undisturbed.

"You know I don't mean all my teasing, don't you?" Ross said.

"Yes, you do. You mean to tease, that is." Leeroy said. "I know you don't mean any harm. People in this occupation are too hard on each other, you know?

"Aren't all guys kind of hard on each other?" Ross asked. He expected to get one of Leeroy's philosophical discourses and was not disappointed.

"There is probably no other occupation where men show each other so little mercy as in long-distance trucking," Leeroy said. "The nature of this work creates rugged independence. Only men who can work well unsupervised are able to do this job for long. Travel is difficult for anyone, even in modern times. A trucker has got to be able to think for himself and make sound decisions repeatedly to minimize his difficulty. When a man gets good at doing something like this on his own, it gives him a lot of confidence. On the CB radio he's pretty well anonymous. If he wants to criticize one of his fellow drivers, he can do it with little fear of getting a poke in the nose."

"I guess you're right, Leeroy. A lot of these guys talk like they're experts about nearly everything. I guess it's easy to have a big mouth when nobody can see who you are."

Ross knew about the kind of derision that could come his way from other truckers. On many occasions, a more experienced man had chastised him for small errors. Being a novice made even unwarranted scorn seem valid, and Ross was slowly learning that some truckers harassed greenhorn drivers like himself as a sort of sport. Running with Leeroy would ensure that anything negative coming his way would be countered by the words of a better and more accomplished man.

The two friends drove out into the afternoon, conversing on the radio with a mixture of jokes and serious conversation. Ross told his friend everything there was to know about the weekend, the baby and Shelley.

They reached the 28 mile-marker and both men remembered the wreck they had driven past the preceding Friday. "See those fresh marks there?" Leeroy said.

"Sure do," Ross said. There was no mistaking the additional gouges. "Fresh ones on top of old ones. A lot of stories in those marks, I guess."

"Yep. It's the way the road is curved there. I guess it just doesn't bank enough. If you aren't holding her into the turn, she just drifts out into that median there. By the time a driver feels his wheels leave the road and looks up, it's too late to get back on track, I guess. Probably they see the pier right there and freeze instead of trying to steer back. Who knows? Some places you nod off, you can get away with it. Not here, though."

"Heard that!" Ross quipped.

Leeroy's voice got more and more solemn as he spoke of the wrecks he had seen. His voice even got an angry tone now. "You know, there's no such thing as an accident, don't you?"

"Whatta you mean?" Ross said.

"I know they call them accidents. Mostly though, things like that happen because somebody wasn't paying attention or thought they could do the impossible. That driver, probably all those drivers, knew they were getting sleepy. They just didn't want to shut down. Maybe they were behind schedule and were trying to make up time. Maybe they thought they could prop their eyes open with caffeine. Or maybe somebody told them they would be in trouble if the load were late, a thousand maybes. Thing is, when you're sleepy, you're sleepy. Bed is the only place for you. Remember that, Laddybuck."

"I think some old-timer preached that to me for a week

or so when I was being broke in a couple years back," Ross said with mild sarcasm in his voice.

"Sorry about that, Ross. Don't mean to be preaching at you." Leeroy sounded contrite now, like a man who knew he had gotten carried away and regretted it.

"No, not at all. I guess you can't remind a guy too much when it comes to stuff like that. I know sometimes I get sleepy and don't want to be. It's real easy to tell yourself it will pass or to open the window and pour another cup of coffee or whatever. I guess it's a matter of pride mostly."

"That's it, Laddybuck. Pride has put more guys in the graveyard than anything else. A man's always comparing himself to other men, always thinking that if he can do it, I ought to be able to do it. Trouble is, men have different talents. What one fellow can do well, another's just wasting his time. It doesn't matter what it is, driving a truck or running a farm or selling shoes, some are just better at it than others.

"A man is lucky if he gets into a line of work where he can use his strong points. Being able to stay awake is an important one for a trucker, but it isn't everything. Most important is this: Get the rig from point A to point B in a reasonable amount of time, without having a wreck or getting a ticket. Do that, and you're a good driver. They'll even tolerate you being ugly if you can keep it out of the ditch. Just ask an expert like me." With that Leeroy laughed, and the conversation took on a lighter tone.

"You said that now, I didn't," Ross said, chuckling.

"You don't have to agree so easy, you know."

"Momma taught me to respect my elders, Leeroy."

"You just keep that up, Laddybuck. Us elders don't see a whole lot of that these days. By the way, what are you going to call your new son?"

The question, the sudden change of subject, caught Ross off guard, and his levity took a nosedive, one he could feel. It didn't make sense. He and Shelley had talked about the name, and it hadn't bothered him much at all. Why did it now? His shoulders dropped a little as the name with all its baggage took center stage. He knew he was hesitating to answer and did not wish to convey any of his true feelings about the name to Leeroy. He stumbled to reply, his voice now clumsy and full of words. "We thought we might just call him Donny, well actually Donald Andrew Martin. Sounds real dignified, don't you think?"

"Was that the name of your father or some relative?" Leeroy asked.

"No, actually it was the name of my best friend in high school."

Leeroy could tell from the sound of Ross's voice that there was gravity associated with the name, and his curiosity was piqued. Leeroy felt a little strange now, but it was not yet full-blown apprehension. He blundered on.

"You say it *was* your best friend's name?" Leeroy said. "I expect he moved away or something?" The pause in Ross's reply was telling. Leeroy suspected the answer before it came.

"He drowned, Leeroy, in 1993."

Leeroy Foust brought his open palm up to the side of his head with a resounding slap. He had been told somewhere along the way about Ross's past. He remembered something, though vague, about that drowning. It had been really hard on Ross, or so he had been told. It was not a subject he should bring up casually. Leeroy had simply forgotten. But wait, if Ross was naming his new son after his old friend, that was a good sign. Didn't such a thing mean that Ross had overcome the experience and was making a statement to that effect by naming his son after the friend? Of course it did. Now was not the time to apologize, but to validate Ross's choice of names.

"Do it gracefully, though, you old fool," he told himself as he keyed the CB mike again. He knew that talking on a radio was an inferior way to communicate, since you couldn't judge anything from facial expression. He should listen closer.

"Oh, I remember reading about that in the paper," Leeroy said. "I didn't know you then, though. Must have been a hard thing for you to take at your age?"

Ross could hear the sympathy and hesitation in Leeroy's voice.

"Well, yes, it was," he said with an obvious drag in the pitch of his voice. He had a desire to tell Leeroy all the painful details about how it had happened, unload the full weight on those sympathetic, fatherly ears. But he said nothing.

There was a pause now in the flow of conversation. As if on cue, a small convoy, maybe five or six trucks, refrigerated units, went around the two H.A. Murphy trucks. The faster rigs were averaging something more than 70 mph, Ross guessed, slipping quickly by in rapid succession and giving both men an excuse for the extended silence. The faster trucks were dressed up with varying amounts of extra lights down the side and along the perpendicular edges of the boxy trailers. It was largess that only a few trucking companies would provide for the vanity of their drivers but a mark of pride to the independent trucker—extra lights were something of a status symbol among drivers.

There were a lot of independent owner-operators who hauled produce, and they tended to stick together when they could, making the most of their gutsy engines on the uphills and holding back as little as possible on the downhills. Always, they kept a sharp eye out for the state police, who hid in any number of good ambush spots with their radar guns. The cops were usually as generous as they could be to these hard-working, self-employed purveyors of lettuce and tomatoes, yet kept some arbitrary limit, known only to them, on their gracious tolerance of excess speed.

While the trucks were passing, Leeroy said to Ross, "Let's go to 19 and see if anything is going on."

"Gone," replied Ross, switching to the channel that truckers commonly used.

The last of the glittering trailers cleared the nose of Leeroy's tractor. He keyed his microphone and with a cheerful briskness, calculated to initiate a response, said, "You missed me, big truck."

"We appreciate that, Hamster." "Hamster" was a slang term recently attached to the Murphy fleet. Something Ross figured they had asked for when they embellished the sides of the new trailers with the bold yellow logo that sported the capital letters H. A. M. "Oh well, it could be worse," he thought to himself.

Silence filled up the new channel just as it had the last. To Leeroy's chagrin, there was no ongoing exchange between him and the produce trucks. He wanted to give Ross some time to forget his faux pas. He knew that among barehanded men, there was an unwritten, unspoken code. You didn't corner another man emotionally. That is what Leeroy feared he had done. The silence got longer and more uncomfortable.

"Like I was saying before, Laddybuck, there is no such thing as an accident," Leeroy finally said. "You take those cowboys that just went by us, not a half-length of space between any of them. You can bet if they pile up somewhere, they'll be blaming it on something else, or someone else. They all know they're taking a risk. They just don't think it will happen to them. If they put a proper amount of distance between them, they might get separated. They can't have that."

Ross listened to Leeroy's cynical voice overtly chastising the drivers in the high-speed convoy. He expected to hear the usual "mind your own business" or other indignant response from the drivers. When nothing like that came, he wondered if maybe the drivers allowed that Leeroy was correct? More likely, though, they were completely nonplussed and didn't care to bother giving the correcting voice any attention. It wasn't normal for Leeroy to talk that way to other truckers, no matter how foolish their actions might be. He sensed that Leeroy was foundering and assumed his usual tone of deference toward the man who had become something of a mentor to him.

"I know what you're saying, Leeroy. Most accidents are somebody's goof; somebody's got their head up their butt, right?"

"You got it. It's always because someone didn't do what they were trained to do or because they didn't use common sense. Sometimes they even let themselves get distracted or try something without thinking of the possible results. The point is, things don't just happen. It's careless people mostly."

When they reached exit 23, the middle of the state and the

place where Ross left the interstate, their talk had degenerated into something neither felt was worthwhile. Yet, strangely, silence was less appealing to them. Ross eased the empty rig down the steep off-ramp onto US 220 and turned south. He was content to say his goodbyes as the intensity of the radio signal faded with the increasing distance between them.

CHAPTER EIGHT

Ross was glad to be away from Leeroy now. The older man's comments about the nature of accidents left him feeling depressed. Ross wondered how much Leeroy knew about his past. Did he know that Ross was responsible for the death of his friend, Donald Andrew Ritts? Why else would he say that there was no such thing as an accident? The charge certainly fit in Ross's case.

Ross felt disappointed. He had always considered his relationship with Leeroy to be something special. The older man's backhanded insult stung Ross. It hurt, but on the other hand, Ross felt it was deserved, and for that reason, he welcomed it, as if each moment of suffering could bring him closer to clearing the debt.

Ross realized then that he looked up to Leeroy the way most young men looked at their fathers. Ross's real father had never done much with him. Gerald Martin had rarely done anything worthwhile at all. He worked a factory job, slept an inordinate amount and spent the remainder of his time in a little bar on the lower side of town.

When he talked to people in his deep, masculine, measured tones of voice, every syllable sounding like it had been cut out with a saw, the words blocked and stacked like so much cordwood, he sounded negative and antagonistic. Only the people who knew him well could ignore the tone and understand it for what it was: a lifelong attempt to seem like a deliberate and self-controlled man, to belie his slavery to the bottle.

The bar was a run-down, brown-shingled little joint that looked like it had once been part of something grand and elaborate, except that the better part had been picked up and carted off to some new location. The leftover space had been converted into gravel parking lot.

Potholes had developed in the lot and had gone without repair for so long that they had become miniature ponds, complete with small tufts of grass at the edges. The grass grew because only the extremely drunken let the wheels of their vehicle get close to the edge; only occasionally did someone too drunk to navigate out onto the street get his battered car saddle bagged on the edge of the holes. Patrons of the bar had given each pothole a name, and it was generally accepted that anyone too drunk to avoid "Lake Superior" or "Lake Michigan" was unfit to drive home anyway. In that case, someone else would offer the tipsy motorist a lift. The car would remain there as testimony to their inability to drive or to handle liquor, or whatever else the barflies might choose to tease them about.

Such a seedy, poorly kept little joint could not have remained in business were it not for a loyal clientele of alcoholics who wished to indulge their cravings in secluded privacy, Ross's father among them.

The place was known as the " Snake Pit," though the title on the dirty glass sign hanging over the door was "The Heritage Hotel." The sign was like the rest of the place—neglected; its illumination, diminished by the lack of working bulbs, scarcely strong enough to contrast the letters in the darkness, seemed to say, "Let me die in peace." The bar's patrons embraced a philosophy not alien to that.

It had once been a hotel, back in the days when that part of town was central. Ross figured that if the rise and fall of this or that district can measure the maturity of a city, then the Heritage Hotel was the part of town in need of hospice care.

Everyone in town, it seemed, knew the roster of patrons of the Snake Pit. Ross had grown up believing he was substandard because of his father's "disease." His mother had said it was a disease, and Ross was unsure whether she meant it or used the notion as a crutch—a crutch she needed often when the ample paychecks his father drew were reduced to little more than a handful of ruffled, dirty bills lying on the dresser on Saturday mornings. Sometimes she would be lucky, and one of them would be a 50. But usually she was forced to get by on little or nothing. Most of Ross's clothing had come from secondhand stores and garage sales. Ross was determined that both of his sons would have better.

Ross reached the factory where he was supposed to pick up a trailer loaded with automotive batteries. It was a sprawling place with acres of room in the back to park trailers. He checked in with the security guard and put his empty trailer in the appropriate spot.

There was another tractor sitting there, and the driver had his window down and looked open and friendly, as if he hoped Ross would make some conversation with him. Probably the man had to sit and wait for his load to be ready, and the time was hanging heavy on his hands. Ross knew what it was like. But today he didn't have extra time, so he only nodded in a friendly way to the other driver and walked into the building.

He had been here enough that he knew his way around. He went to the shipping office but stopped at the payphone just outside of it to call home. There was no answer, of course. Shelley would be at the hospital. He left her a message on the machine so she would know what time he had called and then dialed his mother-in-law, figuring Randall would be there.

He told her where he was and asked if there was any news of the baby. She told him there was none. He asked to speak to Randall. "Hi, Daddy," the boy said. His voice was sad.

"You having fun with Grandma, son?" Ross asked.

"No," the child said, with no apparent regard for the way the statement might affect his grandmother. Ross wondered for a minute if he should tell Randall that his manners were bad and that he should be more considerate of his grandmother but decided it would be best to wait for a better time. He was only 4, and Virginia Clark knew how children tended to be insensitive.

"You miss Mommy?" Ross asked.

"Yeah, I was only home for a little while, and then she brought me back here," he lamented.

"Mom won't be at the hospital all day, sport," Ross said.

"Yes, she will," the boy stated, matter-of-factly. "She already has been." Ross supposed that three or four hours might well seem like all day to a 4-year-old.

"Well, she has to come home soon then," Ross said, filling his voice with the confident reassurance he knew the boy needed. "Tell you what, this weekend you and me can start building your little brother's cradle. You will help me, won't you?"

"Sure, Daddy," Randall said, as if he saw through his father's patronization.

After hanging up, Ross went into the shipping office to see about his load. The clerk, a middle aged redhead, seemed indifferent to his arrival. Truck drivers came and went at all hours of the day and night. Ross was nothing special. He gave her his load number and waited for her response, which came painfully slowly. He was about to ask if she had heard him when she opened her mouth and without looking at him said, "I got nothing ready for Murphy. Check back in an hour or so."

Ross knew he was expected to wait patiently for the load—not an easy task, since there was nothing for him to do with his time. He wondered if the people back in his dispatch office were under the impression that his load would be ready to go when he got there. He called his dispatch office and told them what was going on. He wanted to complain about the delay, but he knew what he would be told.

Wishing he had been more friendly to the other driver he had nodded at coming in, Ross made his way back out to the parking lot. The slow pace of his step must have showed he lacked shipping papers. The other driver leaned out of his window a little and said, "They're making you wait, too?"

"Looks like it," Ross reluctantly confessed. Having to wait like this always brought on the blues.

"I hate it when I have to wait like this," the man said.

"Don't we all," Ross told him. Then he decided to try

cheering up. No reason to spread the misery around. "How long you been here?" he asked.

"Since one. I wasn't supposed to pick up till five, though. Came in early 'cause I had nothing else to do. Thought maybe it might be ready sooner. No such luck."

"You get paid for sitting?" Ross asked.

"Not unless it goes four hours past time," the other driver lamented.

"Me neither," Ross said. Drivers like him were paid by the mile, paid for what they did. They were not compensated for waiting on freight, even if the time were lost out of their day. He would be expected to treat the waiting time as if it did not exist and go to work again when the shipper could provide him with something to haul. Since no one was charged with his time, no one cared whether it was wasted. There was no incentive on the part of his employer or their customer to see that he was busy. The trucking business was supposedly too competitive to allow any kind of payment for a driver's wasted time. Ross knew the real problem was that, for some mysterious reason, truck drivers were excluded from the fair labor standards laws. Therefore, he, like so many other hardworking American truck drivers, was left with no option but to wait. It didn't seem right to Ross. America was supposed to be concerned about fairness and equality. Leeroy called it "institutionalized abuse," but he seemed to have no remedy for it.

"Guess they think we're machines," the other driver said. "When you get your load, they'll expect you to go on and deliver it, too, won't they? No matter how much time you lost."

"Yeah, pretty much," Ross admitted. He resented being treated like a machine. There was nothing he could do about it, though; it was part of a truck driver's life. Drivers complained about it all the time, but it did no good. It was three in the afternoon, and Ross had hoped to be home again by seven or eight. There was no way to know when he would get home now.

"I'm glad it's only a three-hour drive back to the terminal in Heritage," he said. "If I had been expected to go to Springfield,

I would end up driving most of the night, and I haven't slept much lately."

"I hear you," the other driver said. "Even if you're not really capable of staying awake that long, you know they're not gonna allow wasted time while you were waiting on the freight. 'You were just sitting around,' that's what they tell you. Or maybe, 'you should have used the time to sleep.'"

Ross knew it was an unusual person who could sleep at any time of the day, especially if they were not weary. It seemed that truckers were expected to have that ability. He also knew that since he requested that they keep him close to home because of his family situation, it would seem ungrateful of him to gripe for any reason.

"In this line of work, you just have to take the good with the bad," Ross said. "You can make good money as a truck driver, but you sure have to earn it."

"True enough," the other driver said. "This isn't just a job. It's a lifestyle, and most won't stick with it long."

They had only talked about 20 minutes, when the other driver went in to check on his load. It was ready and Ross was left alone in the parking lot. He walked into the building and made a call to Shelley, apologizing for the delay and lamenting the fact that she had been right to fear he would not return as planned. She took it in stride. She had learned to do that. She had picked up Randall after spending most of the day at the hospital, and had resigned herself to another night without his presence.

The empty time stretching out before him weighted him down, and he worried about his newborn son, so many miles away, so fragile and so small that he could fit in a shoebox. Returning to his truck, he turned on the radio and lay down in the sleeper. He could at least relax.

He tuned in to National Public Radio. There was something about those stations. They all seemed to have broadcasters who talked in a measured monotone, as if that segment of the broadcasting field required a distinctive, flat way of talking, devoid of personality, without vitality or drama. If anything would put him to sleep, this was it.

The bubbling sound of Donny Ritts's desperate voice invaded his consciousness, and he started from the verge of slumber. Sitting upright in the bunk, he could still hear Leeroy's words. "Things don't just happen. It's careless people mostly."

He was afraid it would be this way—now he had the judgment of a man he looked up to mocking his efforts to mitigate his guilt. Ross had heard there was such a thing as a subconscious mind. He didn't know how any of that worked, but it must be true. He did know that every so often, something deeper than his thoughts would serve him up things to remember and think about without him ever choosing them.

He could almost picture an open hand, cupped a little to contain another dose of misery, rising up from a dark place inside him, bearing him another portion of guilt, as if he had cleaned up the last helping and it wouldn't do for him to run out. He thought perhaps he should just tell someone. Maybe if he just let the world know what he had done to Donny, he might at last be free from the torment. But he knew he couldn't bring himself to that. Too much time had gone by. He had accepted too much pity and comfort. To confess now would only reveal how long he had kept the truth to himself. No one needed to know. It couldn't help. It wouldn't have mattered then, and it didn't matter now. He couldn't save Donny. He had worked at the rocks until he was exhausted himself. They were too slippery; there was nothing to get hold of. The water was too fast. If he had left him sooner...maybe.

At intervals of an hour, Ross went back into the shipping office to ask if his load was ready yet. Five times it was not. He saw other drivers come and go. It seemed like he was the only one who had to wait.

Finally, he had his paperwork and called the H.A. Murphy office to report in. The shift had changed, and the girl who answered the phone didn't know he had been waiting. Her name was Trudy, and she was new to the staff, though fast gaining a reputation as a smart aleck. She asked, "What have you been doing? It's only a three-hour drive, and you showed out at 1:14."

Ross hesitated, wanting to be both sharp and sarcastic in his answer. But he held the frustration in check and spoke with measured calmness. "What do you think I've been doing?"

"I can't imagine," said Trudy, as if Ross were an annoying child.

"I've been waiting since 4 for a load that was supposed to be ready to go at 3:30."

Trudy showed no sign that she had even heard his answer and came back quickly with, "But it's ready to go now, right?"

"Yes, I've got it," Ross told her.

"Okay, I'll show you out at 9 p.m."

It was already past 9, and it would take him 15 minutes to hook up to the loaded trailer and get on his way, but he didn't say anything. He didn't feel like arguing with an airhead. Ross wondered if she talked that way to Leeroy. If she did, Leeroy would put her in her place real fast. Maybe even have her up in front of old man Murphy for an attitude adjustment.

It was well past midnight when Ross got back to the terminal. He dropped the loaded trailer in the line where it belonged, parked his tractor and turned in his papers. His assignment for the next day was by his name on the driver's board. He was supposed to pick up in Akron, Ohio, at 6 a.m.. If the first run had gone according to plan he would already have been asleep for four hours. "Gonna be a short night, Ross," he told himself. "Gotta sleep fast."

He went back out to his tractor and cranked up the engine so he would have the necessary heat. This time he would not need NPR to help him slumber. He could not go home to sleep. The trip to and from would take too much precious time. He set his alarm clock for 4 a.m. and climbed into the bunk. He wished he could talk to Shelley, cuddle up with her. It was so much easier to sleep when he was with her.

CHAPTER NINE

The rude, intermittent buzzing impinged on a conversation Ross was having with Shelley about the name for their baby. The sound took hold of him, carrying him quickly away so that the image of her face got dimmer and dimmer. Then suddenly he knew where he was.

Aware that he was expected in Akron shortly, he pushed back the thickness in his head. He felt a mild throbbing, surely the first deposit on a debt that later on his brain would have to pay with a steady installment of pain. It always happened like that when he didn't get enough sleep.

He pulled on his clothes, made up the bunk and got into the driver's seat. He pulled on his boots, grabbed his flashlight and got out into the chill air to do a quick vehicle inspection. He made sure there were no flat tires and that the turn signals all worked properly. He was supposed to do a more thorough inspection, but he had gotten into the bad habit of breezing through it for the sake of time.

By 6:23, he was crossing the state line into Ohio. He had time to stop at a fast food restaurant for coffee and some breakfast. He was on time for his pickup.

Loaded at 9:30, he called Shelley before starting for Heritage. She was excited. "He's breathing on his own. I called just a few minutes ago. They tried him this morning, and he's doing it just like he never needed the help to begin with!" Shelley said, as if every star in heaven had Donny's name on it.

"That's great, Shelley," he said numbly. Ross didn't feel as elated as Shelley sounded. He didn't feel much of anything. He was relieved, but somehow he couldn't rejoice yet. He did his best to sound happy, knowing anything less would bother Shelley. "Give him my love when you see him."

"When will you be home?" she asked.

"No telling. I take this one back, then see what they need," he said. It bothered him a little that she seemed to expect his employer to care as much about their problems as they did. He knew it was unrealistic, considering how much work his company had to do. He hadn't been away from her a full day yet. They would surely send him on another run when he got back.

"Okay. Love you," she said, with a slight pout in her voice.

"Love you, too," Ross said.

When he got back to Heritage, they sent him on another pickup, only 90 miles away, to Erie, Pennsylvania. This time he didn't have to wait, but he had to help load, and that took three hours. He got back to the terminal a little before 7 o'clock and was free to go home.

Shelley had a happy look on her face when Ross came throught the front door. "So, was he still breathing okay today?" he asked, looking over Randall's shoulder as he hugged his son.

"Not only that, he's gained an ounce," Shelley said.

"Gained an ounce. I guess that's a lot for somebody his size," Ross said.

"Actually, he's gained almost two since he was born," Shelley said. "You look tired, Ross."

"I drove about 600 miles. And with the loading labor, dropping and hooking trailers and so on, I also worked about five hours," he told Shelley. "I'm tired but not exhausted. It would be nice if they would let me work like this all the time. I could be home every other day."

"When are you going back out?"

"I'm supposed to show up at 7. I don't know if they will send me out or not," Ross said. "He's going to make it, isn't he, Shelley?"

"It looks like it," Shelley said. "Ross, are you crying? Ah, honey."

There was a mist starting to form in his eyes, and Shelley moved to embrace him. Though tears were understandable, she sensed there was something more to Ross's joy. She was more prone to tears than he was, and she had not cried about the baby's progress yet, though she was beginning to now, seeing Ross beginning to weep. "Come on to the kitchen, honey, I saved you some dinner." She tuned in a children's program for Randall and was grateful to see he was willing to stay in the living room.

Ross knew the relief he felt was deeper than he could share with Shelley. He had been thinking, deep down, that their baby might die. If that happened, he knew he would see it as some kind of divine retribution because of the drowning of Donny Ritts. Now that it appeared the child would survive, he felt a strange mixture of relief and guilt.

"I've felt sort of scared lately," Ross said. They were sitting at the kitchen table, and Ross was picking at the plate of food Shelley had set before him.

"Well, that goes without saying. I have been, too," Shelley said.

He looked at her and sighed. "It's like, ever since Donny drowned, I've been afraid that something else would go wrong. I figured this was it."

"Why would something else go wrong?" Shelley asked quietly. She was trying not to let her anxiety show, fearing that somehow, the issue about her carrying laundry would come up.

"I never told you the whole story," Ross blurted. It was as if that subconscious hand were prompting him to finally tell the truth about his friend's death.

Shelley's face was blank for a moment, then softened. She sensed it was time to listen. "There's something I don't know?"

"Something I've never been able to tell anyone," Ross whispered.

"You can trust me, honey," Shelley said, taking his hand in hers.

"Everybody thinks Donny and me were shooting the Devil's Gate and that he got carried away in the fast water or sucked under or something. They never even asked me what happened," Ross said.

"Other swimmers have drowned in the river, Ross. It just happens every once in a while," Shelley said.

"Not in that part. Not in the place where everybody in town has been swimming for God knows how long," Ross said. "Nobody else ever drowned shooting the Devil's Gate."

"I thought that was why they called it the Devil's Gate—because its dangerous," Shelley said.

"It's not as dangerous as it looks. I mean, well it is, of course, but not the way people think," Ross said. "The water is fast, that's true, but only in the place where the rocks squeeze it in. A few feet downstream the current is slow and easy to swim in. Everybody's afraid of it until they've done it once or twice. Then the guys act macho because they had the courage to try it. You don't tell people it's easy. If you're in the fast water you just let it carry you downstream. Most of it, you can touch bottom."

"Okay," Shelley said. "So the fast water didn't get Donny then?"

"The fast water got him all right," Ross said, sobbing ironically. "But not until I left him."

"I don't understand," Shelley said, not sure she wanted to hear what Ross meant by "I left him."

"Donny could swim, but he didn't like fast water. He said it could throw you into the rocks and maybe bang your head or something. I called him a wimp. I shamed him into shooting the gate with me."

"Yeah. You guys did it over and over. You were still doing it when it got dark. That's what I heard," Shelley said.

"Twice. We only did it twice, me and Donny. There were other guys there, too. It was getting dark all right. We had done it once, because I pushed him to try it. I thought if he did it one more time he would get over being afraid. He wasn't afraid, he was just being cautious. But not me. Oh no, not me. It was getting dark. We were edging along the rocks, just kind of easing into the gate, instead of going upstream and hitting the center on the way down. Donny got his foot caught between these two big rocks.

"He tried to pull out, but his foot was twisted. He couldn't get free. I tried to pull him but I couldn't get a grip on anything. I tried diving down to move the rocks away from his foot. That was hard with the water so fast. I got one to move a little, but it slipped. When it fell back down it wedged him tighter yet. The current kind of twisted him around; pushed him between the two big rocks.

"He could lean there against the rock and relax, except that he had to hold his head and shoulders up. I called for help, but the other guys were leaving and I guess they couldn't hear me because of the noisy water. Or maybe they didn't see we were in trouble.

"He was laying there between the two rocks, his foot caught on the bottom, and the water was rushing up over his chest. He had to hold himself up against the current. I couldn't get him loose. I should have left him right away to go for help, but I was afraid he would lose his strength and fall under the water while I was gone. So I kept diving down, trying to get him free. The rocks were so slippery, I couldn't do anything.

"Finally, it was almost completely dark. Nobody was there except us, and I was getting tired. Then Donny started to panic. He thrashed and flailed around in the water, but he couldn't get free. He knew then. He knew he couldn't hold himself up against the water for very long.

"I had to get away from him. Then he went under. I went back to him and helped him up. It was hard. I kept losing my footing on the rocks. They were just so slippery. I got so tired I couldn't hold him anymore.

"I figured I had to get help. But every time I moved away from him, he'd start yelling, "Ross, don't leave me." Then I'd go back and try some more. Until I was so exhausted I could hardly pull myself out."

"I get it. You finally had to go for help. And when you got back with help it was too late," Shelley said. Her face was wet with tears. "Oh, Ross. You poor man."

"It was too late before I ever got out of the water. By the time I left him to get help, he was too weak to hold up against the current anymore. I knew he would drown. But if I had stayed, I might have, too. I got scared.

"So I went and got help. When we got back to the river, he wasn't there anymore. I guess when he drowned, he relaxed, his body went limp. I guess that's all that was necessary for him to get out. The current pulled him out or something. They found him downstream a little way. I tried to explain it to the firemen, but they thought I was too upset to know what happened. I must not have been making sense. Later, I just told everybody we got separated and I didn't know where Donny was."

Shelley was speechless. Ross had clearly been keeping the whole story to himself because he thought it was his fault that Donny had been caught and unable to get free. She could understand why he had such a burden of guilt. He prodded Donny into doing something he otherwise wouldn't have. It was one of those freak accidents that people never see coming.

There was cold, ironic cruelty to the way Donny's body had drifted from the rocks that had held him, after his life had expired and his muscles relaxed. Shelley supposed that it mocked Ross every time he remembered his efforts to get his friend free. If Donny had simply allowed himself to go limp, he probably would have lived, Shelley imagined.

It was fear that had killed him; a level of terror most people never experience had been Donny's companion when the water filled his lungs, after the will to hold onto life had dimmed from the lack of oxygen in his brain. Shelley shuddered as she imagined the incessant coolness defying his efforts to hold his breath, pushing down his nostrils, until the place in his throat that kept food and water going into the stomach could no longer prevent the rush of water into his lungs. She wondered if the terror had dimmed the way the strength in his muscles must have. He would have clung to life with all the strength he had. If he had simply surrendered to his fate without a fight, he might have won the struggle with the death angel.

Being torn between the possibility that Donny would drown if he left and the certainty that he would if he didn't leave had been a cruel choice, the kind of severe emotional trauma that drives people insane. Because of Ross's boldness, the two boys had fallen into an impossible situation. With no good choice, Ross had not been able to choose at all. He held himself responsible, and it was easy to see why. No wonder Ross had been keeping it to himself all this time. The sadness nearly overwhelmed Shelley, yet she pushed the gloom aside so she could reassure her trembling husband.

"Ross. I'm so sorry. I wish you had told me sooner. But I understand why you didn't. I want you to know, you did the best you could. Thank you for sharing it with me." She was kneeling on the floor now in front of his chair, with her arms wrapped around his waist. She wondered if now Ross would tell the story to anyone else. Should she tell someone or keep it to herself?

She decided that for now at least she would keep the secret. In time, Ross might want to open up to others. "If you want to keep it a secret still, Ross, that's okay. But it will be our secret now. If there is anyway I can help besides loving you, I will. You know that, don't you?"

Ross pulled Shelley up from the floor until she was in his lap and laid his head on her breast. The couple wept quietly. In the other room, Randall watched television, unaware.

❧

At each of the two Thanksgiving dinners—one with the Martins, one with the Clarks—the traditional prayer included an appeal for the well being of the baby in Heritage Community Hospital. The couple's somber mood was only partly because of their baby. Shelley let everyone assume it was the whole part. She tried to match Ross's mood, and it was not difficult. Her empathy was a sincere effort to share his torment.

The new knowledge filled Shelley with mixed feelings. If her relationship with Ross had been dependent on his pain, the way she suspected, it was even more so now. To have her relationship with Ross shored up was something she would take any way she could get. Yet it only added to her sense of inadequacy to know that their love was based not on his appreciation for her but on her willingness to help him keep the secret and to comfort him without condition.

She hadn't asked for this new dimension. She had done nothing to draw it out of him. She didn't need to feel guilty about it the way she did their courtship. Ross had been saving it and suffering it alone. Now it had been revealed; it was like a gift he had given her. By sharing his innermost reality, he had reached out for help. And it was her he needed. That was how it should be. But that didn't make their marriage more legitimate. It didn't make their love more real. Not in her view. It only made their false foundation that much broader.

༄

Ross spent most of that Saturday working on the cradle. He didn't have the whole winter to work on it as he had expected, and though he wanted to build it to perfection, he felt compelled to work with haste. He let Randall help him. That meant the little guy got to hang out in the basement workshop with his dad and occasionally hold a piece of wood or hand a tool to him. Ross let him rub some of the pieces with fine sandpaper, so the child could honestly say he helped.

By dinner time on Saturday all of the pieces were cut, shaped, sanded and ready to assemble. They could put it all together the following weekend, perhaps even get the finish applied. After a couple of coats of varnish, final sanding and polish, it would be ready to use. Shelley bought a new feather pillow and cut it down a little to make a custom fit mattress for the cradle. They had a regular crib to keep the baby in at night. The cradle would be placed in the living room and used mostly in the daytime.

The cradle was almost the same color as an antique drop-leaf table they had been given as a wedding present. Ross had tightened up the joints and refinished the table, and it had become the centerpiece of their dining room. They never actually dined in the room because they had no chairs to go with the table. It had become sort of a catch-all. Whenever Ross brought anything into the house, the newspaper or mail or something he had bought at the store, he would put it on the old table initially, until Shelley decided where it properly belonged. It was a bad habit, and Shelley pestered him about it. She tried to keep that room neat, since they did very little in it.

"Better to use the table for something than just look at it," Ross was fond of saying. It was a little disagreement they had, and they playfully argued with each other about it. It didn't really bother Shelley.

CHAPTER TEN

After two and a half weeks, Dr. Riley met Shelley in the hall outside the neo-natal ward. "Ready to take him home?" he asked. She had been expecting it.

"None too soon, I'd say," answered Shelley. "He and I are getting attached to this place. I'm on a first-name basis with most of the staff here. Any longer and I'd have to buy Christmas presents for everybody."

The doctor picked up Shelley's playful mood. "He's progressed in textbook fashion. I wouldn't be surprised if he wants a pony for Christmas."

Shelley immediately went to the phone and called the H.A. Murphy office. Kim, the regular daytime dispatcher, answered the phone. "Hi Kim, Shelley Martin here. Where did you send my man today?"

"I guess he's still in Butler. He hasn't called in empty yet," Kim answered.

"How about trying to get a message to him. I need him to call home. They are going to release our baby tomorrow."

"Oh, that is good news, Shelley. I suppose you want to tell him that, though, don't you?"

"Yeah, don't let on. Even though it won't be much of a surprise to him."

"Oh, look here. A load to Texas just came in. You want me to give it to Ross so he'll be out of your hair for a few days? I could keep him gone for a week with something like this." For an instant, Shelley believed Kim was serious. She caught herself just in time to keep from sounding shocked.

"You would do something like that for me?" she replied, as if sending Ross away were an option she might want to consider.

"No, I don't think I could stand the hangdog look on his face. It's bad enough when he has to go to New England," the dispatcher moaned.

Shelley no sooner got home from the hospital than the phone rang. Evidently, someone had embellished the message somewhere along the way. Ross sounded alarmed.

"Honey, what's up? They said I should call you right away. Is he okay?"

"Ross, he is more than okay. We can bring him home tomorrow!"

Ross felt in an instant as if some great weight had been lifted from his shoulders, yet for some reason he felt weaker instead of stronger now. He felt as if he might faint, although that had never happened to him that he could remember. He didn't even know what it felt like to faint. But suddenly, he was drained.

Shelley could hear the change in his voice.

"That's great, honey," Ross said, almost without breath.

"Are you okay, Ross? You don't sound all that happy."

"No, Shelley, I'm very happy. I just feel, I don't know. I kind of feel tired all of a sudden. I guess I'm just surprised is all, though I don't know why. We figured it would be soon," Ross said.

"Can you be home tomorrow then, to bring us both home?" she asked.

"Let me call in right away, the sooner I let them know, the better. I'll call you right back."

Ross hung up the phone and dialed the toll-free number to his dispatch office. Kim was tempted to try the tease about the Texas load on him, but she knew he would see through it. She told him to take the next two days, Thursday and Friday, which would give him a four-day weekend. As he dialed Shelley again he was beginning to feel better, beginning to appreciate how fortunate they were.

When he told her he would be home that night in time for dinner and would be staying until Monday, she fairly beamed through the phone.

"Ross, tomorrow's gonna be a great day!"

Ross felt like he might even cry. He did not want to look that way to the people he was working with now, though, unloading the truck. He gathered his composure and stood up straighter.

"I'm gonna hustle now and get this truck unloaded, so I can get home. Maybe I can get that cradle finished tonight. Love you, Shelley!"

"Oh, I love you, too, Ross, very much. I can't wait to see you!"

When Ross was finished and on his way home, he felt like the luckiest man on the face of the earth. The truck, now empty of its cargo, felt like it could float all the way to Heritage. The gray sky spit a few little squalls of snow as he headed north across the state highway, but they may as well have been drops of sunshine for all the damage they did to his mood.

He had finally accepted the name they had chosen for his son. Now that the boy had been pronounced healthy, the idea seemed rectified. Donald Andrew Martin, second son of Ross and Shelley Martin, was coming home to take his place. To not only round out their family, but to put to rest—symbolically at least—the death of his namesake so many years ago. Ross felt as if finally he could close the coffin, shovel in the sod and let his teenage pal rest in peace. Maybe now the final bubbling cries would stop haunting him.

Ross finished the cradle that evening, rubbing the final coat of varnish with steel wool and polishing it with paste wax lovingly. He was proud of the project; it looked better than he thought it would, considering how he had rushed through the assembly process. The fine straight grain of the wood seemed to mirror his hands as he worked. It was as good as anything he could have bought in any store around Heritage.

He relished the thoughts of the praise the cradle would bring him as all their friends, family and neighbors stopped in to see the new baby. He would do his best not to enjoy the plaudits. He would simply thank the people for the compliments and act as if such works of art could be produced by anyone, anytime they wished. He knew it would be false modesty but doubted if anyone would see that.

The fact that none of Shelley's friends would be able to buy one like it gave him some added satisfaction. He turned the piece upside down and carved his initials in the corner of the bottom. He even thought of carving the date too, but since carving the initials had been a tricky process he decided not to. His hands were tired from gripping the chisel and he thought he might slip and make an ugly gouge—no sense taking a chance with that. He could always do it later if he wanted, some time when his hands weren't tired.

He carried the piece upstairs to the family room and placed it next to the chair Shelley normally used. Shelley was bathing Randall in the tub when he walked into the bathroom. The boy was surrounded by a flotilla of toys and colorful plastic boats.

"Is this a bath or just an excuse for Mommy to play with your boats?" Ross queried his son seriously.

"Mommy likes to play with my boats," the child returned in the same serious tone.

Shelley cast Ross a sideways glance that implied, "Just wait, buddy." She was smirking but trying to keep it hidden from Randall. She loved to play with her son in the water. It was a special time for the two of them. They lingered over his evening bath, especially on the nights Ross was away. Ross's comment made her feel strangely sheepish, as if some highly intimate place inside her had been exposed. It made her feel closer to Ross, too, at the same time. Her emotions flushed with a warm joy, and she sensed that this evening was something special, that this would be one of the times of her life she would treasure.

"So, is it done?" she asked.

Ross tried to sound casual. "Yep."

"Did you bring it up?"

"It's in the living room," Ross said.

"Come on, Randall, let's finish up and go see little brother's cradle. Will you put some film in the camera for me, Ross?"

"Don't you want to wait until we have a baby in it to take the pictures?"

"I'll get lots of pictures that way, too, don't worry." Shelley laughed.

The three of them went to their family room then and made such a fuss over the handmade piece of furniture that Ross began to feel a little ridiculous. He was glad that no one outside of their home could see how silly he was acting.

Shelley ran her hands over the polished wood and set the cradle rocking gently with a push. She nodded approvingly at how smoothly it swayed.

"Thank you, Ross. It's beautiful. I love it." Shelley's voice had a soft, husky tone to it, as if she were ready to weep.

That night it was almost a chore for the Martin family to go to bed. The anticipation they felt was almost palpable. Except for Randall. He was not really looking forward to the next day, but his mom's enthusiasm was contagious. Shelley had done her best to convince the little fellow that having a younger brother would be a fun thing. He was beginning to parrot the things his mother said. He could sense she wanted him to agree with her.

Ross and Shelley lay awake for a long time talking about their family. Shelley was lying on her side with her head resting on Ross's arm. She liked lying there in the dark, talking to him, the best. She could look straight at him, and he could not see her face well enough to distinguish the spot. As she relaxed and their talk slowed, the depth of their conversation grew. She paused for a long moment for effect and then spoke gently to Ross.

"Do you know how happy you've made me?"

"I hope I've made you as happy as you've made me."

"Thank you, Ross. Thank you for becoming my husband." There was a husky mist in her voice. With that she rolled toward him, and their lips met. Soon their desire for sleep yielded to a greater desire. Afterward they drifted off to a sound sleep, where Ross dreamed of a quiet river flowing past a mountainside of autumnal forest—the crisp, clear air letting the sun reflect the oranges and the yellows and the dappled red of the foliage from the rippling surface of the water so bright and beautiful it made his eyes hurt. And there were no bubbling calls for help to disturb him.

CHAPTER ELEVEN

Shelley's sister Helen called early the next morning.

"Do you feel up to a little party on Saturday, or is that too soon?" Helen asked.

"What kind of party?" Shelley asked, as if she didn't know.

"Well, you didn't give us the chance to throw you a baby shower, you know. We all want to see the baby. Why don't we just have an 'open house' kind of thing at your place on Saturday? That is, if you're up to it?"

"Thanks Helen, that sounds so nice, I would really like that."

"You don't need to do much of anything, Shelley. Mom and I can bring some food, and you know we'll stay afterward to clean up any mess we make."

"I expect that this is pretty much a done deal. I suspect everybody already knows and is ready to come. Am I right?" Shelley asked.

"Pretty much so," replied Helen. "I just need to make a couple calls to confirm it with the gang."

Ross had been sitting at the kitchen table finishing his coffee when the call came, and he could gather from one side what was going on. He had been expecting something like this. He knew that a baby shower was certain to be another "hen party." Shelley and her mother and sister went from one day to the next it seemed, looking for any excuse to have some get-together. These things always centered on family, and they were always a little overdone for his taste. He knew the other men felt the same way. None of them would dare speak a word of dissent to the women, though. They knew better.

Ross and the other men would usually slip off to some male domain, maybe Ross's basement workshop. Sometimes it was the television, if there was a game to watch. The family gatherings grew tiresome and repetitive, not the kind of thing men got excited about. But it was an opportunity for the men to talk—something they liked to do, but would never, of their own initiative, bother to make time for.

"So let me guess, there's going to be a party here on Saturday?"

"How did you know?" she asked with mock surprise in her voice.

"Let me guess, a baby shower?"

"You're just amazing, honey!" Shelley said.

Ross slowly shook his head from side to side. It was a subtle way of expressing his masculine bewilderment about women. Leeroy had once told Ross that when he was younger, men never went to such gatherings. It was a result of the change in culture, Ross supposed. He didn't have to be present, but he knew Shelley would be annoyed if he wasn't. He could see on Shelley's face that she knew what he was thinking, but he didn't try to hide the way he felt.

"Now, Ross, don't sit there looking like a condemned man. You know you'll enjoy it." Ross and the other men were a mystery to Shelley. They would all grumble about going to the party. Then, after they had been together for 10 minutes, they would be laughing and talking together with enough liveliness to make anyone think they were having a better time than the women were. The women would hear them and give each other knowing smiles. It never failed.

Ross grinned. He knew she was right. "Are you ready to go?" he asked.

"As soon as I get Randy dressed," she replied.

"I'm gonna warm up the car."

Their eyes met, and the sense of anticipation magnified as they held each other's gaze. They both knew that words could not express what their eyes were saying to one another.

"Go!" Shelley blurted quietly. Ross turned to the door.

They dropped Randall at Grandma's house one more time, promising to pick him up when they had his little brother in the car. Ross drove carefully across town, feeling a sense of joy mixed with a weight of responsibility. He had felt it before when Randall was born, so it was familiar. His mood was sober as he parked the car and walked around to open Shelley's door. Somehow, he felt like he had arrived, like he had reached a goal or achieved something profound. He was happy about it, but there was a sense of uncertainty along with it.

They walked into the hospital as if everyone of the staff members knew who they were and why they were there. They felt like they were the only people in the world just then and that the hospital must have been built solely for the purpose of sheltering their baby.

Ross remembered how he had grown to dislike the atmosphere in the hospital on the day of Donny's birth. He thought how good it was that they would not have to return to this place of doubt and tension. His family was healthy; even this newest addition was stronger than average. The vigorous way the child had laid claim to life after his premature birth was proof of that. He gave a glance of thanks heavenward as his nostrils embraced the sweet and sour smell of antiseptic, or soap or whatever it was.

The nurse who had been with them during Shelley's labor, Michelle, saw them and gave a quiet wave. Ross wondered if the woman remembered how much distress Shelley had been in under her care? Michelle should speak to them, he thought, show more regard for such a successful family unit. But he excused her; perhaps she could not afford to be distracted from her recording of vital signs or medication. Or perhaps she chose to ignore them, sensing they might see her as having let them down on the day Shelley was in her care. In any case, Ross knew he and Shelley might never see her again. They could just forget her part in that difficult experience.

Ross knew he was indulging in a bit of vanity, looking down on this mousy little nurse and feeling superior by comparison. He told himself to stop it, but the high mood he was in countered that thought as if it were unworthy. He was the father of two now, a whole carload of people. They were a well-rounded family, and he was the "breadwinner," the "daddy." Surely, a little condescending behavior was appropriate for a man of his station.

Then, finally, Shelley had the baby in her arms and not temporarily this time. Mother and child were pushed to the elevator with father trailing behind. The layers of blanket seemed too thin to protect him from his first experience with anything below room temperature. Shelley folded the top of the blanket down over his little face to shield him from the cold. The car was much warmer than the outside air. Ross had turned the heat the whole way up to quickly make things more comfortable for him.

They drove to Grandma's and picked up Randall. Shelley's mother came to the car to take a peek at the bundle, smiling broadly, with her head through the open window, the cool breeze rustling her fluffy hair and revealing how gray it actually was.

"Let me know if you want any help, honey," Grandma said.

"Thanks, Mom, for everything," Shelley said.

Then they were home. Ross felt somewhat let down now. The excitement was past. Now began the work of caring for and raising the baby. He knew it would be an adjustment for all three of them. He determined not to let Randall feel neglected now that his mother could not be so devoted to him. Fortunately, there was a chore for the two of them to do, one that would ensure he would not feel that way soon. Christmas was only a couple short weeks away, and it was long past time to decorate the front of the house.

"Randall, will you help me put up the Christmas lights?"

"Okay, Daddy, are we going to get a tree, too?"

"Of course we are. We need to get most of this done today, too. There's going to be a party here tomorrow, and we want things to be ready, don't we?"

Ross and Randall spent the afternoon stringing lights across the front porch and hanging them from the gutters. It was not difficult work, only time-consuming, even more so because Randall had developed a knack for tangling the strings of lights. Ross struggled to keep from growling at him. Before dinner they had gone and bought a tree and set it up in the living room.

That evening Shelley supervised the decorating of the tree. Ross could hardly believe how fussy she could be about each light, each ornament. Every strand of tinsel mattered to Shelley; even the side of the tree that no one could see was treated like some important work of art. "I've never seen an ugly Christmas tree, Shelley," Ross said, making fun of her fastidiousness.

"I have. And they were all decorated by men," she countered in a tone of voice that was not playful. When the painstaking job of decorating the tree was finished, they sat down to survey the room. Though their living room was spacious, the tree crowded the other furniture. The new cradle was across the room from the tree, next to the wide doorway that opened to the dining room. Donny was sleeping in the cradle.

"It's kind of poetic, don't you think, to have a tiny baby as part of the decorations," Ross said.

"Sure, Ross, it's poetic." She was sarcastic, and it struck him as out of character for her. He began to wonder if he had said something careless. Shelley sat stiffly in her chair, looking into the cradle with eyes that should have been filled with pure wonder. But Ross saw something else in her eyes. It was similar to the look he'd seen in her eyes the day she came home from the hospital and the company had put him to work right away. Ross could usually comprehend her moods, but not this time. He supposed that whatever the mood was, it was the reason for her sarcasm.

From his position on the sofa, Ross could see the antique table in the dining room. He marveled at how well the table and the cradle matched, although they were not intended to. The slight difference in color of the two woods was barely visible in the daytime, but with the lights on at night you could not tell the difference. They looked like a set. Ross thought about putting them together somehow, so that they might compliment each other.

"Hey, Shell, what do you think about arranging things so the cradle and the table are together. Have you noticed how much they look alike?"

"Now that you mention it, you're right. They look almost like they were made for each other. How are we going to do that, though? There's not enough room in here for the table."

"We can put the tree on the porch," Ross offered. He ducked as a pillow came sailing his way. He was relieved that she had become her old playful self again. "Maybe they can't be used together, but I'd like to at least take a picture of them together somehow. What do you think?"

"Why don't you do it tomorrow?" Shelley said. "The light will be better; we'll be taking pictures anyway, and maybe other people will want a shot of them, too. Besides, that will give you more time to think about how to arrange them. A table and a cradle really don't go together that well. Now, a rocking chair..."

❦

The next morning, Shelley was up at 6 in spite of getting up to take care of Donny several times during the night, eager to get going on the party preparations. Ross got out of bed, too, though with reluctance. He was a little ashamed that his wife had more energy than he did.

He made a trip to the grocery store to pick up the things Shelley needed to get through the weekend. There were a couple of inches of snow on the ground; the world looked clean and fresh. The sky overhead was clearing with the exception of one enormous cloud spilling its contents onto the streets of Heritage.

The sun bounced off the new snow and shot straight into Ross's eyes. The snow was melting quickly, and Ross knew that by the time he got home his pickup would be covered with the filmy winter grime.

The snow floated slowly, delicately down through the quiet morning air. It hung on the whispers of the wind, like small tufts of milkweed floss in the fall, its myriad members hesitating before they finished their downward progress, as if their sole task in the universe were to serve as an instant of decoration, an image of fleeting beauty. The flakes gathered in little tufts. More flakes came and spanned the distance between the tufts so that the tufts gathered together. It became a bright, clean blanket on the earth, soft and unspoiled.

But then the tires plowed through it as it lay helplessly on the pavement. They thrust it outward toward the gutters, onto the shoulders of the road, where it mixed with the sand and coated the litter. Then the drier air or the relentless heat of the sun would vaporize it, send it skyward once again, to repeat the cycle. So perfectly pure, so brief, so fragile. There was a heavy sadness in snow, Ross thought.

CHAPTER TWELVE

The people started dropping into the Martin house just after lunchtime. By 1:30, the house was full. They all carried some gaily wrapped parcel, their offering for the new baby. They marveled at the tiny size of Donny and how fortunate Ross and Shelley were to have such a perfect child in spite of his premature birth.

"It's supposed to get cold this afternoon," Ross advised his guests, to make conversation, as they pulled off their coats, scarves and hats and handed them to him to hang in the closet.

Shelley's mother and sister Helen brought several plates of cookies, brownies, vegetables and dip, along with crackers and a cheese ball. They made coffee, tea and punch, and someone brought eggnog. The guests formed into the same predictable clusters that Ross noticed whenever there was a gathering. Most of the women were in the living room, hovering near the cradle.

Victor Clark surveyed the new piece of furniture that everyone seemed so impressed with and asked, "Did you build this cradle from a kit?"

"No, from a picture. Shelley saw one like it in a magazine and asked me if I could make one." Ross tried to sound nonchalant, supposing his father-in-law was seeking some way to minimize the praise Ross's handiwork was getting from most of the guests. Victor nodded as if paying a compliment to Ross required nothing more than that.

Little Donny was held by all of the women and some of the men during the afternoon, and he hadn't fussed much about it. He was in the cradle, sleeping, his unusually small body looking very much like a doll. All the women were talking in hushed tones, as if the baby's sleep were particularly precious.

Helen got out her camera and began to take snapshots of the people in the house. Shelley looked at Ross and said, "better start getting some pictures, huh?"

Ross could sense that the little party could break up at any time now. He knew Shelley wanted to get photos before the people started thinking about leaving. It was time to get the pictures of the cradle he wanted to take. The afternoon light would soon begin to fade.

Ross eased Donny's cradle away from the wall toward the center of the room, gently, so as not to disturb him. He had his parents and then Shelley's parents pose by the cradle, with their hands on the headboard as if they were rocking it. He took a half-dozen shots of Shelley rocking it, some from her chair, some standing, kneeling.

Helen took Ross's camera and took shots of Shelley and Ross together. They got Randall into the act, taking shots of him rocking his little brother, and so on.

Ross's father mentioned that the antique table "looked like it were made to match the cradle." Gerald Martin had been quiet for most of the visit, which was normal for him. The pride he felt for his new grandson, along with his son's handiwork in making the cradle, rallied his pride, and he came out of himself somewhat.

Ross welcomed his father's comments. It gave him a reason to talk about the cradle. "They do look alike, but that's just coincidence. I didn't even think about that when I was building the cradle, but I'm glad it turned out that way. Maybe I can make some more pieces to go with them.

"You ought to try making a rocking chair to go with it," his father said.

"Shelley mentioned a rocking chair yesterday, too," Ross said. "I'll have to think about that, I guess."

"I wanted to try and get a shot of them together, the cradle and the table. How can I arrange them so they look okay together?" Ross asked to whoever might want to offer advice.

"Just put them side by each, see what it looks like," Gerald said.

Ross gingerly slid the cradle, still containing the sleeping Donny, across the carpeted floors, through the archway between the two rooms and aligned it with the antique table.

"What are you doing?" Shelley asked, as if Ross's actions were untoward.

"No big deal, honey. I'm just positioning the furniture for another snapshot." Ross's answer was a little defensive. He knew that his desire to photograph the two pieces of woodwork was due mostly to his vanity and that it might be showing. He didn't want to undo what he had arranged, though, simply because his wife thought he was overdoing it. Hadn't she suggested yesterday that he do this today?

Ross wished she would not speak to him in that tone of voice when there was company present. He always got awkward feelings when Shelley's family was around. He often wondered if the presence of her relatives, with their proper lives and their decency fairly dripping from them, made Shelley feel superior to him, since his father was an alcoholic, and his parents' poverty was so obvious. She always seemed to find just the right time to subtly ridicule him—when no one else who was present would sense it like he did, when she could do it and appear innocent.

"Just don't wake him up, okay?" Shelley whispered with measured tone. She was obviously annoyed that Ross would choose to move the cradle while the baby was sleeping in it.

Ross wished now that he had waited for a better time. Shelley was probably not the only one who thought his actions were inconsiderate of the baby. "Oh well, nobody's perfect," muttered Ross quietly to no one in particular. He gave his dad a half-sheepish smile and got a similar one back. He decided to get the shots quickly and make sure that his son was sleeping soundly before he moved him again.

The view of the two pieces, through the lens of the camera, was unsatisfactory. Ross knew that the precise matching of the color wouldn't show very well unless one end of the cradle was allowed to blend with the broad face of the tabletop. The lack of contrast would show how well matched the two were. He decided to set the cradle on top of the table.

Ross gave his dad the camera to hold for a minute and bent down to pick up the cradle. He carefully set it on top of the table. This proved to be no good either, because the cradle had to sit sideways to fit on the table, and sitting that way, you could not see the ends. The only answer was to raise the drop leaves of the table and turn the cradle perpendicular to the tabletop.

After returning the cradle to the floor, Ross knelt down and raised the front leaf. He slid the support beam out of its slot and tried to wedge it under the leaf. The beam wouldn't slide out the whole way because the leaf would not turn up the whole way, like it was supposed to.

"What are you doing now," Ross heard Shelley ask over his shoulder; with a sigh that suggested she was losing patience with him.

"Bear with me, honey, this won't take long," Ross said, knowing he was on the verge of sounding angry with her for making this protest.

Shelley turned and went back to her seat in the living room with the other women, who were trying to ignore her discomfort. She was flexing the muscles of her motherly instincts, they knew.

Ross realized upon closer examination that the contoured edge where the leaf hinged up had a hardened drop of varnish along it. This kept the drop leaf from coming all the way up. He had evidently never tried to raise the leaves after he had refinished the table. If he had, it would have been obvious that the excess varnish needed to be removed.

Ross was chagrinned. He felt bad enough about taking the pictures now and about Shelley being annoyed with him. He wasn't about to announce to everyone that his beautiful, antique, drop-leaf table wouldn't work right because of an oversight on his part. He would just wedge the leaf up and jam the beam in for now. He could fix it properly later. It only needed to be up for a few minutes anyway, while he took a couple of snapshots. He forced the beam into its place, as far as it would go anyway.

He heard a mild cracking sound as he did so, the sort of noise you get when you stretch any wooden joint. It didn't really mean anything.

The surface of the tabletop was broad enough now with one leaf raised, so he didn't bother with the opposing side. It wouldn't show in the photo anyway, he reasoned. The raised leaf looked almost perfectly level with the main part of the tabletop now. No one would notice any deficiency, Ross felt certain. Surely it wouldn't show in the picture.

Ross hoisted his son aloft again and tenderly set the cradle on the table. The footboard end of the cradle with its rocker rested on the drop leaf now. Ross backed away and surveyed the effect. The little cradle rocked very gently, side-to-side.

"Better watch, those rockers might scratch your tabletop, son," advised Gerald Martin. Ross stifled the urge to glare at this father.

The little boy, nestled soundly in his puffy blanket, didn't seem to notice the motion. Shelley was making a fuss for nothing, Ross was sure. He took the camera back from his dad, who had turned his chair a little sideways now, so he could be a part of the conversation in the living room. Ross was on his own taking the pictures now, he realized.

Just like the old man, to abandon me when I need someone on my side, thought Ross. Or perhaps his father had not noticed that Ross was in any distress. A difference of opinion with a woman was nothing new to him.

Ross backed away from the table now and put the whole table and cradle in the lens of the camera. He focused it and turned the flash back on. He checked the dial to see how many shots remained on the roll. There were six. Ross was happy to be nearly finished.

He wasn't sure if he had backed up enough to get a good perspective in the first two shots. He backed as far as he could into the living room, until the intervening wall threatened to impinge on the view. His body was slightly behind the wall now, and he leaned a little to the side, enough so he was slightly off balance.

Ross was aware of how awkward he must look to the other people, but he had the shot framed well. Just as he was pressing the shutter for what would be the last picture, he heard the crack.

It wasn't exactly a crack, but a gristly, drawn-out tearing sound, as if wood were slowly giving way. He realized then, to his absolute terror, that it was the beam that held the drop leaf up. It was giving way. As the brilliant light of the flash intruded into his consciousness, he saw the end of the drop leaf fall. The cradle and little Donald Andrew Martin were falling too.

Ross lunged. If he had not been slightly off balance, he might have been more graceful, but as it was he fell in his desperate attempt to close the distance between him and the table. It was only about six feet—he could have fallen that far—but caught as he was with his hands up and his body teetering sideways, his movements were clumsy.

A little cry of fear and surprise passed Ross's lips as he dropped the camera and threw himself toward the cradle. It pitched forward almost, as if the sudden loss of support had taken it by surprise too. Ross could see the soft, bald head of his son being catapulted forward as the back of the cradle came up, gathering speed as the bottom of the cradle met the top of the table with a bang and rocked over. Donny's head was directly under the top of the headboard of the cradle as it met the floor, and Ross's fully-grown torso fell on to the rocker bottom with disastrous finality. He realized as he was falling that he had tripped on the cords for the Christmas tree lights.

Ross could feel the glued joints of wood rupturing as the headboard gave way under his weight. He could feel the softness of the blankets and mattress yielding to the inertia of his fall and something else: a sickening sense of something that was neither cloth nor wood, was neither hard nor entirely soft and the ever-so-subtle sensation of something popping.

Ross could hear Shelley behind him, her voice desperate, terrified and angry. He hesitated there, the way he had fallen, knowing that whatever had happened under the pile of rubble that was once his shining pride was something he did not want to face. It was as if some monster had leapt out at him, caught him by surprise and was standing there laughing, unseen by anyone in the room but him. It shook him now, and its putrid breath ripped into Ross's nostrils and pushed out not only his own breath but also his soul. It settled back into the corner then, as Ross forced his mind to take the action he knew he must. But it waited, it lingered, rocking in sadistic glee, muttering bubbly words of derision, like Donny Ritts's voice echoing from the past. Its hideous grin told Ross that it had him now and that it would win.

The shimmering surface of the Sugar River sent little flickers of light into Ross's consciousness, and the strangled, desperate bubbling sound of Donny Ritts's last words punctuated the sound of rushing feet in the house so sharply that Ross was sure the others had to hear it. "Ross, Ross! Don't leave me, please."

Shelley was beside Ross now, frantically pulling at the pile of shiny wood. Ross wanted to tell her to go slowly, to be gentle, lest she make things worse with frantic haste, but he could not make his lips move to form a word. He slowly got hold of the mattress and rolled it to the side, then helped Shelley remove the inverted bedding. Donny was there, face down, his tiny legs pulled up in the fetal position. Since babies often slept that way, Ross allowed himself the luxury of hoping that the boy had endured the fall like the rough-and-tumble lad he promised to be. Yet, deep within him he knew it was not so.

Shelley got hold of herself now and assumed her gentle nursery manner. She wrapped her two hands around Donny and turned him over, to support him with her palms spread as widely as she could stretch them.

The horror of it dug into her, yet the feeling was so foreign to her, so absolutely new and strange, that there was no response from her. She could tell he was dead. There was no mistaking the lack of substance between his body and head. She began to raise him off the floor, and her fingers extended to the back of his head providing the required support. The voice rose from Shelley's throat, slowly and tremulously at first. It gathered speed and strength as the word formed. There was no mistaking the intent of the cry, for the tone of it expressed her absolute need for refuge, and she went for it without hesitation. "Moooooother!"

On his knees now, not because the work of uncovering his son had been accomplished that way, but in total loss of his sense of purpose—as if to assume the universal position of contrition, Ross could feel his lips curling, his teeth gnashing, the hot tears coming forth under pressure.

Ross was alone now, alone in his flesh. In the corner, yet everywhere, without form or sound, he could sense the familiar company he thought he had finally escaped. It was nothing, yet it was everything. It was loneliness, in all its miserable presence. The quiet tormenting solitude of a man who has no place of refuge, no source of comfort, no company but his own accusing thoughts.

Shelley's mother was there now. The others had come to life also. There were excited voices, with voices of reason and deliberation mixing in as well. "Call the ambulance!" "Dial 9-1-1!" "Take it easy, lay him down, let the medics handle it." Over every other sound, the haunting voice of Shelley's wail lifted, overshadowing the other sounds in the room, incessant and continuous, as if it would go on forever.

But there was no voice in the din that was directed toward Ross. It was as if the group of people in his home had decided he was suddenly insignificant. They huddled over the remains of the cradle as if to shelter Shelley, who was in the center. Then they began to rise, almost in unison, as if their movements had been choreographed and rehearsed, and he was not a part of it. They moved apart now, each one having chosen some course of action.

Shelley's father took charge of things. Calling on some long-ago first-aid training, he checked for pulse and respiration. Finding none, he coaxed his daughter to surrender her child into his hands.

"Let me have him, honey, we need to try and get him to breathe. The ambulance." He stopped then in mid sentence, realizing that the hospital was close enough to drive to. They could take the baby there much faster themselves.

"Oh, hell, lets just take him in. Ross, let's go." He turned and looked at Ross, who stood still, mouth half-open, his eyes on the small, limp body.

"Never mind," Victor said. Then to his wife, "Ginny, let's go!"

Time seemed to freeze for Ross, who could think of nothing to do or say. His camera lay there on the floor, alone in a field of green carpet. He wished he could somehow exchange the photos he had taken for the moments they represented, to somehow reverse the flow of time and gain the opportunity to set things right.

Ross's mind whirled now. He came to his senses enough to realize that it was wrong to assume there was no hope. He pushed his way to Shelley and the baby, now being held by his father-in-law. "Yes, let's get him to the emergency room as fast as we can."

He stooped down and gathered up the blue blanket, then fumbled with it, trying to shake it out so he could wrap his son in it. He realized how senseless that was as Shelley's dad began to stride purposefully toward the door with Shelley right beside him.

Virginia waited with her car keys in hand. She swung the front door open, and the trio went out in a rush, leaving the rest of the group hurrying to find their coats and preparing to follow them to the hospital.

Ross stood there with the blue baby blanket hanging limply in his hands, knowing that it should have been him carrying his child to the hospital, him taking charge of the situation, him taking the lead. But he couldn't do anything except stand there alone, wishing he hadn't been so proud of his woodworking skills. Wishing he hadn't tried to take pictures. Damning himself for being so stupid.

Randall had been overlooked in the confusion as well. He came up to his daddy now, eyes full of tears. He knew something tragic had just happened, but he wasn't sure what. He was crying from confusion more than for any other reason. Ross reached down and pulled the little boy close to him, seeing a source of warmth and hope in the tender eyes. He picked Randall up and hugged him. "Come on, buddy, we gotta get to the hospital."

PART TWO

...But the tigers come at night,
With their voices soft as thunder.
As they tear your hope apart,
As they turn your dream to shame...
  I dreamed a dream. From the musical "*Le Miserables.*"

CHAPTER THIRTEEN

A frigid blast of air came from the north and caught the melting snow, midway between its original form of white perfection and degraded slush. The meteorologists liked to call the air an "Alberta clipper," because it usually seemed to gather in that mountainous western province and come pushing down across the states in a southeasterly direction. A huge mass of dense, sub-zero winter that bulldozed cruelly across the American Midwest toward the Mid-Atlantic, dominating any weather system in its path. It crushed the spirits of anyone who purposed to enjoy the outdoors, and those who must work outside were forced to upgrade their winter dress to the heavier parkas and boots they normally saved for January.

Weather this bitter in December was unusual for Pennsylvania. Though no one expected it to last long, maybe only a couple of days, its unseasonable arrival made it more unwelcome. It turned the slush, which would otherwise have been cleared from the roadways and sidewalks by traffic, into a rough, chaotic sculpture. The frozen ridges of ice made grooves and tracks for tires to follow. By the time Ross got to the hospital, the ridges of ice were beginning to take shape. He had to proceed slowly through the streets of Heritage to avoid having his path chosen for him by a high ridge of ice that threatened to deflect his front wheels and toss his pickup off course.

Ross felt like a condemned man walking the last mile. The other family members were already at the hospital, and he was coming along slowly now, with Randall beside him on the seat of the pickup.

Something inside him would not allow him to cling to the wishful pretense he knew the others were employing—that Donny might somehow still be alive, that the good doctors could somehow mend the frail body and put breath back in the tiny lungs.

Ross knew that Randall had some idea of what had happened. Surely the little boy was curious about the confusing events at the family gathering, yet, as if to protect his daddy as much as he could, the lad said nothing. He sat quietly on the seat of the pickup, his neck straining with the attempt to see out over the dashboard, as Ross drove carefully across the roughening streets to the hospital.

It was as if the core of Shelley's family had gelled when the cradle had fallen, and as if Ross's family had disbursed. He assumed that his father and mother had gone to the hospital with the rest of the crowd. He knew that if they had, they would probably be by themselves, whether sitting or standing. The Clark family would circle their wagons against outsiders, especially such substandard outsiders as the Martins.

It pained Ross that his parents had not rallied to support him in the minutes after the tragedy at his home. He supposed they, too, were indulging in the hopeless fantasy that somehow their grandchild was still in the land of the living.

Ross's mind was in familiar territory now. In the days after the death of Donny Ritts, Ross had found a state of mind he could withdraw into. It was a sort of deliberate stupor. He held the ground in the forefront of his thoughts by sheer will. He let nothing that he did not need to think about push its way into his consciousness. It was a survival mode, a trick of his psyche.

Yet the truth was there, just offstage in his mind, like the dying, gurgling voice of Donny Ritts. It was a monster, the same vicious creature that had appeared minutes before in the dining room at his house. They were one and the same, the truth and this manifestation of the ugly reality that was his life, some insane creature from a perverted laboratory in hell, prancing around the events leading up to the fall of the cradle as if to examine them, to determine how best to use them in its effort to torture Ross. It paused every so often and put its jaws around some aspect of the event, sinking its teeth as if to test for a grip. Then it would slowly raise its head and stare at Ross with cold yellow eyes. Ross could keep it at bay if he ignored it. As long as he refused to make eye contact with it, it had to stay out there. As if another world existed outside of reality, and the two could change places—the imagined becoming real and vice versa.

Ross found the place in the parking lot where the rest of the crowd from his house had parked. It was a little cluster of vehicles, all familiar to Ross. He parked with a space between him and them. It was an unconscious acknowledgement that he considered himself estranged now.

He carried Randall across the icy parking lot, walking slowly and carefully with all his weight directly over the soles of his feet, balancing his son as if he were his last remaining treasure. They entered the warm confines of the hospital through the double sliding doors that opened and closed automatically for them. He remembered the last time he had come through these doors, when he brought Shelley in on the day Donny was born.

The nurse seated at the admitting desk seemed to know he was a part of the group that was already filling the waiting room. She nodded at him as he passed, as if to say "It's all right, go ahead."

He turned the corner, and the first thing he saw was the face of his father. There was a look of detachment on his dad's face, as if Gerald Martin was trying his best to stay aloof from what had happened. Ross supposed his father felt some measure of responsibility for what happened, since he encouraged Ross to arrange the cradle and the table for taking the photographs. Ross knew his father was marking time, doing his best to fill the role of grandparent, while it was expected of him. Later he would retreat to the Snake Pit and handle the sorrow of this day in the same way he always handled sorrow.

His mother was there beside his father. The look in her eyes was both apologetic and sympathetic. She wanted to speak comfort to him, Ross could tell, but her mind could not find fitting words. She stepped forward and offered her arms to him.

They had rarely embraced since Ross was small. Her comfort felt strange to him, and it was awkward, since he still held Randall high in his arms. Yet he lingered there, longing for the refuge he knew he could not find there. His stomach was churning now, tightening.

Ross stepped back then and put Randall down. He knelt beside the boy and said "You stay with Grandma for a while now, okay. I gotta find Mommy."

His mother took Randall's hand as Ross swept his eyes across the faces of the others in the little waiting room. He couldn't find anyone who would make eye contact with him. They were all doing the best they could to keep emotion in check, trembling slightly in their winter clothing, as if they were not inside a warm building. Each person's mind was trying to put the incredible horror they had witnessed in some context so that it might make sense.

Ross was not sure where Shelley and her parents might be, though he was sure they would all be together if possible. He began to phrase the question to his mother. She tossed her head down the hall, as if she preferred not to speak, and Ross took a step that way. Just then a door to one of the treatment rooms came open, and the contorted sob of Shelley's mournful wail came cascading out. There could be no mistaking what it meant. Anyone who still clung to his or her dubious hope now dropped it.

Shelley and her parents came out of the room now, a trio of bodies, the separate people only distinguishable by the contrasting color of their clothing. They held each other tightly and walked slowly together back toward the rest of the group.

Shelley looked up at Ross, and her face was wet and wrinkled and so anguished that Ross would not have known her. He knew his own face was drawn up together around his mouth. He wanted to cry, yet he could not until he knew whether or not Shelley would let him be with her. For a long space of time they stood there, Ross and Shelley facing each other, not able to form words. Then, with a stiffness Ross could not understand, she began to stretch out her arms toward him, uncoiling them from the embrace of her parents reluctantly, Ross thought, as if only duty compelled her to reach for him.

"I'm sorry, Shelley. I'm so sorry." Ross's voice, laced with short sobs, was almost staccato. His diaphragm was tight in his chest, and it was a strain for him to breathe. He gripped his wife tightly, but her body was lax and she did not return the embrace in the way Ross hoped she would. There was something missing. He slowly sensed that Shelley was not sharing the grief with him. She would allow herself to be bolstered by her parents but not by him. The only possible reason for this, Ross knew, was that she held him responsible for the death of their baby. "And why not?" he asked himself. He *was* responsible, completely responsible.

The embrace that Ross and Shelley shared was only a few seconds long. Ross could sense nothing from Shelley in it. The hug was empty, like some enormous dark cavern. He knew they had lost something, and with that knowledge came the opening the monster was looking for. He pounced on Ross then with eager teeth and bit crisply into his soul.

Ross, certain then that his worst fears had been realized and no longer able to hold off his tormentor, let go of his self-control. He dropped to his knees and sobbed in unspeakable agony.

CHAPTER FOURTEEN

Victor Clark paced the waiting room of Heritage Community Hospital until his feet began to ache. A nurse, wearing a sympathetic expression, tried to cheer him. "You want a cup of coffee or something?"

"No, but thank you."

"You really should try to get some rest. Your daughter won't be awake for several hours yet," said the nurse.

"Yes, I'm sure you're right," he said.

He remembered what was once a standard television scenario, the expectant father pacing the waiting room floor. That was in the days before men were admitted to the delivery room when their wives were giving birth. If only that were the case, he thought, and sighed.

Shelley and Ross were both under sedation. The hospital staff had admitted Shelley, fearing an unpredictable response to the grief. Victor was determined to stay close by, in case she woke up. Ross's parents had taken him back to his home, where they would sit up watching him. Victor thought administering medication to the couple was overdoing things a bit, but he could hardly question the hospital staff. The two of them had made enough noise in the emergency unit to wake up half of Heritage.

"I can't believe what happened today. Three-week-old babies are supposed to be made of rubber. That's how I always thought they were when the wife and I were raising kids," Victor intoned sadly to the kindly nurse. "More than once our kids had some nasty falls. They can tumble in ways that would injure adults, with no more consequences than tears and fright.

But then, I never saw a full-grown man topple onto the body of a baby before. It's just incredible."

"I know what you mean," said the nurse. "It's sort of freaky. Some of the worst accidents are."

How could anyone be as unlucky as his son-in-law Ross, he wondered? Twice now the young man had lost someone dear to him. Ginny had been uncomfortable when the couple chose to name their baby after Ross's teenage friend.

"It's just doesn't seem wise to me, Vic," she had said privately to him when they first got word the baby was named. "After all, the doctors don't even know how healthy this baby will be. If he has problems, they are going to think maybe they asked for it somehow. I just don't like it. Why can't they just pick some other name?" But she had never breathed a word to Shelley about her misgivings.

Victor knew his wife had some strange ideas. Although they were both devout Christians, she still had a streak of superstition in her. Victor usually found it amusing. Now he wished Ginny had tried to dissuade their daughter from using that name. But it was too late for that now.

To make things worse, the hospital was obligated to report any unusual deaths. The coroner's office would probably want to question Ross and Shelley about what had happened. Perhaps Victor could head that off, since there were so many witnesses to the event. He wasn't sure Shelley could handle the trauma of it all. He would make a call tomorrow. He knew a couple of guys in City Hall.

Shelley had told him Ross still struggled from time to time with the death of his friend in the river, so long ago. He wondered how much a young guy could take before he had a nervous breakdown, anyway? Victor didn't know, but he supposed that Shelley and Ross would need to see a shrink before they were okay. Or maybe one of those grief counselors he'd heard about. He had no idea how someone could be counseled out of grief. He suspected such people were a sham, but then he didn't know everything.

"They say losing a child can ruin a marriage," Victor said to the nurse, breaking an uncomfortable silence that had grown between them. The nurse did not seem inclined to return to her duties, for whatever reason.

"It happened to my brother and his wife," she said. "Baby had some rare blood disorder. Even Johns Hopkins couldn't help."

"You mean they broke up after the baby died?" asked Victor.

"Not right away, but yes. Things were never the same between them. I guess there are just some storms people can't weather."

The nurse's voice was soothing, and Victor felt himself opening up. "Did you see my daughter's face?"

"I know your daughter, sort of," the nurse said. "Oh, I haven't met her, but when she was in…when the baby was born. Well, you know…everybody talked about her. It was kindly, though. She is distinctive. And she's so nice. People notice that more when someone has something like her, you know? She's really special. It doesn't seem fair."

Victor nodded and absently touched his own cheek. "Her Port Wine Stain is one reason she is so sweet," he said, his voice taking on the strain of a man who was close to tears. "I guess she's always felt like she had to be nicer than other people. No, it isn't fair."

"I'm very sorry for your loss, sir. I'll be praying for your family," the nurse said. She reached out and patted Victor's arm.

"Thank you," Victor said. He lowered his eyes and half-turned away from the woman, hoping she would take the hint and leave him alone with his thoughts.

He couldn't help but wonder how much Shelley or someone like her could put up with. Shelley had never had any self-confidence. Watching her struggle with her affliction had broken his heart so many times through the years.

How many times had he felt like the worst kind of hypocrite, since he could never reconcile himself to the cross his daughter had to bear? He could never be free from the anger he had toward God. But he had pretended. Oh, how he could pretend.

How many times had he tried to convince her that the coloring of her face didn't matter? Looking back, he supposed he had overdone it, and that was why she had seen through it. Around age 6 she stopped asking him about it, going instead to her mother, who was better able to face the reality of it unflinchingly. Had Shelley been able to tell at that tender age that he was tormented by it and that his efforts to convince her were really efforts to convince himself? Had she kept her worst feelings to herself out of pity for him? He was sure of it. And he knew that his daughter had grown up without the positive affirmation a father was supposed to give her.

He knew he had failed Shelley. They had become detached emotionally. What he didn't know was how badly it affected her relationship with Ross. Had she married so quickly and so young because she yearned for the kind of male acceptance he had never truly given her? The weight of his guilt nagged at him like the chronic drip of a worn faucet. He stiffened his face against the tears, thankful that he was now alone in the room.

He didn't really feel a great loss about the death of the child. He supposed he would have if his emotions hadn't been so dominated by concern for his daughter. He had trouble keeping his composure when he remembered her cries after Ross fell on the baby.

Truth be told, Victor had a fair amount of animosity toward Ross for being so careless. He'd been more interested in taking pictures of his precious woodwork than allowing the baby to rest comfortably. He realized that part of his anger was rooted in the jealousy he had for Ross's craftsmanship. He had never been able to build much of anything. Though his father and both of his brothers were blue-collar, do-it-yourself types; he had never been gifted with those skills. He spent his whole life working with paper, in the insurance business. He had been an agent for 20 years and then moved up to a management position. He knew how those barehanded types looked down on "pencil pushers" like him—his brothers always had. It didn't matter that Victor's job allowed him to make a better living than either of them.

Ginny had even made a fuss over how capable Ross was. What with driving a big rig all around the state and doing woodwork on the weekends, Ross had that raw, hard-man, outdoorsy mystique about him that most women went for.

He thought Ginny even found Ross attractive sometimes. He could see it in her eyes when they were visiting the kids. He had never mentioned it to her, though, partly because it would embarrass her and partly because it would make him seem insecure. They had been happily married for too long to let something so trivial come between them. He had certainly taken more than a few lascivious looks at the young women who worked in the office. "Lusting in his heart," the preacher would say.

Victor remembered how he was alarmed when Shelley first began dating Ross. He found out about Ross's father and would have forbidden his daughter to see Ross if he could have done so with a clear conscience. It was not fair or Christian to hold the children in contempt for the sins of their parents. Or maybe he did not have the courage to try to steer his daughter after allowing so many years of detachment to isolate her from his best affections.

There was no point in expressing any displeasure now. The remorse Ross would have to face would be more than enough punishment for the young man's carelessness. Victor would not have wished his worst enemy into Ross's shoes. Ross would have to live the rest of his life remembering the day his vanity took the life of his baby boy. Could Ross keep his sanity after this? Could anyone remain sane after this sort of thing? Victor shoved back a wave of pity for his son-in-law. If push came to shove, he knew which side he would be on. Too bad about the baby, though. Too bad.

CHAPTER FIFTEEN

"He's not sleeping very well," whispered *Wanda Martin.*

"I'm surprised he's asleep at all," replied Gerald. "We're not sleepy, and it has to be worse for him."

"I don't like it, them giving him a shot."

"They had to do something for him, Mother," Gerald said.

She didn't really object that strongly; she just needed to talk. "We won't be able to keep him company that much. He's going to need company."

Wanda and Gerald had brought their son back to his house to rest after the staff at Heritage Community had given him an injection of some kind. She knew it was supposed to settle him down after the horrible reality of what happened sunk in, but it did a poor job. Ross tossed and turned on the bed and started from time to time fitfully, as if something were stabbing at him in his sleep. Wanda knew something was.

Gerald was sitting on the floor of Ross and Shelley's bedroom, quietly weeping. He craved some liquor, but his conscience would not let him go and get any—not when Ross was in such a bad way. "He doesn't deserve something like this. He's always been a good boy. I don't understand." He didn't know if he was speaking loud enough for Wanda to hear or not. But he didn't want Ross to hear.

"It was an accident, that's all," Wanda said. She reached out and smoothed the cloth placemat on the night stand between them, trying to punctuate her statement. She was full of nervous energy, despite her fatigue. "Sometimes accidents happen. They just happen, and you can't see them coming. It wasn't his fault."

She smiled at Gerald weakly. "I'm glad we're both here, though. I appreciate you sitting with me."

She had mixed feelings about it. Part of her was glad he cared enough to stay, and part of her wished he would go. He would be more like himself if he had a few drinks in him.

She had never felt so helpless. Watching her boy double over in gut-wrenching agony tore her mother's-heart out. And the awful accident that had taken the lovely grandbaby was too much. At first she refused to believe that such a freak thing had happened. Yet it had. She had seen it with her own eyes. The way Ross had lost his balance when he tried to get to the cradle played through her mind again and again. It must have been that his eyes were focused through the lens of the camera and when he tried to rush he got disoriented somehow. He was never a clumsy person. Maybe he just couldn't think fast enough to get his feet in the right place. He was sort of leaning around the wall while he took those pictures. And didn't his foot get caught in the cords of the tree?

"This will be a focal point in all our lives," Wanda whispered as much to herself as to Gerald. "It is going to take awhile to even get our minds to wrap around what happened. Then there will be some hard, depressing days for Ross and Shelley."

"He'll live it down," Gerald said. "People have been through worse. Remember that Amish family. They lost all four of their kids in a fire."

Wanda remembered. "They had the sympathy and support of every church and volunteer organization in the valley," she said. Though the Amish community usually kept to itself, that particular tragedy was an exception. There had been a lot of publicity. People all felt their loss and pitched in. There were auctions and fund-raisers to benefit the family. It was heart-warming the way everybody helped. "It won't be that way with Ross. This isn't the kind of thing people see the need to get involved in. And it's only one child, not four or five."

Wanda sat there in the darkness and wondered what all of this would mean for her son. She had feared he would become suicidal after his friend Donny Ritts drowned. And she was never satisfied that Ross had gotten over what had happened back then. She would catch him sitting alone sometimes and could tell he was thinking about what happened that day on the river. But Ross always seemed to find a way to bury his miseries. Gerald could bury his in a bottle, though they were not really buried, but somehow transposed by the alcohol onto the lives of the people who were close to him. Ross might even be better off if he could salve his pain with alcohol. If it could buy him a little peace, she would be willing to suffer the same kind of pains from Ross that she did from Gerald. But she knew there was no good to be found for anyone in liquor. The fact that she even entertained the thought showed her how desensitized to its decadence she had become.

She had tried to get Gerald to go to AA meetings for years and then had given up. She had found the strength to go on for the sake of the family by getting involved in Al-Anon, which was a branch of AA for people like her, who must live with someone who has the disease. It was comforting to think of it as a disease. That way she did not have to consider her husband to be some kind of bum, which is what many did indeed think. He was such a good-hearted man—just weak, she thought.

She knew that since Ross had grown up in an alcoholic family, he considered himself to be more or less inferior anyway. It was something she knew before the people at the meetings let her in on it. He had learned to compensate for it somehow, to adapt, the way she'd adapted to the uncertainty of Gerald's character. How much compensation would he have to muster, though, to ride this out? The local newspaper was sure to print an account of what had happened. Everyone in town would know about Ross's misfortune. Could he live it down the way Gerald said? Would he even want to?

And what about Shelley? Would she hold it against him? If their marriage broke up, then perhaps Ross would turn to the bottle the way his father had. And what would that do to Randall, such a sweet, sensitive little boy? Would there be anyone who could remain detached from what happened to help the little fellow make sense of it as he grew up? She could certainly do her best, but it was no secret that there had been a wall erected between Ross's family and hers. A tacit barrier built and maintained to insulate Ross and Shelley from the alcoholism.

They would resist any effort she might make to help them.

❧

Shelley awakened slowly. She knew where she was but at first could not remember why she was not at home. She knew in her foggy mind there was a good reason for it, and soon she would remember why. She was content to lie quietly and stare at the soft light coming from the hallway. Way off she could hear voices. There were two people, women, speaking slowly. She could not tell what they were saying.

Something was beginning to creep into her consciousness now. She knew it was something ugly, and she made a determined effort to keep it away. It did not need to be addressed, she told herself. It was better left alone. But she was even more awake now, and the veil that had clouded her thinking had holes in it. Ragged punctures that let small bits of pain tumble in, one over another until suddenly the whole miserable heap was there to behold.

She remembered the table with the cradle perched on top of it, on display, as if her precious baby boy were an accessory to Ross's handiwork. She remembered him fussing over the difficulty of taking a good photograph and how annoyed she was that he had to do it then, while they were trying to have a celebration. But then the terrible cracking sound had started, and she knew that the old wood of the drop-leaf table was not going to support the weight of both cradle and baby. She had pushed Randy off her lap hurriedly and made for the kitchen. She had just reached her feet when she saw Ross lose his balance and, with his foot caught in the light cords, go sprawling headlong on top of the upturned cradle as if he were trying to pile on, the way football players sometimes did on a man who had been tackled. She heard again the hideous cracking sound as the glued joints gave way and the spindly structure of the little cradle was demolished under Ross's 180-pound frame.

She remembered her hysterical crying the night before when she had first come to face the awful truth. She saw the face of the emergency room physician as he turned to her. He spoke deliberately and slowly, like a man who does not know how to handle what he must do and so, must feel his way. "I'm sorry, there's nothing we can do. Your baby is gone. His neck is fractured. I'm...very sorry." She remembered clinging to her mother and father, felt their strong arms lifting her so she did not need to trust her wobbly legs to support her weight.

Shelley's heart felt like a pile of mush inside her. She remembered a verse from the Psalms that she had always thought strange but that she could relate to now, "my heart is like wax; it is melted in the midst of my bowels." The tears were flowing again now. She could feel them tracking down the sides of her face as she lay there on the bed. And she heard a sob. A sob like so many she had made the night before. And the pain of the cracking skin of her tight, dry lips told her the sob was hers.

❧

Ross lay still, watching the halo of light grow brighter around the drapes. He was wide-awake now but wished he were not. There could never be any reason to get out of bed again, he was sure. He had killed his son. If only he had not tried to take those pictures. What had been so important about taking pictures of that stupid cradle?

He felt repulsive to himself, as if he had been emptied of everything that was good and worthy, only to be refilled with ugliness and evil. Part of him wanted to cry again, but the tears would not come. It was like it had been that day on the Sugar River. Allowing himself to cry would give him some comfort, and he knew he did not deserve any. He would own the pain. He would pay what was due.

He was alone now. As totally alone as any man had ever been. Though he was in the company of his parents, and soon enough Shelley would come back to their home, things would never be the same. He knew it was so.

There was no one he could share the distinction with. No one he could point a finger at, even secretly in his own mind, to give him comfort. No way to mitigate this guilt. No rationale he could employ that would diminish the terrible truth.

He was numb, yet he ached. He was angry yet reserved. He was like a coiled spring of grief, ready to vault into the fires of hell if any offer of escape were given him. He kept hoping that he would wake up and it would all be just a dream, an unspeakably cruel and tasteless nightmare.

He had always known that Shelley's parents considered him to be beneath their daughter. They had never really treated him with the proper warmth when he was dating her. Even when their romance got serious and everyone knew they had an understanding about the future, they had treated him like someone they could do without. Oh, they never said anything negative to him. It was the things they didn't say, the tone of their voices, the look on their faces when it was only him they could make eye contact with. He could tell they did not want him for a son-in-law. Now they would not be able to hide their disdain for him. Now they would cleave to Shelley and shut him out, he could tell. They would seize the opportunity. Who could blame them?

Ross began to slowly torture himself. His thoughts drifted back to the day when he first found out he would be a father. The day she told him about Randall. He remembered the look in Shelley's eyes. She had been nearly as swollen with pride and joy when she first told Ross as she was swollen with water and flesh nine months later. He remembered the intense feelings of wealth he had when he could see her belly growing. Knowing that it was he who had planted the seed, his tender love and glorious desire for her that had caused the miracle to begin.

From the first day of prospective fatherhood he had boarded a train. A train of love that focused everything he did on Shelley and their baby. It had grown each and every day. Every increase in the girth of Shelley's abdomen had been as if another car had been added to the train, so the joy grew and lengthened. It stretched into the past to obscure the misery of his childhood. It blanketed the memory of that dreadful day on the Sugar River with a thick cloud of smoke that softened the dying cries of Donny Ritts. There was less room in his mind for that pain, so thick was the anticipation, so endless the train of joy.

When Shelley first felt movement in her womb, she had been like a kid with a new toy, squealing with delight when the first moving bulge had lifted Ross's hand on her belly. They had lain so many nights with Ross feeling for the movement as if he would never get enough of it.

When Randall was born, Ross had gone home from the hospital and collapsed on the kitchen floor, struck suddenly by a gigantic heartthrob that left him sobbing out his gratitude to God for the marvelous wonder of a son.

When the second child had come along, he had experienced almost as much happiness as the first time. But the joy of it had all suddenly turned on him. It had turned, the way life had turned on him when he led his friend to the middle of the Sugar River and set him up for a frustrating and terrifying death.

He thought about little Donny. How hard the boy must have fought for the chance to grow up. There was surely some level of consciousness in the mind of a baby, though he could not speak or even think in words. Though he could not have remembered it, even if he had been able to mature, the child had experienced life. He knew the soft warm touch of his mother's cheek. He had drawn the nourishment from her breasts and been satisfied with it. He had felt love and known that there were those who desired his presence. But he had been denied the opportunity to grow because of his father's stupidity. It wasn't right. It wasn't fair. If anyone should have been killed, it was Ross. He had put the innocent at risk for the sake of his pride. Just like that day on the Sugar.

How could he ever rectify this? If he were to spend the rest of his life working and paying and suffering, it would never balance the scale. How could he ever look Shelley in the eye again? Though he was Donny's father, it was not the same. He had never known the fullness of gestation; he had not suffered the sickness and the discomfort for nine long months. He had only marveled at the level of agony Shelley had endured in giving birth and been glad that he did not have to suffer such torture. He had not only wronged the baby, he had wronged Shelley, and nothing he could ever do would make it right.

Ross knew then what he would do. He would pay the price; at least what he could—but not yet. This was something that required preparation and care. He drew a little ease for himself knowing that justice would be served. He felt better knowing that there was an out for him. The future was fixed in his mind, though it was not as yet clear enough for him to act upon. He sensed that when the time was right, he would know and follow through. The knowledge gave him a little measure of peace, enough to stand lightly upon. Enough to get out of bed and put one foot in front of the other, enough to keep the monster at bay—at least for now.

CHAPTER SIXTEEN

Dr. Albert Myers, chief of medical staff at Heritage Community hospital, usually held a meeting each week to discuss sensitive cases with his underlings. When he heard about the death of the Martin baby and the unusual circumstances, he held the meeting a day early. The staff could see right away that the boss was troubled at the lack of discretion by so many people in his institution.

"You all know that our job is not only to heal the sick, but to 'do no harm.' That's part of the Hippocratic oath. Since the Martin baby was pronounced dead here the other night, this hospital has been worse than a junior high school with unnecessary conversation about the event. Idle conversation in a professional healthcare setting is bad enough. But the amount of speculation and gossip I have heard is appalling to me, even though I'm sure that most of the people watch their tongues when I'm around. How much worse it must be when I'm not around?

"From this moment forward, I want no more talk about the incident unless it is between people who have some part in the Martins' care. This community is quite able to drum up more than enough careless and malicious gossip on it's own. This institution does not need to contribute to it.

"This couple could benefit greatly from counseling. Some of you probably think I'm being a little too pro-active in this case. Well, maybe I am. The fact is, I feel bad for the couple, especially for the father. I've never heard of such a bizarre twist of misfortune. It's like something Stephen King might dream up.

"My concern, I must confess, is not completely born of compassion. Hospitals are being sued every day for things they are not responsible for. Some shrewd lawyer will probably see an opportunity for a charge based on the fact that we released a preemie so early. If this Ross Martin is as much of a basket case as most of us would be in these circumstances, he will be looking to ease his pain by blaming someone else. The bloodsucking lawyers can smell an opportunity like this a mile away."

One of the other physicians seated at the table took Dr. Myers to task. "Don't you think you might be meeting trouble halfway with this tactic? What makes you so sure these people will consider holding us responsible in some way?"

Dr. Myers looked over at Dr. Zilafro. "Tell them what you told me about the delivery, Henry," he said with some resignation, as if he had not wanted to reveal this part.

Dr. Zilafro cleared his throat and began slowly, even more reluctant than Myers had been. "Shelley Martin experienced an unusually high reaction to the medication we used to stop her labor, or rather tried to stop. She lost some autonomic function—had trouble breathing. If her husband had not complained so strenuously we might even have lost her. Her pulse was beginning to slow when I got to her. I fear the man may be somewhat prejudiced toward us because of that."

The consensus was formed quickly then. Everyone present agreed that the hospital needed to play this one carefully. They also knew that Myers' admonition to keep quiet about the tragedy was essential. The hospital did not need another lawsuit.

Young Dr. Riley left the meeting dripping with cynicism. Later he entered the physician's lounge and found another doctor there, Roger Fleischmann—someone he knew he could be candid with. "At the risk of sounding youthfully idealistic, let me translate the chief's rhetoric for you, Fleischmann: The medical profession keeps to itself about the close call Shelley Martin had. The couple must never know how close she came to death or how her husband's insistence on Dr. Zilafro's presence actually saved her life, which might go a long way in helping him cope with the guilt we are so concerned with. But no, it's more important that we cover our collective ass."

"And you had your doubts about the low road being the pathway to success," Dr. Fleischmann said.

CHAPTER SEVENTEEN

Pastor Fred Sawyer got the call from Virginia Clark while he was in the middle of his morning prayers. He had just finished thanking God for the health of the Martin boy. He usually repeated his gratitude for such a complete answer to prayer for a week after he got it. But since this was Sunday, when he needed to concentrate on his sermon, and since his list of concerns was so long with the Christmas season coming on, he had crossed it off early.

Still on his knees, he stretched to reach the phone. It was his personal number, and only the members of his church had it. There was an understanding that it was not to be used unless something serious had happened. He had a secretary and an answering machine for any church-related business. He knew this would be something he had better take while on his knees. Virginia was clearly upset.

"There was an accident yesterday at Shelley's house," she said, her voice shaky.

Sawyer's calm, comforting instincts kicked in. "Go slow, Virginia. Tell me what happened."

"The baby was killed. Ross fell on him." She was sobbing now.

"Did you say Ross fell on the baby?" he asked, trying not to sound as shocked as he felt.

"Yes, he made this cradle for the baby, and he was trying to take pictures of it. It fell off the table; it was an old rickety table, and the cradle fell onto the floor. Ross tried to get to it, to catch it before it fell. But he tripped and landed on top of it. It broke…and the baby was crushed underneath him." She let go with unrestrained sobbing.

Although Ginny seemed to have a penchant for melodrama, her distress was understandable this time. All her problems were usually reserved for his ears, he had come to believe—even the little ones she exaggerated to evoke his sympathy. On the surface she was a resolute, stoic matriarch who kept a strong front for her husband and family, but she fell apart on a regular basis in his office, usually for some trivial reason. Some fancied slight had wounded her feminine pride and toppled the unstable stack of pains she had piled up inside her like so much cordwood.

He liked being a pastor, but sometimes he resented the people he was called to serve. Why should he be called upon to do the job that was rightly Victor's? He had supposed at first that this was another such moment. Then the incredible story of Ross's fall and the baby's death unfolded, and he felt awful for thinking so lowly of the woman.

"This happened yesterday?" he asked.

"Yes. We had a little baby shower for them yesterday. It was about 4 o'clock, I guess, when it happened," Virginia said.

"How are Ross and Shelley?" he asked.

"I don't really know for sure. The doctor gave both of them something to calm them down and help them sleep. It was pretty strong stuff. Shelley slept for 12 hours in the hospital. Victor was with her when she woke up, but she is pretty bad off. Ross went home with his folks. They haven't called yet."

Sawyer arranged to find a replacement to teach Virginia's Sunday school class and to visit Ross and Shelley later in the day.

"Don't worry, Virginia," the pastor said. "Remember, all things work together for good, for them that love the Lord."

He slipped the phone back into its cradle and straightened up. His eyes fixed on the slanted line he had drawn through the notation "Martin baby." It was as if the Almighty had been waiting for him to cross off the name before he got the news. He wondered what that meant, if anything.

Ross Martin had become little more than a face in the

crowd to Pastor Sawyer. That was going to change now. He had counseled the boy after the death of Donny Ritts, but that was when Ross was in high school, and he couldn't even remember what year that was for sure. He made a mental note to check his diary before going to call on the Clarks and Martins that afternoon.

He had married Ross and Shelley, but Ross was like so many young men when it came to religion—not really committed. Shelley came to every service she could, usually without Ross. He knew that Ross's job as a trucker for H.A. Murphy took him away sometimes on Sunday, but he suspected that Ross missed as many sermons as he could while still keeping his wife happy.

Sawyer continued praying then. He soon reached the end of his list, but he lingered on in meditation, waiting and ready for any insight he might get on the day's ministry. The matter of Ross and Shelley's misfortune dominated his mind. He hoped it would not crowd out the other important things he needed to remember for the day.

The scripture he quoted Virginia Clark about all things working together for good went through his mind again. He used that verse a lot, even suspected that he might have overused it to the point that it had become trite to Virginia. He knew that it was not out of the realm of possibility for God to take a child from parents. He could use the pain of it to drive them out of their worldly comfort, into the place where they could take a fresh look at life and their souls. People never learned anything from pleasure and usually got less holy when life was easy. He was careful who he shared such truth with, knowing that some folks would see it as a cruel philosophy. Whether God had caused it to happen or simply took advantage of it was beyond him anyway. He just knew that the coming months would be a window of opportunity for Ross Martin's salvation. He prayed for the wisdom to use that opportunity well.

❧

Pastor Sawyer picked up Victor and Virginia from their house early in the afternoon. They sat together in the back seat of his car, clutching each other as he drove through Heritage. The streets were streaked with ice, the remnants of the previous day's snowfall now pounded into a ceramic glaze.

"Better to drive on than slush," noted Victor from the back seat, in a wasted effort to relieve the gloom. He wondered what words of consolation their man of God might have for this particular situation. He wouldn't have traded places with the man in the front seat for anything now. There were some times in life when there was no way to bring comfort to people, and all one could do was perhaps show up and declare by your presence that you cared. More would be expected from Pastor Sawyer, Victor knew, especially from his wife. She had a look on her face since the pastor had arrived that he couldn't quite understand. She saw something in this soft-spoken man that she desired in him but had to do without. He had seen it before. "Well, a man can't be everything, can he?" Victor mused in quiet resentment, there in the solemn car.

Virginia saw a clergyman as something above life, somehow detached from it and therefore able to reach into it and repair hurts, the way an auto mechanic might reach into the cramped spaces under the hood of a car and work some mysterious magic. Victor supposed that in most cases the magic happened in the minds of the people. The minister simply offered a vehicle for it, gave people an object they could focus their hope on. However it worked, Victor was grateful that here was someone who would at least try to help his little girl put her life back together.

When they reached Ross and Shelley's house, Sawyer asked, "What are the names of Ross's parents again?" They weren't people he knew that well, since they did not attend his church.

"Gerald and Wanda," Virginia said.

"Oh yes." Having checked his diary, he also remembered now that Gerald had a drinking problem and was a regular at the Heritage Hotel.

It made things harder for Ross and Shelley, he knew. Not just because of Gerald's alcoholism but because there was a social gap between Ross and Shelley—the kind of gap that he tried to eliminate as a minister. People like Victor and Virginia viewed Ross's parents with some measure of disgust. They were supposed to show the love of God toward everyone, even alcoholics. Sawyer could hear, however, the mild change of inflection in Virginia Clark's voice, even with the momentary speaking of the names. She was subtly letting him know that Ross's parents were not on a par with them. Sawyer pursed his lips, glad he did not need to look her in the face just now.

They knocked on the door, and Wanda opened it at once. She had seen them pull up and met them at the door. The mood inside the house was too somber for any one person to handle alone, and Wanda was grateful for the company. She had run out of things to say to her son and daughter-in-law.

Gerald was seated on the couch with Randall, watching a children's video on the television. It was an odd thing for Gerald, who had never taken any part in child rearing. Keeping the little boy occupied was something worthwhile he could do just now, a fulfillment of duty.

Ross and Shelley were at the kitchen table. There was an agonizing pause, an uncomfortable silence that punctuated everyone's awareness of the bitter event. Everyone knew the purpose of the visit, but nobody knew how to overcome the intensity of the grief long enough to say anything. Finally, the pastor broke the ice

"Ross, Shelley, I'm sorry about your baby." Shelley's face slowly contorted into the same drawn-up picture of agony she had displayed the night before. The sobs wrenched her frame. She turned and faced the man, and he moved to take her in his arms.

"There, there, I know. I know," he let the tone of his voice convey what words could not.

He moved his head up a little and made eye contact with Ross. Ross's face looked every bit like the illustrations he recalled from a copy of *Dante's Inferno* he had in his library. The artist had done a good job of depicting hopeless misery on the face of a man, and seeing that look, so stark in Ross's face, shook Sawyer in a way he had not prepared himself for. He realized then that no tragedy he had ever tried to console had been as pointed and focused on one individual as this one was on Ross Martin. He buttressed his courage, telling himself that this was what he had wanted when he went to seminary—to help people who needed it. He knew that no one was better prepared to help than he was. Yet he could not shake a feeling of inadequacy. He had felt that way before, he reminded himself—he had to go on in spite of it.

When Shelley got a little control of herself, Sawyer sat her down again and moved over to embrace Ross. The man was stiff. It was as if the hug was not so much accepted as it was tolerated. Strange that Ross could remain deliberate and controlled in the face of what had to be self-contempt. This man wasn't acting the way Sawyer expected him to—probably some defense mechanism; sorrowful people were unpredictable.

"Ross, are you okay?"

"No, I'm not okay. Thanks for coming, pastor."

"We need to talk about this," Sawyer said. "I can't say I know how bad it hurts. I can only imagine. I only know it is more than anyone can handle alone, and you don't have to."

"I killed my son." Ross's voice was matter of fact, but trembling.

"There was an accident," Sawyer said.

"I caused it," Ross said.

"They told me about it. You couldn't have known it was going to happen." The pastor's argument seemed weak, even to him.

"I built the cradle; I restored the table. I put the two together." Now Ross lost control as the words came out. Almost tumbling over one another in a mixture of child-like sobs. "I... fell...on him."

Now the man of God took the truck driver in his arms the way he had Shelley. He was releasing his emotion now, and Sawyer felt better. Ross was acting like a normal human being now. Crying was called for, and the man was crying. Sawyer got a mental image of the tremendous weight of sorrow that Ross carried inside him. He wished to open himself up and take on part of the load himself. It was a way of helping; it was what he had been called to do for people. But he sensed the burden was not free to go where it would. It was chained down, like the heavy coils of steel he saw passing the window of his study on the beds of trailer-trucks nearly every day. Sawyer supposed that his mind had conjured up the imagery somehow because Ross was a trucker.

"What happened to you is something incredible, Ross. I can only think that God has some incredible purpose for it all. Maybe that sounds trite to you, like it's what you would expect me to say, but it's true."

At his words, others in the room began to wail. A long time went by. The group of people hugged and cried and comforted each other without shame or reservation. Even Randall was holding onto his family members one at a time, hugging each as if in his innocence, there were a capacity for sorrow and compassion the others lacked.

"Go ahead everybody, this is the right thing to do," the preacher reassured them.

After a prolonged period of mourning and sharing of grief, the people settled down somewhat. Wanda and Virginia went to the kitchen to make coffee. The pastor resumed his counseling. "I think we should pray. Let's all join hands round the table and ask the Lord to help us get through this."

The older women returned from the kitchen, and the group bowed their heads. The preacher let go a deep sigh as if he were laying down something heavy.

"Lord, you know how hard it is for us just now. You know all about the terrible accident that took little Donny from us. You know how much we hurt, and you know how hard it is for us to understand. You know the future. And we believe that you have little Donny on your lap right now. We trust that he is in a better place.

"But Lord, our trust can't make the painful feelings go away. We can't help in our humanity but have doubts, fears and guilt. We suffer from what has happened in a way that no amount of each other's sympathy can completely wash away."

The preacher could not quite find the right words. He

felt himself come to an end almost in his ability to articulate anything of value. He knew he must press on, so he let the words come out and endeavored to construct sentences on the edge of his tongue. The result was surprising to him.

"Lord, we can only ask for strength. We ask for the strength to love each other in the midst of this pain. We ask for strength to trust in your goodness in spite of accidents and tragedy. We ask not so much for relief from this agony as to see your face and to feel your presence in it. Help us to see this time of chaos and loss as an opportunity to lean more heavily on you, to trust you for the grace to go on. We know that the pathway of growth in this life is a mixture of joy and pain. Help us to believe that the happiness to come will be more intense than the misery it replaces and that the meaning we gather, as we trust in your mercy, will make us more like you and your son Jesus. Most of all Lord, help us to get through this one day. Give us the peace that passes understanding, and glorify yourself in us. Give the words of our prayers the power to sustain us, until a time of understanding comes for us. In Jesus' name we ask this. Amen."

Ross was able to take some comfort from the man's words, much as he did so many years before after the death of the other Donny. But he knew the little comfort would not be lasting and that there was no way he would be able to "sustain," as the pastor had prayed. For now he could hold himself together, and for the sake of Shelley and Randall, he would. But eventually there would come the day of reckoning. He could wait till then. There was more comfort available to him, he could somehow sense. But he would not take it.

"I know that prayers may seem inadequate to you now," the pastor said, addressing everyone in the room. "What I can tell you is that time will make this easier. I know that God's mercy is sufficient to see all of us through this. The hands of God don't always work in the way we wish them to. We can't expect to avoid the hard things in life. What we can expect is that God will see us through, one day at a time."

His face and voice were soft now, as he tried his best to

share the pain of these people, to mix the reality of faith into the reality of life, so that the blend would make sense to people.

Spiritual work was frustrating. No way to measure whether or not you were doing any real good. The pretensions of people, their ability to effect a relationship with God, at least until times like this, made him wonder sometimes about the value of his work. But he understood more clearly now that times like these were essential to his work. Maybe the only time he accomplished anything was when people's lives began to fall apart. He checked that train of thought, though, as he had so many times before. Negative thinking was one thing he could not allow himself if he were to be an effective minister.

The pastor caught the eyes of Wanda momentarily, knowing that the "one day at a time" thing was used in group therapy for families of alcoholics and that she, no doubt, was familiar with the concept. He wondered if Gerald was active in AA? If so, he would be equally familiar with it. It was a nice "feel good" concept to most people. But to some, it was a method of survival. Maybe the experience with alcoholism would have a positive effect on this situation. Ross and Wanda were experienced at coping with chronic misery because of Gerald.

The look on Ross's face scared Sawyer. His grief would naturally have an unusually sharp edge to it, and he could not tell how aware the others were of it. He approached Ross. "Can you and I go somewhere and talk privately?"

"Sure," Ross said, but his face looked anything but eager. He led the man down to his basement workshop. Sawyer noticed there was some sawdust on the workbench. It was probably fresh from the cradle Ross had built only a few days before.

Ross put one foot up on the workbench and leaned his elbow on his knee, facing Sawyer. The muscles on his face, tight under his skin, wrinkled his brow and made him look years older than he was. His eyes drooped at the corners with sadness, yet there was a grim determination in them. It glared out from the sockets as if it would bore through steel. The crooked line of his mouth spoke of a soul ready to collapse under the weight of remorse. Yet his jaw jutted out slightly, like a man possessed by a grim purpose.

The mixed look on Ross's face disarmed Sawyer for a moment, and he had to look away in order to collect his thoughts. When he looked back, Ross's face had softened a bit, as if he had known he was projecting something personal and secret and now thought better of it.

"Ross, I know this is especially hard for you," Sawyer said.

Ross stared back, unwilling to drop the drawbridge. "It's hard for everybody," he said.

"You know what I mean," Sawyer said softly.

"You mean because I caused it."

Sawyer rubbed his chin with his hand and searched for better words. "You can't look at it that way," he said.

"I know you mean well, pastor, but don't expect me to lie to myself," Ross said.

"That's not what I had in mind. What you need is some time to put this thing into perspective. It's normal to feel guilty about what happened. You're not the only one who will feel guilty," Sawyer said.

"I'm the only one you wanted to talk to in private."

"Fair enough. But I know how you felt about the death of Donny Ritts. It hasn't been that long ago. I wonder if you might feel an unreasonable share of guilt." Sawyer was treading carefully now. "I'll be honest with you, Ross. This could affect your family badly in the long run. I know it might not seem fair for me to ask you to be the strong one now, but you're going to have to be. Whether you know it or not, Shelley and Randall will need you to support them. Not Randall so much. Thank God he's too young to get a good hold on this. But what happens between you and Shelley in the next few days and weeks will resonate in your memories for years to come.

"You might see yourself as responsible for what happened, but I don't think they do. But they will be looking to you to set the tone of their lives for a while. I won't kid you. You've been given a lousy hand to play. But it's yours to play. You're the man of the house. They need you to be strong."

"Who do you think you're kidding?" Ross spat out, his voice venomous with the bile of inner demons.

"What, you think I'm putting you on?" Sawyer said, taking a step back from Ross's blazing eyes.

"I think you want me to feel good about myself, and you'll use anything that will work for you. I appreciate it, but I can't escape the fact that I'm the one at fault. You think they don't see me as the one at fault? Get real, pastor," Ross said.

"You don't understand. Being strong for them doesn't mean you deny whatever share of responsibility you might have. What it means is that you find the courage to go on with life, to refuse to let the harsh world you guys are going to be living in defeat you. You're the only one who can show them that. And maybe they will see you as the one at fault. They might even say so.

"I won't kid you, it's gonna be hard. Probably harder than anything you've ever done. It's something I doubt most people can handle. But if you are willing to face it and make the best of it, you can minimize the damage this does to Shelley and Randall and ultimately to yourself.

"You say you see yourself at fault. I say you'll feel differently in time. I think you'll be able to forgive yourself for it. But it will take time, lots of time. You can't afford to let Shelley and Randall be without your strength because you feel guilty. The last thing you probably want to do is go on as if you had no more to do with the accident than anyone else. You probably feel like that's shirking your responsibility or something. Am I right?"

"Yep."

"What you need to see is that you've got a higher responsibility now. The need your family has for you has to trump everything else, at least for a while."

"I don't know," Ross said. "I don't feel like I can do anything good for them."

"Let me give you a thought, Ross," the pastor said. "If you really feel like you are to blame, then you want a way to make things right. The best way to use that desire to make things right is to give Shelley and Randall all you've got in the way of faith and hope and strength. Anything less will lead to more pain and misery. Trust me on that."

Ross was looking down at the floor now, slowly trying to digest what the minister had told him. Something glimmered in his mind, a small ray of hope, a sense that maybe the pastor was right. He looked up and nodded.

"Ross, when something like this happens in a family, the husband and wife usually do blame each other. I don't know why, but they do. Often it leads to a divorce. The statistics aren't good. That's why I'm being honest with you right from the beginning. If we work together on this, you and me and Shelley and Jesus, maybe you guys can beat the odds."

"I just..." Ross began to weep. The sobs came then, strong and wracking. He struggled to keep the sound under control, not wanting the people upstairs to hear him.

"I know," Sawyer said. "It hurts like fire." He put his arm across Ross's shoulder. "This is gonna take a tough man, Ross. I think you're up to it."

CHAPTER EIGHTEEN

The funeral was private, and only family members were present. Pastor Sawyer kept his remarks brief and appropriate for the brevity of the child's life. When Ross and Shelley got home after the funeral, there was a message on their answering machine from H.A. Murphy, asking Ross to call in. He promised Shelley he would not leave that day, even if that was what they wanted. He dialed the number. Kim, the daytime dispatcher, answered.

"Hi, Kim. Ross Martin here. Thanks for the flowers," Ross said.

"You're welcome, Ross. Everyone here is very sorry about your baby. How is Shelley doing?" asked Kim.

"She's holding up okay. She's a tough person, I guess," Ross said.

"I need to see if Mr. Murphy is available," Kim said. "He wanted to speak to you. Can you hold?"

"Sure," Ross said. He felt uneasy as he waited on the line for his boss. An upbeat piano tune played on the hold line, overlaid with a sales pitch Ross could nearly recite in his sleep. The looped recording played through twice. Ross looked at Shelley, hoping for some reassuring look from her. But her eyes and features were as bland and unexpressive as the faces on her collection of ceramic dolls resting on a shelf above the telephone table.

Finally Murphy came on. He cleared his throat and mumbled a clumsy expression of sympathy. Ross wasn't sure if the man was finished speaking, so he did not respond. But Murphy shifted quickly to the main reason for asking Ross to call. "Ross, I don't have to ask you how you're feeling. I can imagine how badly I would be feeling in your shoes. I wish there was something I could do," Murphy said.

"I appreciate that, sir. We'll be okay. We just need time," Ross said.

"That's what I think, too. You need time. I hate to do this to you Ross, but I'm going to have to take you off the road for a spell. Just until you've had some time to adjust and get over your sorrow some. I'm not talking anything permanent," Murphy said.

"I guess you don't think I can concentrate on driving, huh?" Ross said.

"Do you think you can?"

"No. Probably not the way I should," Ross said.

"I appreciate you, Ross. You're one of my better men, and I wouldn't want to see anything happen to your driving record. It's too easy to have an accident, especially this time of year. I'll tell you what. You come in tomorrow at 7 o'clock, and we'll put you to work in the warehouse. The pay isn't as good, I know, but I'll let you work some overtime if you want. I'll try to keep your wages up close to what you're used to. You think you can do that for me?" Murphy said.

"I guess so," Ross said, as if he had no opinion at all on the matter. When he hung up he turned to Shelley. "They want me to work in the warehouse for a while, load trucks and stuff. It will be all daylight shifts anyway. That's one good thing."

"So you won't be going away at night for a while?" Shelley asked.

"That's right. He thinks I'll be too preoccupied because of what happened." There was a bemused look on Shelley's face. He longed for her to be her old self for just a few moments. He felt awkward and unwanted.

Shelley felt strongly disappointed that Ross would not be returning to the normal way of things. Ordinarily she would have been delighted to have him home every night and would have done anything to prolong that time. But she felt differently now. She looked down at the floor, keeping her face away from Ross's so that he might not read the way she felt.

Shelley was torn internally. She could not muster a positive feeling toward Ross. All she could see was him with that stupid camera, traipsing around the dining room, taking pictures and laughing at her for being so concerned about the baby. She knew he was hurting, too, but whatever there was in her that normally responded to his pain was broken, severed like a watermelon cut cleanly in half and rolling apart. And all the former joy they had shared together meant nothing to her, less than nothing.

She saw her reflection darkly in the bright surface of the coffee table and remembered her usual preoccupation with the purple spot on her cheek. How ironic could it be that for the first time in her life she was able to forget about her face? It was something she had wished for so many times. Now the horrendous price she'd had to pay mocked her desire to forget her discolored face. It was as if God was angry with her for disdaining his one reckless moment in her creation and wanted to teach her a lesson. Well, he had taught her a lesson all right.

❧

When Ross reported for work the next morning, Jack Dobbs was waiting for him. Dobbs was the dock foreman and Ross had worked for him in the past. "He told you?" Dobbs asked.

"Yeah," Ross said. "I guess I'm gonna be helping you out for a while." Dobbs slapped him on the back.

"I'm real sorry about what happened to you, Ross. I just want you to know how highly we all think of you around here. People want to look out for you, you know?" The man was clumsy with his sympathy, but Ross thanked him for it and tried to smile at him.

"It'll be just like old times," Dobbs said.

That day was hellish for Ross. Even people who knew how to be tactful had a hard time expressing their sympathy for him, so bizarre was the nature of his son's death. Some of the people, especially the men, just sort of clammed up around him, not knowing what to say. The best he got was a pat on the shoulder, a lingering, caring touch that conveyed what words could not.

Some of the women hugged him. There were a few sympathy cards left in the slot where his time card went.

Ross went through the motions of doing the old familiar job. Some things had changed in the years that he had been driving, but there was nothing he couldn't adjust to. Nobody really seemed to care how well he worked anyway.

Ross longed to be out of there—to be back on the road, where no eyes could fall upon him, to be alone with his thoughts and grief. The sympathy and pity he saw in the eyes of his co-workers only served to punctuate the lump of misery that had twisted his stomach up into a knot, as if his entrails were being wrung out like a soggy bath towel.

Christmas came and went. Ross and Shelley handled the holiday mechanically, going through the motions just like they had in previous years. But this year when the season was over, Ross could hardly remember any of it. When people at work asked what gifts he had received, he had to stop and think. Ross neglected to turn on the colored lights on the porch many nights, and Shelley did not ask him to. Even Randall did not bother to point out the lack of illumination. It was as if the Martin house itself were in mourning.

❧

Pastor Sawyer stopped by the Murphy terminal one day and asked to see John Murphy. They fetched the boss from his office. Sawyer extended his hand.

"Mr. Murphy, I'm Fred Sawyer. I'm Ross Martin's minister. I'd like to speak with you privately if you can give me a few minutes of your time.

Murphy motioned the clergyman back to his office, which was spacious but cluttered and smelled a little musty. Sawyer noted the lack of windows.

"You want coffee?" Murphy said.

"No, thank you. This won't take long. I'm sure you're busy."

"I guess you have concerns about Ross?"

"Yes. I just wanted to talk to someone he works with. I'm

afraid he might be distracted, you know, maybe have an accident or something?" Sawyer said.

"I understand. I have those concerns, too," Murphy said. "That's why I'm not going to send him out in a truck for a while. He worked in the warehouse out here for a long time before he started driving. The pay isn't as good, but he'll have less stress. He's not crazy about the idea, I can tell, but I have to do something like this. There is no way he could keep his mind off his troubles when he's driving. If he works here he'll have to use his head more, keep thinking about what he's doing. I think it's best. A truck driver is supposed to keep alert, to keep his mind on the road, but anybody who's ever done it knows that you don't always. The road gets monotonous, and you are free to think. He doesn't need to think right now."

Murphy leaned forward in his desk chair, wanting the pastor to see from his posture, his face, and his words, that he was sincere.

"I'm glad you're doing something," Sawyer said. "I've been calling on him and his wife every couple of days now. I know they appreciate it, but I'm not sure I'm doing them any good. They've got so much pain, and they are just too young to know how to handle it, I guess. Oh, they know what they're supposed to do; they know how they're supposed to act, but I don't think it is sincere. They both have feelings of guilt, especially Ross." Sawyer paused, debating whether to bring up Ross's earlier burden of guilt. "Did you know about what happened to Ross when he was in high school?"

"You mean his friend drowning?"

"Yes."

"I heard the story. You think there's some connection between the two?" Murphy said.

"I think Ross feels guilty about both of them. Put yourself in Ross's place for a minute. He can't help but feel responsible for the baby's death. If he has any lingering guilt about his friend, well...I just don't know what it might do to him. And the situation between him and his wife isn't good. It rarely is when there is a death of a child. Things like that sort of pull the rug out from under people. They lose something, something they maybe never get back."

"So tell me, what usually happens in situations like this? Divorce, I suppose," Murphy said.

"All too often. I guess what I expect to happen—maybe what my guts tell me will happen—is that they will have a huge fight where they each pour all their negative emotions out onto each other. They are keeping that all bottled up because they know it is the right thing to do—be forgiving and all," Sawyer said.

"I don't mean to be disrespectful here, but what I'm getting here is that religion doesn't have all the answers?" Murphy spoke in a way that implied triumphant cynicism.

Sawyer sensed Murphy's implication and nearly sighed outwardly. He had secretly feared something like this. He reminded himself not to sound defensive. "No, of course we don't have all the answers. If we did, there would be no room for faith. God wants faith, Mr. Murphy. It's hard to grasp in times like this, I know. But the essence of Christianity is most real when people are going through these painful times. God uses things like what Ross and Shelley are living through to shape them into better people. I suppose that sounds, well…cliché to you."

"Not at all," Murphy said.

"I don't mean to preach, but hey, that's what I do."

"That's all right. I didn't mean to imply anything bad. But you and I both know this thing will do the two of them more harm than good."

Now Sawyer did sigh outwardly. "It won't, Mr. Murphy. I have to believe—no, I do believe—that God will bring them through this into something better. That's what he does."

"Okay. Fair enough. But you still want me to what, keep my eye on Ross?"

"Well sure. Just be a little more considerate of him than you might otherwise be. I know I don't have to tell you that. I guess I just feel a little bit inadequate for this trouble. I'm trying to hit every part of Ross's life. I hope you understand."

Murphy looked at Sawyer with new respect and a measure of compassion that surprised both of them. "Of course I do. I don't blame you for feeling that way. What happened isn't your everyday accident."

The two men nodded to each other, acknowledging that there was no more to say. Sawyer rose, and they shook hands. "Let me leave you my card," Sawyer said. "You call me if anything happens you think I or his family should know about. Would you?"

"I'd be glad to, pastor." The tone of Murphy's voice had no trace of cynicism now.

After Sawyer was gone, Murphy pulled Leeroy Foust off to the side. "You know Ross about as well as anyone here. How do you think he's doing?"

"I really haven't been around him that much since the accident. Ross isn't the kind to talk much about his troubles. I figure if it was me, I'd want to be left alone," Leeroy said.

"His preacher was in to see me. I think he's worried about Ross's mental health or something. I thought you might be able to shed some light," Murphy said.

"Why don't you just try to put Ross and me together on a couple runs. That way I'll get an idea of how he's really doing," Leeroy offered.

"Maybe that's what I'll do when he goes back on the road. I have him working the docks until the first of the year. I figure it might be safer for him." Murphy looked out across the warehouse as if he might find some answers hanging in the rafters.

"I bet he doesn't like it much," Leeroy said.

"No, I think he feels like I don't trust him."

"It's bad enough, what happened with his baby. Now you don't want him to do his job. You could be making things worse for him, you know," Leeroy said, pushing his cap up on his head so he could have a better view of Murphy's eyes.

"Thanks a lot, old timer, that's just what I wanted to hear," Murphy said. He looked discouraged and concerned.

"He'll be all right," Leeroy said. "Just don't go back on your word about letting him drive when the time comes."

CHAPTER NINETEEN

Ross rolled out of bed and turned off the alarm clock that was buzzing insistently by the bedside. Though the buzzing was more than enough to wake Shelley, his wife lay turned away from him. She did not stir. As he went about the business of dressing and getting ready to leave for work with no effort to be quiet, she remained still and silent as a lump of clay. Before the accident she would have gotten out of bed to fix his breakfast and see him off.

As Ross shaved he had a vision of driving endlessly with the windows open. The dry wind ripping and flailing about in the cab of the truck, beating on his heart as if it could sponge away his pain the way it dried up pools of water left in a field after a soaking rain. He would drive relentlessly, until there was no moisture left in him to become tears, until his soul was parched and dry, and the sting of his guilt became part of a greater pain and less distinct, less focused on his heart. Maybe he could bear it then.

Ross walked around to the other side of the bed and leaned over to kiss Shelley. It was hard for him to follow through with it, since he knew she was totally indifferent to his affection. Pastor Sawyer had said they should go on acting as if things were normal. If they were patient, then in time things would begin to feel normal.

There hadn't been even a mention of sex since the accident, though before that they couldn't get enough of each other. Now Ross could tell Shelley didn't even care if he touched her. Not that it mattered. He had lost all interest in sex. He just didn't think about it anymore. It had been crowded out of his consciousness by the sorrow, he supposed, like every other good thought.

"Gotta go, Shelley, give Randy a hug for me, okay?"

Her response was something like a gentle grunt, as if she were forcing it out, which Ross supposed she was. He left the bedroom and slipped quietly down the carpeted steps and turned on the light in the kitchen. The coffeemaker was nearly finished filling the pot, the timer having turned it on at 5 a.m., the same time as his alarm upstairs.

Ross poured himself a bowl of cereal and added the milk. He filled his thermos with coffee and poured a mug for his breakfast. He was just reaching to set the pot back into its heated nest when the wave of emotional pain struck him. He did not know whether he had let his guard down on purpose or if it was simply that no one could hold up such a pretense full time.

He sobbed so suddenly and violently that he did not even realize it was about to happen. His knees buckled, and he sank sideways onto one of the kitchen chairs. The crying was as if someone had opened a dam. The walls of his stomach heaved and wrenched as if they were a pump pushing the tears out through his eyelids. The saltiness stung his eyes, and though he squinted in an effort to control things, the strain on his eyelids only accentuated the sting in his guts. He bawled and heaved and sobbed so long that his throat began to hurt.

Ross had heard about people having nervous breakdowns. He didn't know what took place when that happened, but he figured it must be something like what he'd just experienced. He was glad it happened when he was at home and alone. He wondered what would happen if he broke down like that on the job?

Ross sat down at the table and shoved his spoon into the now soggy cereal. It did not matter if his food was appetizing or not, he had no appetite. He ate out of habit and necessity. He was losing weight. His belt was now buckling on its tightest hole.

As he chewed his soggy breakfast, Ross mused about

his situation. He remembered the hours he used to spend contemplating suicide after Donny drowned, how the idea found a permanent place in the back of his mind during the months following that event. It was never very far from his thoughts. It was an option he wanted to hold on to, a possibility of escape that gave him comfort. There would always be a way out.

He would gladly swallow a whole bottle of aspirin, but that was out of the question. If he were to bring any good out of his death, he would have to make sure everyone thought it was accidental. He would need to think over everything really well before he followed through with it.

Ross knew his suicide would hurt Randall and Shelley. There was a certain stigma attached to a family whenever someone took their own life. In his case, people would probably expect him to consider suicide. He would have to convince people that he was all right before he did it. That meant he must act normal for a while.

But what was normal for a man in his shoes? Maybe suicide was the normal thing? Did insurance companies pay if a person committed suicide? Ross didn't know, and he couldn't ask his father-in-law, their insurance agent, about it. That would just tip them off to what he was planning.

Ross knew he had at least $250,000 worth of insurance. He had purchased that much coverage right after he and Shelley were married. The Murphy Company carried some on him, too. It was part of the benefits package. He did not remember how much. It had been too long ago, and Ross never expected to be asking these questions. Then he remembered that when he first started at Murphy they had given him a folder with all kinds of information about hospitalization and other benefits. He could probably find out how much the coverage was if he still had that folder. He could not remember where it was or even if they had saved it. If it had been saved, chances were that Shelley had put it away in the file cabinet. He would have to try and find it as soon as he got the chance. Someday when she was out, he would search for it.

Ross left his house and drove across town to the Murphy terminal. This would be his first road trip since the accident. He was eager to get back to some semblance of normalcy. Perhaps his spirits would pick up some today.

He got to the terminal and found his truck. It was in sad condition. Not mechanically speaking—the garage took good care of that part of it—but the interior. Obviously, they had been using the truck while Ross was not driving. He knew that would happen. But he had not expected that anyone would let it get so filthy inside. There was mud tracked onto the floor. The mud had dried and been ground into fine dust, and there was a layer of the dust over everything. There were enough fast food wrappers and coffee cups to fill a small trash can. It was disgusting.

The sleeper berth was nearly as bad. The bedding was mussed, and Ross wondered if other guys had slept in the bed. He knew he would have to wash the sheets as soon as he got the chance. For the time being he would prefer to sleep on top of the blankets.

He spent a good half hour just cleaning the truck enough to make it fit to work in. He knew he was a little fussier than most of the men, but he didn't think any of the guys were this sloppy. There had probably been a lot of different drivers in and out of the truck during the time he was off. None of them would have had any incentive to clean it since they would only be in it for a short time.

He finished cleaning the truck as well as he could in the predawn darkness and then drove it over to get his loaded trailer. The trailers with cargo on board were parked separately from the empty ones. He found the one that had his load, matching the number on the nose of the trailer to the number on the bill of lading.

He backed the fifth wheel of the tractor under the front of the trailer and eased the tractor backwards until he felt a solid bump and heard the satisfying clatter of the hitch mechanism closing its jaws around the kingpin. He put the tractor in first gear then and tried to pull away from the trailer, to test the coupling. The tractor bucked a little but could not move since Ross had yet to connect the air lines, which when pressurized from the tractor's air system, would release the parking brakes.

Ross turned on all the lights and flashers and got out of the cab to inspect the unit. First he connected the light cable from the back of the tractor to the receptacle on the front of the trailer. He followed that by connecting the two air lines that controlled the brakes on the trailer. Then he went to the crank on the side of the trailer and raised the dolly legs that supported the trailer when it was not hooked to a tractor, "landing gear" as it was called.

He always looked at the hitch by shining the beam of his flashlight up into the cramped space behind the fifth wheel. Satisfied that all was secure, he made his way slowly around the rig, checking lights and tires, making sure the unit was roadworthy.

He climbed back into the cab and started filling out his logbook. The law required drivers to account for their working and driving time on a graph that showed every hour of the day. A driver was either off duty, in the sleeper, driving or on duty-not driving. Most of the time Ross simply filled in something that was close to what he had done. He didn't know anyone who filled out his log with the thorough diligence the law required. To most truck drivers the logbook was simply a nuisance.

Ross was nearly finished with the logbook when he felt the truck shake. Leeroy Foust was standing on the steps of the truck looking in at him through the window glass. Ross hadn't noticed Leeroy approaching because his nose had been buried in his paperwork.

Ross lowered the window, and they stared at each other awkwardly for a few moments. Finally Leeroy broke the silence.

"Good to have you back, Laddybuck."

"Thanks, Leeroy."

Ross lowered his eyes back to his paperwork. He felt like he might lose control of himself again, the way he had earlier. If it had been anyone else but Leeroy, Ross would have been able to act normal. Leeroy was hard to pretend with, for some reason. Leeroy put his hand in and squeezed Ross's shoulder slowly, gently.

"Are you okay, Laddybuck?" he asked.

Ross could not answer. He sighed and wet his lips with his tongue.

"I guess I asked a stupid question, huh?" Leeroy said.

"I guess it depends on what you mean by 'okay.'"

"Look, Ross, I don't want to stick my nose in where it isn't welcome, but my guess is you need someone you can trust to talk to. I don't want to pressure you, and we need to pay attention to what we're doing here, but if you need a friendly ear, you've got it. Now, what do you say we hit the road?"

Ross nodded his head repeatedly, his lips pursed as an indication that he did not wish to speak. Leeroy walked back to his truck, and soon the two rigs were heading out the gate and toward the highway.

Ross felt a little better. Maybe he should pour out his soul to his friend. He had never done that with anyone. It simply didn't feel comfortable to let others see how he really felt, know what his life was truly like.

He never told others about his father's drunkenness or the times he heard his mom cry herself to sleep late at night. There had even been times when the evidence of his father's problem was more than he could hide. Like the times when Donny Ritts saw Gerald passed out on the floor in the middle of the day. Donny had allowed Ross to pretend as if nothing were wrong, even acted as if he could not see the old man. It was that kindness, that generous acceptance of Ross, in spite of the obvious, that had held the boys together. It was what made Ross love Donny the way he had.

The alcoholism that Ross grew up with was something he had learned to live with. It was just there, the way his nose was just there. He lived with it, ignoring it as much as possible. Only when something happened to bring it into focus, did he bother to deal with it. Then it was usually one sort of denial or other.

The ability to ignore and overlook the obvious was a

survival technique Ross had come to understand. When he had accepted the responsibility for Donny's death, he had just tucked the matter in beside his father's drunkenness. He could handle it the same way. He wondered if eventually he might be able to fit this new guilt into that space, too.

Ross pushed those thoughts out of his mind now, to concentrate on driving the rig.

The truck felt clumsy to him after the three-week hiatus. He longed for the confident feelings that being alone in his truck gave him. They were absent now, shadowed by the unfamiliarity his limbs felt because of being so long absent from the truck. He went through the gears with his own clumsiness compounded by the thickness of the transmission grease. It denied him the feel of the gears that would be there when the prolonged torque had generated enough heat to drive out the mid-winter chill. Then his left arm and right foot would enjoy the intricate ballet of RPM and timing that his brain had developed over countless thousands of gear changes.

Leeroy's welcome voice broke into his thoughts through the speaker of the CB. "Does your radio work, Ross?"

Ross's microphone was hanging from the ceiling by a bungee cord. He pulled the device down to his lips and pressed the transmit key as he spoke into it. "Yup. Sounds good. Do I sound okay?"

"You're coming in loud and clear. Let's take it up a couple."

The two men moved their radio channel setting from 19, which was the usual channel used by interstate drivers, to 21. They could talk here without annoying other truckers with their private conversation.

"You make it?"

"Sure did."

Soon they were at the onramp to Interstate 80. Ross pushed his throttle down to the floor even though there was a slight downgrade to the ramp. The stiffness of the lubricants, the dense winter air, the cold rubber of all 18 tires bulging under the payload, gave way only to the additional horsepower his foot was commanding. The two trucks merged into the light flow of eastbound traffic and moved through the early morning darkness as if they were connected together with an invisible chain.

For a while they rode in silence. Leeroy usually liked being quiet, even when he was running with somebody, but this was not a comfortable silence. What could he say to Ross? What was helpful and supportive? He decided that even small talk would be better than no talk.

"So, what did you get for Christmas?"

"Well, let's see. The usual: some clothes and some tools. How about you?"

"I bought myself a new TV set."

Ross realized then that Leeroy probably had a lonely Christmas, since he was now a widower; his wife had died the previous spring. He had a son and a daughter, but they both lived in the South and had families of their own.

"Your kids must have sent you something."

"Yeah, my daughter made me a shirt. Nice enough shirt. Didn't need it, though."

"You should have taken a week off and went to see them."

"I thought about it. But I decided it would be better to stay home and get used to being alone on holidays. I didn't want them to think they needed to worry about me. Figured I'd show them I was okay by spending this year on my own."

"Must have been pretty lonesome, huh?"

Ross realized he had given no thought to Leeroy during the Christmas and New Year holidays. The guy could have used a dinner invitation or some kind of company the first year since his wife died. A "Shelleydinner," as he called them, would have helped Leeroy pass at least one lonely evening. But then Ross had enough of his own misery to cope with. He wouldn't have been able to help Leeroy much. Shelley might have gone along with the idea, but not with any sincerity, he guessed

"You'd be surprised, Laddybuck. It isn't as bad as folks make it out to be. Don't get me wrong. I miss her pretty bad, but if a man doesn't bother to feel sorry for himself, he does all right. Most folks hear someone say they're going to be lonely or whatever, and so they are. It's the same way with handicaps and such. Years ago people just took things in stride."

Leeroy realized that he had just blundered into the very thing that might be helpful to Ross. He decided to give it a try.

"Let me tell you a little story. When I was a kid, we lived beside this fellow who had a wooden leg. He was a carpenter. Lost the leg when he was a teenager. Old boy worked every day, though. Kept up with the other guys, too. He couldn't climb ladders, of course, but he made up for it by seeing what the other guys needed and staying a step ahead. Sometimes he'd have the boards cut and ready to hand up to the guys before they even knew what they needed themselves. He used his head more than a guy with two good legs would. He had to, I guess.

"Most men don't like to do the thinking on a job like carpentry. That means if the job gets done wrong, they have to take the blame. This fellow didn't have to fight anybody for the privilege of thinking, so he probably ended up better off than if he'd had two good legs. Eventually he had some other fellows working for him. You don't see that kind of thing much anymore.

"These days, a guy like that would be on partial disability. Probably be entitled to the handicap parking spaces at the mall, too. Somewhere along the line people started feeling sorry for themselves anytime life gave them an excuse. Started to take advantage of every hardship. That carpenter fellow made do with what he had because nobody ever told him he was handicapped. There were lots of people like him. Not all missing a leg mind you, but handicapped somehow. Most of them made do."

Leeroy paused to see if Ross would comment. He did not. Having a conversation like this on a CB radio was hard. You couldn't read the other person's face to know how they were receiving what you said. Leeroy thought he could help Ross see that he could take the bad thing that had happened to him in stride. But he really couldn't tell; maybe Ross thought he was foolish.

"You still there, Laddybuck?"

"Yeah, Leeroy. I was just taking in what you said. I think I know a few people like you're talking about. Guys who try to get all the slack they can."

"Sort of like that. What I mean to say is that people are more able to survive trouble and injury than today's society gives them credit for. People are always blaming their parents or their poor childhood for the weakness in their character. Always making excuses for doing trashy things.

"Used to be people rolled with the punches when bad things happened. It didn't break them like it does today. Maybe people were tougher then, but I don't think so. Seems to me, we don't give people a chance to overcome things. Maybe we're too quick to feel sorry for them. Or else we let them feel sorry for themselves. Self-pity is comforting Laddybuck, but it's cheap comfort."

Leeroy decided he'd said enough. He would give Ross a chance to think about it. If Ross brought the subject up later, then maybe he could say more. He waited to see if Ross had anything to say. After a few minutes, he put up his microphone and switched on the FM. He kept the volume low, though, in case Ross came back to him.

Ross tried to keep his mind on the road and watch his speed and lane position—all the things that a driver usually does without thinking. He needed to guard his thoughts anyway, lest he get wrapped up in thinking of his troubles and do something stupid. He knew Leeroy was trying to help him with the philosophy he'd just expounded. He didn't think it applied in his case, though, or hoped it didn't.

Suddenly the solution to his problem appeared to him out of the gray morning mists. He wondered why he hadn't thought of it sooner. It was so obvious. It seemed like just yesterday when he had spent an hour driving past this point in the rain. Only then he had been going the other way.

It was the bridge pier, the one that had stopped the produce truck just before Thanksgiving week. It was right there in front of him as he and Leeroy approached the 28 mile-marker, wearing the pattern of scars it had gathered through the years from collisions. It waited ambivalently for the next sleepy driver to let the inertia of the straightaway carry him to the high side of the curve, where only a precise steady pull on the wheel would defy Newton and cause the vehicle to follow the painted lines instead of the established motion.

It was the threshold of eternity. It was the answer to how Shelley could collect on his life insurance. All he had to do was wait until he was going east sometime. Sometime when he had been running hard and could be expected to be drowsy. He could do it so easily. The speed limit was 65, and he could easily be doing 75. He could just relax at the right time, close his eyes, and he would never feel the end coming. Had anyone even suspected suicide when the last truck crashed?

Even if Shelley or someone else thought he was suicidal, there would be plenty of room for doubt. It was perfect. It was easy. Everyone knew it was just a matter of time before another sleepy trucker "bought it" at the 28 mile-marker. It may as well be Ross Martin.

CHAPTER TWENTY

There was dryness in Ross's mouth, a finality in his spirit now that he could see his end. But something told him to buck up. This was what he wanted, what he had determined he must do.

The warmth he used to feel between Shelley and himself came to his mind, as if to torment him with the briefest memory of happiness. But it fled away then, like dry leaves in a high wind. In its place was the dull heartache he continually suffered, as if his soul had been sunburned and the layers of skin were peeling away slowly, with a grueling, relentless itch. Growing on the rawness was another pain. It was a stinging sensation, a sharp tormenting anguish, a sense of loss.

He would never again share a tender moment with Shelley. They would never again cuddle together and fall asleep on the couch the way they used to, each of them content with nothing more than the closeness of the other. They would never again make love with their lips hungry, kiss tumbling over kiss like the out-of-step strides of an army rushing into battle—losing control of their mouths as the greater sensations consumed and overwhelmed them.

The memories were almost palpable. Yet the physical sensations were no longer pleasant. They had been twisted somehow so that the flesh of Shelley's sensuous mouth gave him pain. He never got over the delightful softness of her lips the first time they had kissed. He did not understand what "tender" was until then. But even those memories had been perverted. As if the justice that demanded its way had found a passage into his psyche with the power to deny him even a happy memory. The collected profundity of the universe corrupted in the splinters of a collapsed wooden cradle.

≈

Leeroy was trying to figure out what to say next. He wanted to find out what was going on in Ross's head but knew it required being tactful, something he was never good at. It wasn't really fair to accuse Ross of self-pity, was it? Wasn't a man who suffered what Ross had entitled to a little bit of self-pity? Wasn't that a normal part of the grieving process? Leeroy's mind was never comfortable when it came to this kind of subject. He was from the old school of manhood—be tough and quiet.

Most young guys were willing to open up and tell how they really felt. But Ross was an exception. That was one reason Leeroy liked him so much—Ross was content that the depth of feeling between them could be conveyed in the private nickname "Laddybuck."

"You falling asleep up there, Laddybuck?" barked Leeroy into the mike.

Ross had a notion to answer "not tonight," but thought better of it.

"No, not at all. I guess I just don't know what to say. I appreciate your help, Leeroy. But tell me, do you think I'm pitying myself?"

Leeroy felt a little sick now. He wished he had just kept his mouth shut. There was no way to change the subject without implying to Ross that he did think the younger man was indulging in self-pity. He decided to try and get out of this as quick and easily as he could.

"I guess I almost wouldn't blame you if you did. Maybe that's why I thought of it, Ross. I only know about self-pity because I've done it myself a time or two. I guess the thing is, some people can get sort of addicted to it, so to speak. The harder your troubles are, the better it feels. But it's a kind of trap, Ross. It begins to feed on itself, like a drunk trying to ease their sorrow with more booze. Sometimes they think the only answer is another drink."

"You didn't answer my question," Ross said, with a tone of detached matter-of-factness that made Leeroy even more uncomfortable. Ross had a way of pinning a man down with words; the kid should have been a lawyer, Leeroy briefly mused. He figured Ross was getting angry with him.

"You're right. I'm sorry. No, I don't think you are. But I get the impression that you aren't being completely honest somehow. As if you know something the rest of us don't."

Leeroy could hardly believe his own mouth. What had ever possessed him to say that? But now that it was out, he realized it was true. Rather it was what he thought was true, deep down where denial keeps a man from staying long enough to get hold of anything.

Ross's behavior had not been as sorrowful or openly remorseful as he might have expected. Ross seemed to be "stoic." Was that the word? But then, how could Leeroy really know what Ross was like when he spent so little time with him? The denial had its way again.

Leeroy knew Ross would be mad now. He had reason to be. Leeroy started trying to think of some way to apologize when Ross's voice came back on the air.

"I don't know any more than you do, partner." The voice was resigned, as if Ross had no real concern for his friend's opinion and was subtly transmitting that thought. But it was a lie, and Leeroy knew it. Maybe he should try to pin Ross down.

"I guess that's not exactly what I meant. I mean that you must be holding things so deep inside you that the people like me who want to help you can't get our fingers around anything. I feel frustrated. I guess I figure you're blaming yourself so much that you feel like you should suffer all alone.

"But I'm sorry, Laddybuck. I said I wouldn't try to stick my nose in, and here I go with my whole face. I'm just an old fool who doesn't know when to keep his mouth shut. Don't pay me any mind."

"I don't think you're any such thing," Ross said. "But I do realize, now that you've said it, that people are watching me. I guess I should have known they would be. Maybe I'm watching myself, too. One thing I know for sure, I feel like I'm in some strange world. I hate myself for what happened, but I don't know how to make it right. There isn't any way. I guess people want me to fall apart or go crazy. Maybe end up in the psych ward, huh?"

There was a quiver in Ross's voice that Leery could hear through the radio transmission. The guy was obviously upset. Maybe he shouldn't be driving yet after all.

"No, Laddybuck, nobody wants anything like that. Maybe we feel as helpless as you do. Maybe we're frustrated that we can't do anything either. When people get frustrated, it comes out of them in strange ways sometimes."

"Maybe."

"I told you before that I was on your side, and I meant it. I just don't know how to help you with this. I know how to drive a truck, and I'm pretty good with tools, but damned if I know how to straighten up a fellow inside. I think you should talk to someone who does. A preacher maybe?"

"I'll think about it."

Ross was surprised at the older man's candor. Leeroy played the part of strong, silent type almost with a passion.

Ross thought about what Leeroy said. Maybe it would help to talk to some preacher. He knew Pastor Sawyer was eager to get involved and help him sort it out. But Ross didn't feel comfortable with him. He was a nice enough man, no doubt a good preacher, but Ross didn't like the idea of opening up to someone who knew his family so well, especially someone who also knew Victor and Virginia so well.

The idea that his deepest thoughts might occupy the same turf as those of his in-laws terrified him. There was no way to insure they would not see who he really was, no way to keep them at a safe distance. He would have to find a minister who would talk to him privately. Someone who Ross could share his whole heart with and then walk away, back into his real life and leave it all behind.

There was one place he might find such a man. There was a little trucker's chapel in the parking lot of a truckstop in the eastern part of the state. Ross only stopped there once in a while, and he had never bothered to go into the chapel. A converted semi-trailer actually, it had a tiny living space at one end and a miniature church at the other end. A chaplain lived in the thing year round.

As far as Ross could tell the chapel had few visitors. That was just fine with him. The chaplain, whoever he was, would probably have lots of time to talk to him. Probably have plenty of interest in helping him. He didn't know if he could be helped, but it was worth a try. A man had to start someplace.

Ross and Leeroy could only run together until they reached the junction of interstates 80 and 81, in eastern Pennsylvania. From there Leeroy turned north toward Scranton. Ross continued to follow 80 east. He crossed the Delaware River at the Water Gap and drove another hour until he reached the edge of the New York City megalopolis that began in New Jersey—the collection of smaller municipalities so tightly packed together that he could not tell when one ended and another began.

Ross made three stops to offload his cargo, which was auto supplies and parts that H.A. Murphy had picked up, sorted and put on pallets for easy delivery to department stores. The first two deliveries went directly to the stores, and the remainder of the pallets was given to a local drayage company who would peddle them along with other freight to the remaining locations as it was convenient for them.

When the trailer was empty, Ross drove to another warehouse facility in Jersey City. He parked the trailer he had pulled from Heritage and hooked up to one that was full of imported automotive supplies. He would take that back to Heritage, where the freight would be unloaded, sorted and reloaded for delivery to stores all over the Northeast and Midwest.

The day was coming to a close as Ross left the warehouse. The traffic of commuters clogged the highways as he attempted to get back to Pennsylvania. It took two and a half hours to drive the 73 miles back to the Pennsylvania state line.

If he could find a parking spot in the congested truck stop where the chapel was located, he would have a couple hours to talk to the chaplain before turning in for the night.

CHAPTER TWENTY ONE

Ross pulled into the truck stop about 7:45 that evening. He circled the parking lot twice, looking for a place to park his rig. There were a couple of other drivers doing the same thing. They were cruising like predators, each hoping to be the first to spot the next opening. There were maybe a hundred trucks parked here—some pulled into spaces, some backed in. They weren't all staying the night.

As Ross cruised the lot he mused about the occupation and lifestyle he had chosen. He was often frustrated when people who knew nothing of the trucking industry assumed he worked some kind of regular hours, or that most truckers did. The truth was that many factors beyond the control of the drivers forced them to work and rest on a schedule most people would find intolerable. The stories some people told about overworked, sleepy truckers were only mildly exaggerated.

It was a complaint Ross heard from other truckers a lot, but it seemed they were all powerless to change. Many trucking companies routinely abused the hours-of-service regulations, pressuring and sometimes even rewarding their drivers to go farther between rest breaks than the law allowed. They put not only their drivers at risk but the motoring public as well. Unrestrained competition in trucking, though a boon for the industries it served, sorely compromised safety.

There was always a newly started company willing to bend the rules to provide better service. Many shippers would choose them over the more conscientious carriers because highway safety was not a shipper's concern.

Ross considered himself fortunate that his employer was

not as demanding as most. How H.A. Murphy had managed to maintain their customer base when so many others had lost theirs to cheaper carriers was a mystery even to Leeroy, who often commented on the business savvy of the Murphy family. He had advised Ross to stay with the outfit as long as he could.

Ross was just about to give up his search for a parking space when just ahead of him he saw the flashers on the rear of a rig come on. The driver began to come out of the space slowly, tentatively, since he couldn't see what was behind him. The driver would have taken a look around behind his rig and then run to the driver's seat and begun to back out, hoping that some other driver would assure him on the CB that he was backing safely out of the tight spot.

Ross seized the opportunity. He wheeled his unit into position to stake his claim on the space. He keyed his CB mike and spoke reassuringly to the driver.

"Come on back there, big truck, I got my eyeball on ya. You're doin' fine."

"'Preciate the help there, hand. This place is like drivin' in a sardine can," the other driver said.

"I was just about to give up and go on down the road. I musta circled this place three times waitin' on somebody to leave," Ross said.

"You'd think this place had good food or somethin', the way all these trucks stop here."

It was a standard joke, one Ross had heard many times. There is an old adage about truck drivers knowing the best places to eat. In truth truck drivers must eat in places where there is room to park. Quality of food makes no difference. Most truck stop restaurants would never make it if they had to compete with the ones only cars have access to.

Ross walked past the brightly painted chapel trailer on his way to the restaurant. There was an antique tractor still hooked to the front of it, but the rig hadn't actually moved in years. The chapel had a plate glass door, so that passers-by could see the inviting interior. Ross didn't see anyone inside, but then, he could only see a little of the inside since the door was in the side and the converted semi-trailer was only about eight feet wide. He went into the restaurant and got a seat at the counter. There was a telephone at each seat so drivers could take advantage of the time while they were waiting for their meals to come.

The waitress was showing signs of strain after a long shift. Strands of her bleached hair were hanging down across her cheeks, evidently slipped from the pins she had used to keep them away from her face. Tiny drops of perspiration glistened on her upper lip.

She gave Ross a real smile as she poured him his coffee and took his food order. Ross had noticed when he was just a kid the difference between a fake smile and a real smile. In places like this most smiles were pasted on, and they looked like it.

She was pretty but not glamorous. A lot like Shelley. Ross felt drawn to her. He wished he could take her aside and buy her dinner. Maybe sit with her and tell her his troubles, but she was too busy, and he was just another driver, another face in an endless parade of strange faces. As sincere as the smile looked, Ross supposed that it was practiced and professional, a necessary affectation for success in this woman's trade.

It was the best time of day for a waitress to make tips, Ross figured. There was a steady stream of drivers like him who would come in for a meal. They wanted good service, a smile and if they could get it, wit and a sense of humor from a waitress. They liked someone who looked or acted like their wives or mothers, not starchy and formal but homey and comfortable. It was a daunting task with so much food to carry, coffee to pour, counters to wipe, checks to total up, etc. But the reward for doing it all with good cheer was a tip rate that tended to be higher than in other restaurants. Most truckers left a dollar tip, even if they only had coffee. More than 15 percent was common. If you could laugh at that off-color joke you'd already heard three times, you might even do better.

There was good selection on the menu, but that didn't matter to Ross. He hadn't really tasted anything he had eaten since that bleak day in December. There was a meatloaf special that looked good. You could usually expect the special to arrive sooner than the other menu items. Though Ross knew the meatloaf would probably have crisp edges from too much time in the microwave, he ordered it anyway.

Ross forced himself to pick up the phone and call Shelley. Before the accident, she had lived for his calls at the end of the day. Now he could have forgotten entirely, and she wouldn't have noticed. He supposed she dreaded the conversation as much as or more than he did.

The phone rang on Shelley's end five times before she picked it up. It was as if she were trying to ignore it entirely, hoping it would go away. There was a time when she had answered as if she were waiting by the phone, often on the first ring. Each ring punctuated the rift between them. Ross knew it was Shelley's way of communicating her true feelings to him—feelings that her religious conditioning would not allow her to embrace directly. Even her greeting was calculated to be cold and disinterested, Ross guessed.

"Hello."

Ross realized just then that this was their first phone conversation since the baby's death. He had been working in the warehouse, and there was no need for a daily phone call to Shelley. He hesitated, feeling suddenly deflated. The contrast from the joyous anticipation that had once rung in her voice upon getting his calls, to the obvious detachment she now expressed was another message. It dug deep in his gut and twisted.

He became self-conscious then, knowing that his face was contorting and hoping the waitress would not see the pain the phone call was giving him. He hadn't even spoken to Shelley yet, and already she was ready for the call to end.

She should have repeated the "hello" by now, since he had not responded, but she did not. Ross guessed that even in that was a message. He sighed noticeably, then wished he had not. Certainly she would take that as a message.

"Hi, Shelley, how was your day?"

"Oh, hello, Ross," Shelley said, as if she were mildly surprised. "My day was all right. How was yours?"

"It wasn't too bad. I got all the stops off and got out of Jersey with my backhaul. How's Randy?"

"He's fine. Do you want to talk to him?"

Ross could barely hold back his tears. Before, she would never have passed him over to Randall until she had spent the necessary time letting him in on the highlights of her day, unloading the information as a way of keeping him involved in her life. Now she seemed to feel there was nothing between them but the child.

Suddenly, Ross realized he had been indulging in some kind of foolish fantasy that everything would somehow be okay between them when he returned to the old routine. He wanted to plead with her to tell him about something, anything that she had done, to share some news from her side of the family; even the mundane details of her housework would have been welcome in his ears. He missed the warmth in her voice that had made any faraway truck stop feel like home.

Before he could think of anything appropriate to say, she passed the phone off to Randall. Ross could hear her voice, cheerful now, as she spoke to the child, her desire to avoid him implied with every syllable.

"Here, talk to Daddy, Randall."

Ross determined not to convey any of his misery to the boy. He quickly mustered an upbeat tone and greeted his son with the appropriate excitement, even as Randall was drawing a breath to speak.

"Hi, buddy, how's my boy doing?"

"Hi, Dad. Fine, how are you?"

"Just great son. What did mommy fix you for supper?"

"Chicken stewp with smashed taters."

There was a bouncy good humor in the boy's tone, the playfulness they used when talking about food. Shelley's chicken soup had big chunks of carrots and celery in it. The rich broth was good over biscuits or potatoes. Ross always told Randall it was more like a stew, and they had conspired to call it "stewp" as a way of teasing Shelley. She pretended to be annoyed at their foolishness, though she actually loved it, or at least she had.

And as far as Randall knew, "smashed taters" was the proper nomenclature for mashed potatoes.

"I wished I had me some chicken stewp and smashed taters," Ross said, slipping into the deliberate bad grammar he used to entertain Randall. "I gotta eat this old chewy truck stop meatloaf. It will probably be colder 'n fish lips by the time it gets here and just as hard to bite through."

Talking crude, with a backwoods accent, was his way of playing with the boy on the phone. Shelley always acted annoyed at that, too, saying she would have to train all of that bad grammar out of Randall or run the risk of raising a "hick." Ross guessed the boy knew the difference, though. Even if he didn't, Ross got a big kick out of the giggling it evoked from Randall. That was too precious to part with.

"Yuk! Daddy, you always eat that nasty old truckstop meatloaf. Why don't you try something else?"

"It's cheap, boy. Besides, if I can't have Mommy's cookin', nothing tastes good to me."

There was a painful truth in what he had just said, he realized. He would not think about it now, though. He would wait until the talk with Randall was over. They went on that way, the content of their words completely inconsequential, the tone of love toward each other everything. Finally Ross said goodnight to Randall and asked him to put Mommy back on.

"I'm back," Shelley said.

There was less coldness in her voice now. Perhaps the delight that Randall had shared with Ross had touched her somewhat. Ross wanted to tell her how much he loved her and wanted things to be okay between them again, but he could not broach the subject for fear that she would revert back to the coldness. He felt helpless and clumsy, as if he had to win Shelley's approval somehow but did not know how to start. He impulsively decided to be candid with her.

"I miss you," Ross said.

"I miss you, too."

"I don't mean just because I'm away from home. We haven't

"Don't cry, Mommy."

Shelley took her son in her arms and pressed her face into the bony space on top of his shoulder. It was strange, and she felt that it was wrong somehow to take comfort in his innocent pity. Shelley wondered how much of this she could indulge in before she caused some emotional damage to the boy. The thought that the grief might cause her to give this fine little boy some "complex" nagged at her. But she couldn't help it. It hurt too much, and there was no one else.

CHAPTER TWENTY TWO

Ross sat at the counter and stared at the back of the telephone receiver he had just hung up. He wanted to cry, but there were too many people around him. It was just as well. He had spent entirely too much time feeling sorry for himself. What was it Leeroy said, "cheap comfort?" Maybe Shelley would never care about him again. He had to face that, had to work with what he had. He was determined to follow through with his plan, unless there was another way.

Leeroy had spoken as if he should try to make the best of things. Ross didn't know how he could make anything good come out of this. He only knew that he had always had within him a vague sense that something wasn't right. He had felt that way since he was very small. He could never quite put his finger on it. He had grown so accustomed to the feeling that he had completely forgotten it was there. It faded into the background of his life, became such an integral part of who and what he was that he only took notice of it on those rare moments when he could detach from himself and get something like an outside look. He had that perspective now, and for a fleeting but very real instant it spoke to him. It seemed to want him to take another look. It was as if he were supposed to see that he had missed something. Maybe the chaplain knew something. Ross couldn't imagine why, but he suddenly wanted to talk to this stranger.

Ross realized he had built up an image in his mind; this chaplain had become an imaginary friend of sorts. Not exactly a friend, maybe his last hope for a friend.

"You're really losing it, buddy," Ross whispered to himself as he dug his fork into the now-cooling meatloaf.

When he finished his meal, it was nearly 9 o'clock. He paid his check, left the waitress a generous tip and walked out into the cold night air. There was a light snow falling, the kind of snow that doesn't come and go upon the land with some weather system but rather seems to hang in the air, a living accessory to winter. The way leaves and green grass live in summer.

He could only see the snow because he happened to gaze upward, into the halo of one of the outside lights circling the grounds of the truck stop. It gave Ross the impression that it would never stop, the way the pain in his heart would never stop. It would drone on and on, slow and unceasing, like this relentless falling snow. It would not advance quickly, lest it reveal its evil intent and cause him to begin to dig his way out from under it. Slowly and gradually, like a stealthy, patient enemy it would overwhelm him.

The chapel was sitting there in front of the rows of parked trucks with their glowing marker lights. The glass door emitted a welcoming light onto the short staircase that bridged the gap between chapel and pavement. Ross walked toward it casually, noting the lone set of footprints in the fresh dusting of snow making their way from the shadows to the staircase. Bold, bright letters were centered on the door: WELCOME.

When Ross entered, two men looked up at him from the table that was centered in the room. At first their faces were cautious and curious, as if anyone who lives behind an open door must be prepared not only for friend, but foe.

They quickly nodded at him and reached out to pull one of the other chairs back for him to sit with them at the table. Ross could tell which one of the men was the chaplain because he was wearing a blue cardigan with Chaplain Jim embroidered on the chest.

The other man's voice quickly shifted. He was out of time and had to "get on down the road." There was a quick introduction, merely an exchange of names, a quick handshake. Then the other driver was gone, out into the darkness. Ross got the distinct impression they had been waiting for him to arrive.

The chaplain was clearly pleased to see Ross. The smile on his face was genuine, and his handshake — repeated now as a way of reinforcing the earlier one, which had seemed superficial to both of them — was solid. Ross might have felt intimidated by such a strong handshake, but the eyes and the weathered face put him at ease.

"Nice little place you have here," Ross said, unsure of how to begin.

"Thank you. Most of the credit goes to the truck stop, though. They've adopted the chapel. They provide the electricity and other utilities, and the restaurant feeds me. They pour coffee free of charge for my table any time I bring a driver in to talk.

"It's sort of a symbiotic relationship. The chapel makes the place look more respectable in the eyes of the community, besides giving the drivers some spiritual aid. There have been some runaway teenagers who have trusted us enough to allow me to contact their families. The stories got into the local paper once or twice. Good for the place's image."

Ross nodded, but said nothing.

"So tell me a little bit about yourself, Ross." The man's eyes were a piercing blue, and they seemed out of place on such an old-looking face. Not old really, but "used" was the word that came to Ross's mind. This man had lived some, Ross could tell. He'd likely spent most of his days working outside, Ross figured. His skin had that leathery, raw look.

"Well, I'm from the other end of the state. Ever hear of Heritage?"

"Sure. I spent 30 years running the big road. I've even fished in the Sugar River once or twice."

Ross felt that was a good sign, though the mention of the Sugar River gave him a moment of pause. He told Chaplain Jim whom he drove for, which got an impressed and approving nod from the older man. He could tell the man had a lot of questions on his lips and that they would come spilling forth as soon as he felt comfortable. But the man threw Ross a curve.

"You're the reason I'm here, you know."

"What do you mean by that?" asked Ross, taken aback.

"You're in a bad way," the chaplain said. "I could see it as soon as you walked in. You've got a real problem. You're hurting inside, son, hurting bad. Not everyone can see it like I can. It's sort of a gift I have. I don't spend my time here just so I can preach the gospel to truck drivers, though that is the main reason for this chapel. When I was on the road, I saw so many guys get bitter on life. It's hard working alone, off by yourself in a truck. A lot of guys lose their way somehow. They get into drinking or drugs; they end up cheating on their wives. Long and short of it, they mess up their lives for the sake of making a living. It always seemed unfair to me, almost wicked that it should go that way. I want to make a difference for people when life is ready to beat them down. I'm glad you're here. I hope I can help you."

Ross looked incredulously at the man, uncertain of what to say next.

"Aw, don't pay any attention to my little speech, Ross. I don't usually talk like this to drivers." He paused for effect. "I'm right, though, aren't I, about you?"

Ross felt both relieved and cornered by the chaplain's candor. A fleeting thought came to his mind that maybe such a perceptive fellow really could help him see what he had been trying to pin down all his life.

"Yep."

"I've got all the time in the world. Tell me about it."

It took Ross a few moments to gather up his courage. When he spoke, his voice was subdued and barely audible.

"I killed my son." Ross expected the man to flinch. He did not.

"How did it happen?"

"I fell on him," Ross said through clenched teeth.

"Sounds like you had an accident."

"Not exactly."

"Tell me more. Tell me why you say it wasn't 'exactly' an accident."

The chaplain's voice was even, showing no trace of shock or revulsion like Ross expected.

"I set him up for it."

"How did you do that?"

Ross went through the bitter details of how he had built the cradle, how he had restored the old table and how he had wanted to show off the two pieces of his work. He described how the old wooden beam that supported the drop leaf should have been replaced. How his shoddy workmanship and his vanity had compounded each other to create a trap for his baby boy. And how his clumsy feet had tripped on the wires at the very moment he might have stopped the fall and let him go crashing down on the fragile child's body. He was weeping as he related the events to the weathered face, and his chest convulsed as he finished the tale.

"I'll have to admit, Ross, that's about as hard a thing for a man to take as I've ever heard. I understand now why you look so pained," Chaplain Jim said.

"That's not the whole story," Ross said.

"What else went wrong?" the Chaplain said, even though he was not sure he wanted to hear any more.

"When I was in high school, I persuaded my best friend to go swimming with me in a dangerous part of the Sugar River. To make a long story short, he drowned. Then we decided to name our new baby boy after my friend. So now I've killed two people I loved who were named Donny. I think maybe I cursed the baby by doing that," Ross said.

"No! There's no such thing. At least not in a man's power."

Jim could tell by the way Ross said he had "set him up for it" that Ross held himself completely responsible for the baby's death. He would have to be careful what he said to this man. He decided to shift the focus a little.

"I guess you and your wife aren't getting along real well since it happened either?"

"No. She tried to tell me not to do it. I didn't listen to her."

"What did she tell you not to do?"

"She didn't like me moving the cradle around with him in it. She thought I should wait for a better time. If I had listened to her, he would still be alive. That makes it worse."

"I take it you feel responsible?" the chaplain said.

"I am responsible. There's no way around that."

"Well, maybe not, but the fact remains, it was an accident—a very freak, unfortunate accident. We can't hold ourselves responsible for things we can't help. You didn't see it coming; you would have prevented it if you had."

"Of course I would have."

"So when did this happen?"

"Just a week or so after Thanksgiving," Ross said.

"So you haven't really had time to get over it?"

"Get over it? How do I get over it? What right do I have to get over it?"

Chaplain Jim took that in. He had never known a situation quite like this one. Here was a man who had indirectly caused two deaths. No, that wasn't accurate. He had not wanted anyone to die. He had only been doing normal friend and father things. Still, the tragedies were results of events Ross had put in motion. God must have a purpose here, he sensed. But he had to say something to this young man that would turn his thinking outward.

"Do you not want to put it behind you, then?"

"I don't know. I guess I want to make it right."

"Does your wife hold this against you?"

"I think so."

The chaplain nodded. "What do you mean by 'make it right?'"

"I don't know. I guess I can't do that."

"Have you forgiven yourself?" asked the chaplain.

"What good is that?" Ross said.

"It has to start there. I take it you haven't thought about forgiving yourself?"

"No. I don't see what difference that would make."

"Ross, do you know the Lord?" asked Chaplain Jim.

Ross knew that such a question would come up. But the direct way the man put it took Ross off balance. "I'm a believer. Would I be in here if I weren't?" Ross replied.

"You'd be surprised how many non-believers I get in here. I guess what I mean is this: Does your faith make a real difference in your life? Can you remember a day when you made a conscious decision to serve God? I'm not talking about just going to church. I mean really letting your life be governed by Jesus, making your decisions based on his teachings."

"I always thought so, I suppose," Ross said. "I've hung around church since high school. My wife got me started. I've prayed the prayer. I read my Bible. I know most of what's in it. To be honest with you, though, I haven't felt much like God was on my side lately. I don't know why he would want to be."

"Maybe it didn't matter that much up to now." Jim's voice got solemn then, but serious, and he spoke with conviction. "Ross, I'm not a minister. I've never been to college or seminary or anything formal. I've just read the Bible and done some studying. Mostly, I've lived. I've watched people. I've watched what happens when the chips are down. I've seen the difference real faith can make. I'll be the first to tell you there's a lot of what passes for religion that's phony. There are plenty of self-righteous and hypocritical people around. There are a lot of them in church."

"Everybody says that."

"Sure. But I can tell you this: If you'll put your faith, your trust, in God, if you'll believe what Jesus said about seeking the kingdom of God, you'll find the power to outlive this thing. God can give you the courage to forgive yourself and face whatever is coming to you because of what happened. Don't get me wrong here, I can't and I won't pretend that your troubles are going to be over—only that real faith can see you through them.

"A lot of preachers will tell you that if you follow the Lord, everything in your life will get straightened out. Your family will grow stronger and you'll prosper. The truth is that when a person comes to God, they sometimes find out God has other plans. If you've read the Bible, you know the stories in there are about people who had it hard."

Ross found himself strangely captivated by the man's words. He didn't give him the usual pap that Ross often heard on the religious radio stations he listened to in his travels. This guy sounded like he knew what he was talking about.

"Can you tell me some more about yourself? How you grew up, what your childhood was like?" Jim asked.

Ross gave the man a skeptical look. He remembered Leeroy saying how people wanted to blame their parents or their childhood for their problems.

"You gonna help me find some excuse for what happened?" Ross asked.

The chaplain smiled. "What makes you say that?"

"Well, that's the style these days, isn't it? Blame your parents, say you were an abused child?"

"You know why people say that their problems are based on their childhood, don't you?" Jim asked.

"No, why?" Ross said, expecting some joke or witticism.

"Because most emotional and spiritual problems people have *are* based on their childhood. It's overdone, I know. But for the most part, it's true. When you're too small to understand what's going on, you get your thinking shaped. You get used to wrong notions and ways of dealing with life. As long as you get by, you never have a reason to question the way you think. But take what happened to you, for example. You're going to be doing some real soul-searching. You need to consider everything. I'm not saying there is something in your past that's working against you, but you need to talk about it if you can. You need to know whether or not your thinking is healthy."

"I can't see how what happened when I was a kid made me careless with my son," Ross said.

Chaplain Jim thought Ross was being evasive now. He hadn't been that vague in explaining what he wanted Ross to see. The younger man probably had bad memories from his childhood and didn't want to talk about it. The chaplain pressed him to open up.

"That's not what I mean. I'm talking about how you deal with what happened."

"Well," Ross began, "my father drank a lot. He still does. We were poor even though we weren't poor."

"You mean he drank away everything that you needed to feel like a normal human being? Never got the things the other kids took for granted? Let me guess, no baseball glove, no stereo, no cable TV, things like gas and electric got shut off regularly, that sort of thing?"

"That's it pretty much. How did you know?"

"I've seen it. Not my folks, but in my family. You grew up thinking that other people looked down on you. Right?"

"They did. I don't blame them."

"Say that again," the chaplain challenged.

"What? That I don't blame them?"

"That's what I thought you said." Jim shook his head. "What you don't realize, son, is that you weren't able to change the way your father was. Let me ask you this: Do you look down on other people, kids who had to grow up the way you did?"

"No, of course not."

"Why not?"

Ross was trapped now. He wanted to hold his ground, even in the face of this logic. It seemed important that he do so. But he didn't know why.

"I know it was really my dad's fault. Maybe I don't feel right blaming him?" questioned Ross.

"I know. There's a certain loyalty we have toward our parents. Your dad was a nice guy most of the time, right?"

"He still is. He still drinks, too."

"My guess is that you're going to blame yourself for the death of your son, because you're so used to feeling low down, you can't rise above it. You're in a pinch. You have to retreat into familiar territory, where you feel safe. You have to think the way you did when you were a kid. It worked for you then. You think it'll work for you now. But it isn't your dad this time, it's you. You can't see yourself as responsible for your boy's death, the way you thought you deserved your poverty. It's too big of a difference. That's too much for a man to stand. You'll destroy yourself."

Ross stared deeply into the man's steely eyes. He feared that maybe this chaplain could read his thoughts, figure out that self-destruction was exactly what Ross had in mind. He couldn't maintain contact with the penetrating gaze. He foundered then, not knowing what direction he should take in order to keep control of the conversation. Humor seemed to be the default setting on his emotions.

"What, think myself to death, worry myself to death?" asked Ross with a nearly genuine smile on his lips.

Jim was ready for the younger man's shift to humor. He sensed it coming on and met it with the kind of gentle sternness that only someone who knows he has the other's respect can get away with. "You know what I mean, Ross. Don't try to play games with me."

Ross thought he should object to Jim's tone, but something deep inside him responded to it, actually welcomed it. Something primal stirred in Ross. He yearned for the confidence this man had. He felt as if he wanted to plunge in and accept the man's opinion. But he could not. It was too strange, too foreign. He could not trust it, could not allow himself to retreat into it. Rather than remain speechless, he contrived something.

"I think I know what you mean. Can you help me understand it better?"

"Oh, you understand it. You understand it better than I do. You built up a kind of defiant pride inside you when you were small. Oh, you maybe didn't seem like a proud person or act that way. You weren't a braggart or anything like that. You just set up these walls around yourself. You held yourself to high standards, really high standards. You wouldn't let anything happen to identify you with the way your daddy was. You kept yourself separate from it, insulated from it. The only way you felt good was when you acted exactly the way a decent person is supposed to act. It was as if you were going to show the world that you were different, that you were better.

"Well, you showed them. You've been showing them all your life. You're so used to showing people what you're not, you've lost sight of what you are. You can't forgive yourself for what happened because you might have to admit that you're not everything you want to be, that you're not everything you think you need to be. Well, the jig is up, my friend. You're not perfect. Matter of fact, you're seriously flawed. Just like the rest of us."

The chaplain sighed then, audibly, almost with regret. He realized that what he had dropped on Ross was a lot when delivered in so blunt a fashion. He was sure he was right, though. Something in Ross's face as the little speech was being delivered told him that. One of those uncomfortable silences surrounded the two men then, while Ross took in the whole of what Chaplain Jim said.

Ross didn't know how to respond to this. He was shocked that a man who had only just met him would presume to understand so much about him and the secrets of his heart. He certainly didn't think he was guilty of all the pride the man had charged him with. He had always been humble. Didn't people see him as humble? They must have, else he would have had some indication of it by now. He wondered if this was some "canned" speech—one the chaplain gave to every man who came in with a similar problem. What did the lawyers call it, "boilerplate?"

Ross felt a little disappointed now. This was not exactly what he had expected from a man with such a kind and wise demeanor. The thought came to him that maybe coming to see a guy like this was foolishness after all. He had admitted he wasn't a minister, that he had no formal training. The man was just a truck driver like himself, albeit an old one.

"I guess I'll have to think about that some," Ross said politely.

"Yes, you think about that. But please come back and see me again. I'd like to know how this works out for you."

The two men made brief eye contact again, not enough for either to read the other much. Ross felt the desire to get off by himself.

"I'd like to pray with you before you go."

"Of course," Ross said.

The chaplain's voice was kind yet strong as he led the younger man in prayer. His voice conveyed a total acceptance of Ross as a person and his value as a human being. It was something Ross felt deeply as he listened to the man's voice, not his words. Ross thought it strange in light of what the man had said about him only minutes before. He hardly heard what the man prayed. Something about God becoming more real in Ross's eyes.

As Ross walked slowly away from the chapel, he mused in the wintry air that perhaps this feeling was what made the visit to the chapel worthwhile. Was that why all people went to see ministers or chaplains? Was that why there was religion and church and all the trappings that went with it? If that was all there was to it, then it was not worth much, because there was one thing he knew for sure—this feeling would melt, just like this snow, the next time Shelley passed him off to Randall, like she had done earlier that evening, instead of taking time to talk to him. Snow was pretty, but you couldn't hang on to it.

Ross undressed and lay under the blankets in the truck's sleeper. He dismissed his earlier concern about the cleanliness of the bedding. The deep throbbing of the truck's diesel became a soothing background for his thoughts. He knew there was something to what the chaplain had said about the way he handled his problems, about the way he looked at life. He had known it for a long time. He wasn't quite the same as other people in some deep-down basic way. But he had never seen a reason to sort it out and had become used to being the way he was—just like the man said. Was that such a big deal?

The alarm woke Ross at 5:30 a.m. He dressed quickly in the cozy interior of the truck and went into the truck stop building to shave and get some coffee for breakfast. As he was drawing the razor across his cheeks, he realized that he had actually slept that night. He couldn't remember tossing and thrashing about in search of comfort like he had become used to doing. Seeing the chaplain had done that much for him anyway.

He drove the truck slowly out of the lot and entered the highway. It was too early for there to be much traffic. It was one of the reasons Ross liked to start so early in the morning. The snow that fell through the night had been light enough to be blown off to the shoulders of the road by passing vehicles, so there weren't any slick spots. It seemed like, for a few precious minutes, he could have a piece of highway to himself.

The headlights cut through the morning darkness, creating a circle of light that seemed small enough to be secure. It was as if the world had been reduced to a bite-sized portion of itself, a portion a man could manage. Whatever hazards and problems might await him were veiled in a soft curtain of darkness. When it was light outside, Ross never quite felt this way. In daylight he would have to search with his eyes, far out ahead of his truck, in order to see everything he needed to, in order to anticipate what might happen next. It was more demanding, Ross thought, though probably safer, since you could not tell what dangers might lay concealed in the darkness just past the range of the headlight's glow.

Ross realized that perhaps he liked driving within the glow of the headlights because it gave him a feeling of security. The way ignoring what was really going on in his life when he was a youngster had provided a sense of security. Both notions of security were false, even risky. He wished he could somehow begin to ignore what had happened to his son that way. But there was no way to bring a curtain of darkness down over the emptiness in his home and in his wife's heart. No way to veil the truth of his accident.

As the first gray streaks of dawn began to fill and spread across the eastern horizon that appeared now and then in his mirror, the thoughts grew clearer in Ross's mind. He realized that most of what the chaplain said to him was true, or at least partly true. He had grown up denying reality. Not really denying it but learning to cope with it by ignoring it. He had no other choice.

As Ross had learned to ignore reality, and to substitute for it a kind of self-reliance, he had spiraled slowly inward on himself. He had learned to relate to the world and the other people in it as if he were the primary character in some grand play.

He had never been completely himself, had he? There was always that fear that who he was or what he was wasn't quite up to par. And now that he had a real crisis on his hands, he could see how phony to himself he had been. He had never learned to live life, because he was too busy acting life. Ross Martin was lost in his own personal hell, and he didn't know the way out. What was worse was that he wasn't even sure if he was still sane. He didn't know if these strange ideas forming in his head were genuinely true or if they were just the desperate ramblings of his tortured soul. A soul so tormented by pain, so driven by self-loathing that it had no sensibilities of its own to work with.

Ross began to think that perhaps he should reconsider his decision to take his own life. Perhaps if he could continue to discover more about himself, he might be able to handle this burden of guilt in some healthy fashion. Perhaps he could handle it the way other people handled such things. But how was that exactly?

He supposed that most people, most men at least, would make excuses for themselves. They would focus on some mitigating factor about the accident. They would tell themselves that perhaps the baby was never really very healthy to start with and that if he had been healthy, he would have survived the fall. Or they would have blamed the glue that held the joints of the cradle together, deciding that it must have been weak or defective in some way.

Certainly a normal person would find some way to dodge the guilt that was demanding Ross take his life. Wasn't that the healthy way for a human being to think? Survival, after all, was instinctive. Didn't he owe it to himself to accept every possibility that he was not entirely to blame? Didn't he owe it to Randall at least, if not Shelley?

"Give yourself time, Ross," he told himself. If the prayers of Chaplain Jim were to have any effect at all, didn't they need time to work out? Could Ross expect some miracle? And surely Pastor Sawyer was still praying for him.

Ross arrived back in Heritage shortly before noon. He checked the board and found nothing beside his name. That simply meant that his next assignment had not been determined yet. He strode to the dispatch window in hopes that he might be able to select something, since there could be several loads yet unassigned. Seated at the computer terminal was Kim, a woman about his age with whom he was somewhat friendly.

"Hey, Kim," Ross said in a cheerful tone.

"Hi, Ross." Kim gave him one of those warm smiles that suggested she had a lot of compassion for him because of what had happened to him and his baby, as did most of the people at H.A. Murphy. Ross felt a little pang of guilt because he knew he was about to take advantage of the woman's softness toward him and perhaps get a better load assignment because of it.

"I noticed there isn't anything by my name yet. Does that mean I get tomorrow off?"

The grin Ross managed to give Kim was strained and false, and she knew he was more or less joking about the day off. She admired his attempt at humor because she could tell it was hard for him to smile. She wanted to do something nice for him. She had three loads she was working out the details on, and she guessed it would be fair to ask him which one he preferred, since he was right there.

"No such luck. But I can give you a choice. I have two store runs—one finals in Indiana and the other finals in Kentucky. Or you can take a load to Harrisburg. You have to be there in time to sleep and load out at 7 a.m., though, because that one backs up with a straight shot to G.R. You know the drill, Compton Classics."

Ross knew the drill all right. Compton Classics was a fussy customer who shipped "just in time" to General Motors in Grand Rapids, Mich. They monitored their loads as if they were the U.S. Treasury. Any little error on the driver's part would produce some kind of negative feedback. Ross was like the rest of the drivers; he avoided Compton loads whenever he could.

When Kim said the other loads "finaled," that meant they both had a number of stops along the way. It was often a zigzag tour of small towns, but the final was, of course, the last stop.

"I'll take either one of the store loads. When will they be ready?"

"Kentucky can go any time. Take Indiana, and you can wait till morning." By rights she should have given him the Kentucky just to get it moving, but she figured Shelley would appreciate him being home for dinner, so she gave him the option. Chances were, no one would notice she had shown him any favor.

"Indiana for me then," Ross said. "And thanks a lot, Kim." They exchanged knowing smiles. As Ross was walking away he realized that he had just smiled at someone and that it was a genuine, spontaneous smile, not something forced or contrived. Maybe things were really beginning to come around for him. Kim was warm and attractive, though; that made her easy to smile at. Especially when he had not seen a true smile from Shelley in so long.

He called Shelley to let her know he would be coming directly home. He asked her if he could stop and pick up anything to save her from having to go out, but she declined the offer. Her voice was as bland and emotionless as he expected. He almost wished he had selected Kentucky, so he would not have to go home and face Shelley's coldness. That would have seemed strange to Kim, though, thought Ross. She probably had no idea how Shelley was treating him.

As Ross approached his home, he tried to think of just what he might say to Shelley. He couldn't think of anything that offered hope of breaking the ice in her heart.

Maybe he could just take her in his arms and hold her. Maybe she would trust him enough to cry with him. Once, early in their marriage, after they'd had an argument, they had cried together, locked in each other's arms. The incident had proved somewhat therapeutic to their relationship. It was as if they both recognized that the other had weaknesses, shortcomings and points of selfishness. In spite of it they had decided to love and accept each other, to look beyond each one's disappointment with the other.

But that was a long time ago, shortly after their wedding. In fact, it had been their first real fight. Maybe they were both scared when they found out their marriage would not always be bright and cheerful. Maybe they had lost some aspect of their youthful innocence together that day, and the crying was a way of mourning the loss. Maybe if they could mourn the loss of Donny together, things would be okay.

The chaplain's words came back to him then. "I can tell you this: If you'll put your faith, your trust, in God, if you'll believe what Jesus said about seeking the kingdom of God, you'll find the power to outlive this thing. God can give you the courage to forgive yourself and face whatever is coming to you because of what happened."

Ross remembered the small sense of hope he felt when Jim told him his "troubles may not be over, but God could help him live through them." The words had the ring of truth to them, and for that reason they held some real comfort.

CHAPTER TWENTY THREE

Ross walked through his front door into a still house. He thought of calling out to Shelley like he would have done in the days before the accident, but he was afraid to. She would probably take it the wrong way, think him unduly lighthearted.

He walked into the kitchen and spoke her name as if she might be hiding in one of the cupboards. He felt stupid then for doing that. He was letting the awkward way he felt cloud his thoughts and actions, and he determined to think and speak very deliberately from then on. What happened between them in this conversation could be crucial.

He looked down the basement steps, since the door was opened. Sure enough, he saw the glow of the lights. Both Shelley and Randall would have heard him come into the house. Randall usually came upstairs to meet him or at least called out about Daddy being home. He heard nothing.

He stepped slowly and carefully down the steps. He could hear Shelley then. The distinctive sound of clothing being pulled out of the dryer, buttons and zippers making clinking sounds as they brushed across the metal door. He turned around at the bottom of the steps and looked into the basement

Shelley slowly moved her head to look at him. He knew she was anticipating his appearance as much as he was hers. They faced each other without really looking. Ross felt that fleeting desire he'd had earlier when he wished his load were ready to go—the desire to be somewhere else.

"Hi," Ross said.

"Hi yourself."

"Where's Randy?"

"He takes a nap every afternoon," Shelley said, as if she were informing him of something he did not know, and there was a mild sarcasm in her words.

"Yeah, I know. I guess it just seems early for him to be napping."

Shelley concentrated on folding a fitted sheet for Randall's bed, always an awkward procedure. Ross watched her hands as if they both welcomed the distraction.

"Early," Shelley said. "Early." The word made no sense to her. Her mind was blank, and she was searching for something to say. Even as the words came out she had no sense that she was saying them. She looked at Ross as if she were in a trance. "Yes, well it might be a little early. He was sleepy and getting cranky."

"Oh, I see," Ross said clumsily. "And how are you, Shell?"

"How am I?" she said.

Ross nodded. "Yeah, how are you?"

It seemed like the stupidest question in the world to Shelley. She thought it was crass of him to ask it. How could she be? The thought came to her that he too felt awkward. But she didn't care. Let him feel awkward. He ought to feel that way.

Even as the negative thoughts came to her mind, she had a twinge of conscience. She was not being kind to him just now, she knew, but it seemed all right somehow to be unkind to him. It appealed to something inside her. It was vengeance. It felt good. She was hungry for more of it.

Shelley folded another sheet, enjoying Ross's discomfort. He was standing there, his question yet suspended in the mysterious coolness between them. Her eyes flashed a devilish anger his way.

Ross picked up the box of detergent from the top of the washing machine and fumbled with it, then placed it squarely on the shelf where it belonged. He wanted to run, but he couldn't—partly because he resented her attitude and partly because he felt as if he ought to absorb her contempt, which he sensed was about to come spilling out of her.

"What am I supposed to say?" Shelley shifted to their playful, pretended British accent. She used it now to punctuate her sarcasm sadistically. "Oh, I'm just fine, Ross dear. Randall and I have been having a lovely time packing up the baby's clothes and putting all the baby things into a cardboard box. Later we're going to celebrate as we carry it all out to the car and drive to the Salvation Army donation center." Her eyes were wet, and her face contorted now in a mask of abject misery, yet she did not sob or tremble.

"Hell, we might even stop for ice cream on the way home. Won't that be smashing? We can take one of the little teddy bears we got at the shower and wrap it up in the little blue blanket we got at the shower. We'll pretend we have a baby brother. Would you like to come, too, Ross? That would be sooo...delightful. You can bring your camera. 'Oh, just be careful, Randall dear, don't walk in front of Daddy, he might trip!'"

Ross adopted her sarcastic tone but not the British lilt, all the while knowing it was the wrong thing to do. "Thank you, Shelley. That was so very encouraging. You really ought to be a counselor. No, better yet a comedian! Oh wait, even better, a comical counselor. Everyone knows the best way to handle tragedy is to make a laughingstock of the victims." Ross immediately wished he could recall the word "victims."

"Victim?" Shelley retorted angrily, dropping the British accent to show she was serious. "So you're the victim? Oh, pardon me. How could I be so silly? I really thought Donny was the victim."

As the words hit, Ross flinched. Shelley saw that her words were taking a toll. She saw the opportunity to dig deeper by reminding him of the other Donny who had been his victim, but even with all the venom she had to spew, she couldn't lower herself that far. Oh, how she wanted to, though. How could she do it? How to imply it subtly?

"How could I get you two mixed up? I mean, how could I get *the* two mixed up?" With that she took hold of the laundry basket at her feet and as she stood, wrenched it violently against the door of the dryer. The dryer door slammed with a force that made the metal side panels ring like someone striking a gong.

Ross felt cornered now, both by his wife's disgust and by

the monstrous load of guilt that had suddenly come snuffling and slobbering to his side, breathing down his neck. He needed some defense, some weapon.

"Oh, as if you are 'Little Miss Innocence' here! If you hadn't been so stupid carrying these damned heavy laundry baskets, he might have been able to grow into a healthy baby *before* he was born! Who knows whether or not he could have taken the fall if you'd given him half a chance? If you weren't so bull-headed, he might still be alive!" Ross spoke defiantly.

"There it is," thought Shelley. All this time she had wondered whether or not Ross had noticed. She had started to think he had not and that he would never mention it. In reality he had just been saving it, hording it up so that he could use it against her. Even though there was no good reason to think it would have made the slightest difference in the outcome of the cradle's fall, he was trying to shift the blame for the baby's death onto her.

"Good dodge, Ross. Only someone as self-centered as you could come up with that one." She stepped widely around him as she made her way to the steps. Ross stood there unmoving, like some mannequin in a department store. He wanted to beg her for mercy and to throttle her for her cruel words at the same time. He did neither.

As Shelley stomped up the steps, the physical strain of the climb made her feel weak. It softened her attitude a little, and she began to realize how incredibly wrong she had been to speak to Ross that way. But, unlike other times when such remorse had given her the heart to apologize, she simply felt empty, bland, like the tasteless white portion of an egg. Whatever love she once had for Ross had gone into exile or else simply died altogether. She could not care about his feelings. Her own misery was boss, and it was going to stay that way.

Ross stood in the basement watching the washing machine tremble as it entered the spin cycle. His chest felt like everything inside him was coiled around the spinning drum of the washer. The machine was pulling the coil tighter and tighter. It was trying to strangle him inwardly, to draw all hope out of him like the spinning washer drum drew the water out of the wet clothes and sent it forcefully down the drain into the sewers and away from everything that was clean and good and worthwhile.

He sank slowly down, the will to hold himself up gone now as the heavy weight of visceral agony tore at his resolution. The desire to live and breathe as faraway as the stars. He slipped sideways down the exterior of the washing machine until his sides felt the cold concrete floor beneath the throw rug that was lying in front of the washer. His head struck the cement with a dull click that sent a sharp pain through his brain. He didn't wince at the pain or the sick feeling that came along with it. It was dim suffering indeed compared to the mental and emotional anguish. And what did it matter anyway? He wanted to be dead. He longed for it, the way he had once longed for the touch of Shelley's hand or the taste of her kiss.

Ross lay there on the floor for a long time. After a while he noticed that the spinning of the washer was stopping. He heard the clicking of the switches as the electric motor shut off and the spinning ran down. He was beginning to come out of the cloud of despair enough to be conscious of what was going on around him. He could smell, almost taste the dampness of the rug under his chin. It was foul, like the pits of Hell must be, Ross thought.

❧

Shelley fixed her eyes straight ahead and put one foot above the other, climbing the steps with determination. The basket of laundry, still warm from the dryer's heat, radiated into her neck and face, punctuating the strange sense of anger and shame she felt. She breathed in deeply the cozy scent of the fabric softener. She usually delighted in the smell, seeing it as an indication of her success as a homemaker, one of a thousand little pleasures she used to validate herself as a mother, milestones or landmarks in her march toward the wholesome comfortable Christian home and family she had set out to build.

But it did not please her so today. It was all bogus, all a waste of time. The emptiness she felt now was a yawning chasm, a gap so wide that no amount of comforting words, no amount of religious drivel could span it.

It was all a sham. She knew that now. Her whole life she had been taught that God would be with her, would "walk beside her" when things got tough. And she had believed it all, in spite of the agony of having a splotched face. She had structured her whole life around the principles and ideals she heard in Sunday school and church. But never once had she been able to test it, never suffered even the loss of a grandparent or distant cousin, never had a setback of any consequence.

Well, things had gotten tough all right, bitterly tough, unreasonably tough—and where was God?

It wasn't fair for such a freakish thing to happen in the world she had worked so hard to build. It wasn't fair that the child she had loved and suffered so much for had been taken from her by a moment of her husband's stupidity. Was it some kind of tasteless joke? Being a mother was not just some "assignment" she could accept or decline; it was not a job she did—it was who she was, it was what she was.

Could the loving God she had been told to trust in since she was a tot pull such a dirty trick on her? And what about the baby? What good was his brief life anyway? And now to top it all off, Ross had the gall to try and blame her for the whole thing. Well, she didn't have to take this, no way, nooo-siree-bob!

As she raged inwardly, a patient, small voice persisted in her head, as gentle as the stroke of a baby's eyelash yet as certain as the stout wooden staircase that bore her steadily upward. Shelley knew that her attitude and the cold-hearted behavior she was allowing herself to indulge in did not belong in her life.

But she couldn't help it. This was something Shelley had never considered before, something she had taken for granted before she had the experience to know anything about it. Merely believing or knowing that something was right or proper or good did not give a person the ability or strength to do that thing. Knowing and doing were two separate things. How naïve she had been, how judgmental of people she considered weak before she knew how sick and cruel life could be. Well, she knew now. Quickly, the curtain had been pulled aside, and Shelley could see the truth.

❧

Ross had to face it now. All doubt had been swept away, and a little voice told him that it was just what he had expected all along. There was no other way. He could dream all he wanted about how his self-disgust was based on childhood injustice and deprivation, how other people could handle things another way. But for him there was only justice, only the one true way out of this living purgatory. Only paying back Shelley and Randall with the one tangible thing at his disposal would give him any vindication or righteousness.

It seemed important now that Shelley know. He wanted to tell her that he was willing to do the right thing, to pay the price. But he could not do that. He had thought through the thing well enough. His suicide must be kept strictly to himself; otherwise the insurance coverage might be denied them after he was gone.

It wasn't fair, he thought. Couldn't he even have the satisfaction of telling Shelley he was going to take his medicine? It would make him feel better to do that, would give him some measure of peace. But no, he could not risk it. Not if he wanted the plan to work. That little bit of pleasure was denied him also.

He turned his face down to the dirty rug and opened his mouth to taste the vile dampness. He gritted his teeth into the coarse fabric and bit down until he had his mouth full of the sour-tasting cloth. He chewed and grimaced and finally spit it out. Gritty dirt remained on his tongue, and he savored the putrid flavor. He realized it didn't make sense to lie there on the floor and chew the rug like that, but then, what did make sense? And who cared if he did what made sense or not? For him, there was no tomorrow. He reasoned that he was chewing the rug as a way of testing his ability to force suffering upon himself, lest he find out at the critical moment that he was inadequate for suicide, too. "I won't be," he reassured himself in an audible voice.

His thinking was twisted now, he was sure. He was doing things that weren't logical. How long would it be until people began to wonder about his sanity? What if they had him committed?

Ross pushed his body up from the floor and got to his feet. He dusted his trouser legs off a little and wiped the dirty tears from his cheeks. He spit in to the laundry sink until he had most of the dirt out of his mouth and ran the water to hide the evidence. He made his way up the stairs and through the dining room to the stairs for the second floor. He climbed them slowly with his hand on the rail, which he rarely used.

He found Shelley lying on her stomach across the bed. If she was sobbing, there was no indication of it. Her face was buried in her crossed arms. She reminded Ross of a small child hiding from the world by keeping her eyes shut so nobody could see her.

Ross stood there for a minute and stared at her. He mustered up his courage to speak. With a long slow sigh he began. "Shelley, I'm sorry I said what I did down there. There isn't any excuse for it. All I can say is that I accept responsibility for what happened. You deserve better. I'll show you. You'll see. I'll show you."

There was no movement from the bed. Ross went back downstairs, left the house quietly and drove away.

PART THREE

...Ah, up then from the ground sprang I
And hailed the earth with such a cry.
As is not heard save from a man,
Who has been dead and lives again
                    Renascence, Edna St. Vincent Millay

CHAPTER TWENTY-FOUR

Shelley's cheek was numb now. She had been lying still on the bed for so long she lost track of time. Ross had entered the room behind her and rattled off something in his miserable, solemn voice, but she hadn't cared to listen. He had gone away then; she heard the door slam, figured he left the house. She didn't care where he went.

As she heard Ross start the motor in his pickup, she had another burst of anger. Just what did he think he was doing now? Oh, of course. He was just going to drive away, leave her and Randall alone again, the way he did every time a new week started, and there was nothing she could do about it. He got to travel around and see new sights all week long. She had to stay here with the anguish, had to deal with the emptiness that he'd caused her.

She sprang to her feet with the energy of unchecked rage. She had pounded her pillow at other frustrated times in her life, but that wouldn't do it now. She had to break something. She took her stiff forearm and swept it across the top of her dresser, clearing photographs, knickknacks and cosmetics like flotsam before a bow wave. The things crashed against the wall and bounced to the floor, clattering and crashing raucously.

She pivoted on the ball of her foot and brought a roundhouse kick as forcefully as she could against the sliding closet door. The screws that held it let loose, and she could feel the broad side of it pushing air until it met the clothes hanging inside the closet. She shrieked uncontrollably until a wave of sadness caught her in its swell and rocked her wearily down onto the soft bedspread. She coiled her fists around the softness, the same way she had done countless times when waves of sensation had swept reality from her while she and Ross were making love, and the contrast of the two intensities flashed before her mind in cruel mockery of each other.

The feelings of intense anger and the feelings of intense love she remembered were as opposite as possible, yet they had something in common—they each filled the empty spaces in her heart. Anger or hatred filled her heart every bit as fully as love did. And she realized the deadly power of hatred, anger and division in all its various forms. She became strangely pensive now, as if some unseen intellect were directing her thoughts.

She observed that since she had never experienced any really harsh losses in her short life, she had no reference point for what she was going through. She became aware of how close she had come to losing the very essence of her soul, and she breathed a sigh of weary relief as the last vestiges of animosity drained from her mind, swirling and gurgling like dishwater down the drain. There was still a dull, empty feeling, but it was a familiar thing once again. She knew she could handle it.

❧

Shelley felt the soft, warm hand of her son sweep through the strands of tangled hair falling over her face. She realized then that she had completely forgotten him, sleeping in the other room, only the thin wall separating them. She also knew that the rage was past her now. She felt mellow and calm, as if the wind had stopped blowing and the dry leaves of her torment were settling down into a carpet of green grass. She knew that soon the grass would grow thick around them, and they would be captured like flies in a spider's web. Soon enough the grass too would die as all things do in winter. But the springtime would come again as it always did, and with it the vernal breath of life would restore her sanity and her happiness the way Randy's loving caress was soothing her soul.

She turned her wet eyes and face up to look at her son. Her dear, sweet, loving, little baby boy; her firstborn—the fruit of the love that she and Ross had desired and brought to pass with so much joy and eagerness.

His face was a smaller version of Ross's. It wasn't quickly evident, but when you looked close at his eyes, the way they squeezed together on the ends as he grinned, the resemblance was unmistakable, as if it were a secret that revealed itself only to the initiated, only to those who took the time to study it. As if it were a treasure, shown only to those who loved Ross.

She sat up then, wet-lashed eyes flying wide open. She did love Ross. Loved him in the kind of deep-down way that lets temporary animosity cover it from time to time. Her love for him was strong enough to be taken for granted, like the deeply laid stone foundations of their 80-year-old house. It was the kind of love she had wanted for the man she married, the kind that could weather any storm. She knew it now. She would let him know it, too. She had been cold and cruel to him lately, she knew. Well, that was over.

Ross had suffered from Donny's death every bit as much as she had, she recognized. Maybe more, because of the way it had happened. And she remembered then the awful thing that had taken place only a short while ago in the basement; remembered the disregard she had showed for Ross and his feelings and how she had crucified him verbally. She gulped in a huge swallow of air then; she realized how careless she had been with his soul.

CHAPTER TWENTY-FIVE

Ross resigned himself to what he must do. There was no other way to make up for his son's death but to surrender himself to the waves of remorse and give justice its due. He had driven past the bridge pier at the 28 mile-marker for the last time. Today he would end his life.

All he had to do was get back to the terminal and ask Kim for the load to Harrisburg. He could make up some story about Shelley going away for the day if he had to. Kim probably wouldn't even ask him why he was changing his mind about it and not taking the load to Indiana. Not if he put on the sullen face he had been wearing recently and acted as if he wanted to avoid conversation.

As it turned out he didn't have to ask Kim about it. The face at the dispatch window was John Murphy himself. Ross felt better facing him instead of Kim. John wouldn't notice any difference in his mood, since he had not seen him earlier.

"Hi, Mr. Murphy."

"How's it going, Ross?"

"Just fine, sir." Ross rarely bothered to call the man "sir." He wished he hadn't this time either. He was trying to do everything as normally as possible.

"You're here too early, Ross. The load to Indiana won't be ready for a while yet," said the boss.

"Yes sir, but when I was in here earlier, Kim said you had a load to Harrisburg. I wondered if you'd mind if I took that one instead?"

Murphy didn't respond to Ross's query immediately, instead taking a close look at the computer screen and checking something on a clipboard. Ross didn't know what it all was, but the man got a quizzical look on his face and replied, "Why not, if you want it? That will be one less headache for us today."

Ross supposed the boss was wondering why he would volunteer for such an undesirable assignment. Ross decided the safest course was to remain tight-lipped. In a few minutes he had a thick package of papers in his hand and was headed outside toward his truck.

The trailer going to Harrisburg was another multi-stop auto-parts store load, but since the stores were all near Harrisburg, Ross would not make the deliveries to the individual stores. He would simply drop the trailer in Harrisburg, and another driver, someone who lived in the area, would make the deliveries. Whoever took the trailer to Harrisburg was routinely dispatched on the Compton Classics load to Michigan.

It was still early afternoon, and Ross had more than enough time to run the five hours to Harrisburg, then sleep for eight hours before picking up the load to Michigan. It occurred to him that if he were going to drive into the bridge today, it would be hard for anyone to believe he had fallen asleep. That usually happened in the middle of the night.

He decided it didn't really matter all that much. Without some indication from him that he was suicidal, the insurance people would have no choice but to pay the claim. They could and probably would speculate, but disputing benefits to a widow and little boy so soon after the woman had suffered the shocking loss of a child would be perceived as heartless on their part.

Besides, he wanted Shelley to know, or at least to live with the possibility that she had driven him to it. It would be the only way he could let her know that he had done it for her and Randy. Such an act of nobility should not go unnoticed, he thought.

He remembered that he often got a little drowsy in the afternoon anyway, many people did. It was something about circadian rhythm, whatever that was. It was at least plausible for him to fall asleep on a dreary winter afternoon.

As Ross hooked up the lines and raised the landing gear of the trailer, he wondered if he was losing his mind. How could one tell if he was losing his sanity? He guessed that if anyone knew what he was about to do, they would consider him crazy. But he didn't care. All he really wanted was freedom from this incredible torment, to leave behind this wrenching pain in his gut that had been dogging him for so long.

❧

Leeroy Foust pulled into the truck stop in eastern Pennsylvania in the late afternoon. His belly was telling him he should have grabbed something sooner, but the food here was tolerable, as truck stops went. After spending all of the previous afternoon delivering to that ridiculously slow warehouse in Scranton, he had run up into Massachusetts and picked up a load of automotive batteries the next morning. He didn't know how things might have gone for Ross, but he hoped to cross paths with him again, maybe run back to Heritage together if they were lucky.

He parked in the snow-covered lot and made his way toward the restaurant. In his path was the mobile chapel. Maybe Ross had taken his advice and stopped in here to talk to the chaplain about his problems. He looked through the glass door as he walked past and made eye contact with a man seated at a table inside. He was only a few steps beyond the chapel door when he heard a footfall on the steps and a voice calling out, "Say, driver!"

Leeroy stopped and turned around to see the leathery face of the old chaplain smiling down at him. "Can I have a minute of your time?" The man walked down and approached Leeroy with his hand out. "I don't mean to bother you, but I noticed the logo on your jacket. You drive for H.A. Murphy." It was not a question but a statement, since the distinctive jacket was something all Murphy drivers wore proudly.

"That's right," Leeroy said. "What can I do for you?"

"I suppose you know Ross Martin?"

There was a serious look on the man's face. Leeroy guessed Ross had taken his advice and seen this preacher. The man looked a little too concerned.

"Yes. Fact is, Ross is a good friend of mine."

"That's good. So you know all about what happened to him."

"Did he stop in and talk to you?"

"Yes, last night," Chaplain Jim said. Leeroy said nothing then, but his eyes softened, signaling to the chaplain that further conversation would be welcome.

"I expect you're going in to get a bite?"

"That's what I had in mind."

"Can I join you?" Jim said.

"Be my pleasure," Leeroy said with a smile.

The two men went in and sat down in a booth, one with a telephone. Leeroy ordered a meal and Jim just had coffee.

"I don't ordinarily invite myself to somebody's table," Jim said as soon as the waitress left. "Being a chaplain, guys usually think I want to push my religion. I have to be careful not to be that way."

"I understand," Leeroy said. "But you're concerned about Ross. How long have you known him, and what all did he tell you?"

"He told me about the death of his baby boy."

"Did he tell you he fell on the boy?" Leeroy said, grimacing as he choked out the bitter words. Describing the thing to a stranger wasn't easy. He felt almost like he was betraying Ross, but this man probably knew it already.

"Yeah. Tough thing for a man to handle, very tough."

"Is he handling it?" asked Leeroy.

"That's why I stopped you. He seemed almost like he had come to terms with it. But I couldn't help thinking, after he'd gone, that he wasn't telling me everything. I realized that what happened to him is worse than most men could handle. He thinks deeply, that boy."

The chaplain's reference to Ross as a "boy" let Leeroy know the man cared about him. He let his guard down.

"You're right about that, I guess," he said. "I never thought about it too much. Ross always seemed to me to be sort of private. Like he would let you in so far and no farther. But lots of guys are that way. I don't see any problem with it."

"No, not in most cases. The problem I see with this guy is…" Jim hesitated now, looked down into the cooling coffee in his cup, then back up at Leeroy. "Well, I don't want to jump to conclusions or anything, but maybe a guy with this on his mind could get suicidal. Especially a guy that's self-reliant and private, like he is."

The two men sat and stared at each other for a few moments, both uncomfortable with the subject. Leeroy had to acknowledge that the thought had crossed his mind, too. He put his coffee cup up to his mouth and spoke from behind it, as if fearful of addressing the possibility. "Yeah, I reckon he could. I guess most of us that know Ross have wondered about that. Hell, how could a man not think that way, with what happened to Ross? Sorry about that. I try to watch my tongue."

Chaplain Jim chuckled a little at Leeroy's apology for using the word "hell." It was plain to see that this was an old-fashioned man, a lot like he was. "No, that's okay," he said.

"What can we do? I mean, do you think we should say anything to his family? Now that I think of it, I told Ross a while back that I understood how tough the thing could be for him. Told him I would help him any way I could."

"You his best friend?"

"I don't know. I doubt it. We just sort of run together when we can. I trained him when he first started, and we hit it off. I know there's a big age difference for us to be partners, but we are anyway. He probably has other friends outside of work. It's not something we ever talked about. He's close to his wife, I can tell you that."

"You mean he *was* close to his wife," Jim said.

Leeroy cocked his head at Jim's statement. "What do you mean, was?"

"Well, he told me she held it against him, thinks he's to blame for it. But that's not surprising. A lot of marriages break up when couples lose a baby, for whatever reason. I guess they think they have to find some reason for it. They tend to blame each other. Doesn't make sense—but when people are hurting, they don't see clearly."

"With what happened, it'd be easy for her to blame him. Easy for him to accept the blame, too," Leeroy said.

"No doubt," the chaplain said.

"The poor guy. I know he's been hurting. But he seemed to be handling it okay." Leeroy shook his head. "Or maybe I just wanted to think he was handling it okay."

"Can you talk to anybody in his family?"

"The only one in his family I know is Shelley. That's his wife's name if he didn't tell you. I don't really know her that well. You know how it is. I've talked to her a little at the company picnics and when she'd show up at the terminal for one reason or another. She's brought him to work a time or two. She's a fine lady. She thinks he walks on water—or she used to anyway."

"The thing is Leeroy, people need time, lots of time to work through something as painful as this. Something tells me Ross won't give himself that time. You know, don't you, that Ross felt responsible for the death of his best friend in high school?"

The memory of another time when he and Ross had run together came to Leeroy then. Ross had told him about naming the baby after his best friend in high school. Leeroy had been able to tell by Ross's voice on the radio that it was a difficult subject for him, but he didn't know why until now. Wait, that was wrong. John Murphy had told him about that before Ross went back to driving. Leeroy wondered why he had forgotten that part?

Leeroy realized then that there was more to this baby's death than he had wanted to face. Had he been in what they called "denial?" He had always considered the notion of denial to be psychobabble and a lot of hogwash. Then he felt a strange foreboding, not the kind of thing he was at all used to feeling. He began to fear for his friend.

"I guess I never put the two together," he said. "Come to think of it, for pity's sake, they even named the baby after his friend. He told me that, too, but it never dawned on me that the name would complicate things."

"He told me he felt like he had cursed his baby by giving him that name," Jim said.

"Surely, you told him different?" Leeroy said.

"Yes, of course. I told him there was no such thing as a curse. I prayed for him and all, but I don't know how much it helped him."

Leeroy reached for the phone. Without saying a word to Jim he dialed the dispatch office at H. A. Murphy. John Murphy himself answered.

"Boss...Leeroy. I need Ross Martin's home phone number."

"Okay, Leeroy. I would have thought you'd have that. It won't do you any good to call him now, though; he just left here for Harrisburg." He gave Leeroy the number but was curious about what he wanted it for.

"Can I ask what you want to talk to him about? Is everything okay?"

"Well, sir, actually I want to talk to his wife. I'm concerned about Ross."

"We all are, Leeroy. I thought he was doing all right. But you don't think so, do you?"

"I just want to see how they're getting along. I want to get her opinion about Ross. I've been talking to this chaplain out here at exit 46, and he seems to think Ross and his wife are on the outs."

"Ross has been talking to a chaplain about what happened? Seems strange. His pastor stopped in here one day right after the accident and sort of made me promise to look out for Ross. I guess he didn't think Ross could handle what happened very well. I just assumed that he was counseling with his minister."

"That could be. But this chaplain had a talk with him the other night, and now he is worried about him. Frankly sir, I am, too."

"Maybe we should worry about him. Say, does his wife work outside the home?"

"No, not unless she just started to," Leeroy said.

"Funny then. Ross came in this morning and agreed to leave

tomorrow on a parts-store run to Indiana; then he came back in a couple hours later and swapped for the Harrisburg run, the one that gets the Compton Classics to G.R. He left just a few minutes ago. I didn't ask why he wasn't staying at home with his wife tonight when he had a chance. Figured it wasn't any of my business. But this isn't like Ross."

"No, it ain't," agreed Leeroy.

"Okay, old timer. You call his wife. I'll see if I can find the number for that preacher who stopped in to see me. I think he left me a card. Maybe he knows Ross better than we do."

"Okay, John, I'll let you know if I find out anything from Shelley," Leeroy said.

"You be careful," Murphy warned. "There isn't any reason to scare her, you know."

"Sure, I know how to be tactful."

Leeroy hung the phone up and looked into the eyes of the old chaplain. He decided to wait and talk to Shelley before he shared any of his misgivings with the man. He picked up the phone again and dialed the number.

❦

Shelley was sitting on her bed when the phone rang, with Randall sitting cross-legged on her lap. She was stroking his incredibly soft hair and doing her best to keep from crying, now that she had come to her senses and counted her blessings.

At first she considered just letting the phone ring, since the answering machine would get it. The mood she was sharing with Randall was one of those precious things a person must enjoy while they can, since you can never quite bring them back, no matter how much they are desired or how hard you try. Then she realized that it may be Ross calling, and she wasn't going to miss the chance to apologize to him and tell him how much she loved him. She stretched out and took hold of the phone without letting go of Randall.

"Hello."

"Hi there, is that you, Shelley?"

"Yes it is." She knew the voice from somewhere but couldn't put a name with it.

"This is Leeroy Foust calling. How are you doing today?"

That was a huge question for Shelley to answer, and she wanted to unload it on someone, but she didn't think this was the person. She settled instead for the cliché, "Just fine, and you?"

"I'm fine, too, Shelley. You're probably a little surprised to hear from me, I guess."

"Actually, I'm glad you called. Are you with Ross?"

"No, Shelley, I'm still out east here. But I have been thinking about him a lot. That's why I called you." Shelley began to feel distressed. There was something about the tone of Leeroy's voice. She didn't know him all that well, but he had always been cheerful towards her.

"I've been thinking about him, too. Oh Leeroy, if you see him, tell him to call me, will you? I need to tell him I'm sorry. I was really mean to him today. I've been treating him like dirt, and I just now came to my senses." She realized she was understating things a bit but didn't think it was wise to say too much in front of Randall.

"Well, don't be too hard on yourself. What happened with your baby would be a hard thing to take. That would put anybody in a bad mood."

"Thank you. You're so sweet. But really, I need to tell Ross."

"Shelley, I don't want to be nosey or anything, but I'm kind of afraid about Ross's mood, too. Do you think he's gonna be okay?"

The full portent of Leeroy's words fell upon her then. She knew that after the cruel things she said to him, her husband could be capable of anything. He might even be suicidal. It was too much for her, and despite the presence of her 4-year-old, she broke down.

"Oh Leeroy, Leeroy, I just...destroyed him. I said the cruelest things to him. I'm so sorry. I don't know how I could be so heartless, but I was. I even blamed him for the death of

Donny Ritts, after all the times I told him it wasn't his fault. Oh, how could I be so mean?" Shelley confessed, her words tumbling over her sobs. She wanted to pound her fist into the bedding again but restrained herself for the sake of Randall. "Oh Leeroy, we've got to find him."

"Settle down now, honey," Leeroy said in a fatherly tone. "I'll make a few phone calls. I know where he usually stops, and if they don't see him, we can call the yard in Harrisburg. They can have him call you."

"Any time of the night, Leeroy. You tell them to have him call me as soon as he can, no matter what time it is. Please! Oh, I wish he had a cell phone in his truck." The couple had considered getting a cell phone months before but decided against the extra expense. The decision seemed foolish now.

Leeroy promised he would get back with Shelley when he knew something more. He put the phone down and looked deeply into the eyes of Chaplain Jim. He was struck with the sense that his running into the chaplain here was something more than coincidence. He was never a religious man, had never taken seriously any claims of supernatural activity in the lives of people. But he was always respectful of those things, and now as he sat there with this holy man's patient gaze reading his face, he began to wonder if perhaps he had missed something important.

"So what did you find out?" The chaplain's face looked calm, but he was clearly anxious for more news.

"Well, it's not good." Leeroy told Jim about Ross unexpectedly leaving on a run again so shortly after going home and how Shelley had been so hard on him. Also that Shelley wanted to tell Ross that she was sorry and that she'd had a change of heart.

"Better call the boss," Leeroy said. "Maybe he can get hold of Ross somehow." Leeroy punched in the toll-free number to Heritage and related the story that Shelley had shared with him to John Murphy.

"So what you're telling me is that Ross went home to see his wife, and she sort of drove him out again?" John said.

"That's the way it looks. Did you get hold of his preacher?" asked Leeroy.

"Yeah. He told me that the two of them have been putting on a great show for him. He seems like a pretty sharp guy. He visits them regularly, trying to keep his finger on what's going on. He thinks they know all the right things to say to him—basically what they think he wants to hear—but he hasn't been fooled by it. He's close to Ross's in-laws too, so he hears things they don't tell him. But there's not much he can do as long as the two of them continue to play that game. He's afraid Ross could get suicidal. He says Ross keeps too much inside him. I guess he's right. You know Ross."

"I maybe don't know him as well as I should," lamented Leeroy. "Do you have any way to get hold of him?" Even as he asked, he knew it was a stupid question. John Murphy could only make phone calls and leave messages for Ross.

"I left word at the yard in Harrisburg. They'll be watching for him to come in. He'll be told he needs to call us and call home at once. I don't know what else I can do. You got any suggestions?"

"No, I guess not. I'm heading in myself as soon as we hang up. If I see anybody I know bound for Harrisburg, I'll tell them to look for Ross and give him the word. I guess me and this chaplain here are gonna pray for him, too."

"You do that, Leeroy," Murphy said.

CHAPTER TWENTY-SIX

Eugene Wythe had not intended to become a criminal—it just sort of happened. He was intelligent and big enough that no one could pick on him much while he was growing up in Western Pennsylvania. But he had always been moody and unpredictable. Though grudgingly accepted by his peers, he had no close friends in his adolescence. Too short on social skills to get involved in sports or any extracurricular activities, he became a loner and rationalized his solitude by considering himself better than other people. Though he was self-serving and dishonest, he never did anything worse than shoplifting, and that he did mostly for the sport of it.

When he came of age and got out into the working world, away from the comfort of his parent's provision, things changed. When he had to get out of bed and go to a job five days a week, something inside him rebelled.

His employers saw him as shiftless and prone to cause trouble. Never blessed with much ambition, he could find ways to avoid completing his tasks, all the while rationalizing the failures in his mind. He learned to delight in causing people trouble, always telling himself they were stupid, and he was too good to work for them anyway. In time, his condescending thinking became the normal path of his consciousness, and he truly saw himself as superior to others.

His was an extraordinary existence, he reasoned. Since people could tell how smart he was, they naturally felt insecure around him, afraid he would eventually take their job from them. Consequently, people found ways to get rid of him. He would get another job and be willing to start at the bottom, but as soon as he began to learn and suggest ways of doing things better, another foreman's or manager's insecurity would manifest itself, and Eugene would be let go.

In time Eugene reasoned that he might as well take the necessities of life from those who were able to earn them. Perhaps if he saved part of what he stole, he could launch his own business someday and be able to hire others. He would never treat his underlings the way he had been treated but would allow each person to rise as high and fast as his talents would allow. He would be a fair employer, not like the ones he had worked for. But first he had to get enough money to start a business.

He started out with burglary. He picked the better homes in rural Western Pennsylvania and Eastern Ohio, knowing that in most houses there were couples who both worked outside the home. That meant he could have the whole day to enter the house, look over its contents, pick what he wanted to take, move the stuff to an easy spot to retrieve, then load it in his van and drive away.

Lots of well-to-do people lived in the country. Wealthier people had good insurance, and most of them would be glad to be robbed, or at least that was what his twisted mind told him. He ranged over a broad area and avoided establishing any pattern so that the police would not be able to predict where he might strike next.

He even got a part-time job that served his burglary enterprise well. He took a position driving a "honey truck" for a business based out of Heritage. He drove to construction sites, campgrounds, fairgrounds and any other place that used portable toilets and serviced them, which meant pumping out the contents and cleaning them. Sometimes he picked them up, delivered or relocated them. He was able to range over a four-county area, and he worked alone.

His employer knew the job was a hard one to fill for the wages they paid, so they put up with his time-consuming forays to the sites along with the occasional high mileage on the flush truck. The truth was that Eugene was looking for homes to burglarize. The job was good cover. As Eugene worked his way around the area he found lots of houses that likely held pricey goods. You could tell by the way people kept their homes. There were always external indicators of prosperity, if you knew what to look for. If someone saw him in a place he shouldn't be, he could always say he was looking for one of his units to service.

He even had to rent a storage locker to hold all the stuff he'd gathered but hadn't been able to sell yet. Some of the loot he kept for himself.

He had nearly blown the whole thing one time when he entered an old remodeled farmhouse and found it was occupied. The owners of the place were a pair of surgeons who put in long hours and came home late night after night. He had gone in at 11 a.m., convinced that since both Mercedes had driven away, both doctors were gone, too. It turned out the man of the house was relaxing in a hot tub in the basement.

Eugene had jimmied the lock so quietly that he was able to walk nonchalantly into the basement, prepared to take his time lifting the merchandise. He had a theory that if he didn't disturb things much, these busy people might not know he had robbed them right away. He had nearly walked past the man, who was sitting so low down in the water that only his bald head was visible, and Eugene had simply not noticed him until he began to sit up with that incredulous look on his face. "Hey...hey, what are you doing in here?" the man said, with fear in his voice.

At first Eugene was too surprised to take any action. He stammered a little at first, thinking maybe he could talk his way out of the situation. The doctor started out of the tub, obviously not willing to listen, so Eugene decided to run. He was halfway through the door when he realized there might be a better option than flight. The doctor did something that gave Eugene an idea—he slipped on the wet tile as he was trying to get out of the tub. He caught himself and suffered no injury, but for a moment the man was vulnerable—naked, wet and weaponless.

Eugene picked up an aluminum softball bat that was leaning conveniently against the wall and gave the man a quick shot on the side of the head. The physician went down like someone had turned off his switch, and Eugene stood there shaking, staring at the fleshy, motionless body.

Eugene waited for a while, listening for any sound of activity that might indicate the doctor was not alone, but none came. He made a search of the house then, lamenting the fact that something had gone wrong, because this could have been his most lucrative heist. These people had a lot of nice stuff.

He returned to the basement and checked out the doctor as best he could. His breathing was shallow and uneven. Eugene didn't know what that meant. Would the man die? Would he come around and remember what Eugene looked like? There was a bump on the side of the man's head as large as Eugene's fist.

The idea that came into Eugene's head as the man slipped was to bash him on the head and position his body so that people would think he got the injury from falling. Eugene had made the decision so quickly he had no time to ponder whether or not he could actually kill the man. Strangely, he felt no remorse at all now, as the man lay there motionless. But would the man die?

Eugene wished he had taken the time to put both hands on the bat and take a strong swing. As it was, he would have to hit the man a second time. Would the police be able to tell about the second blow? Surely if he hit hard enough to crush the bone deeply the first evidence would be covered, he reasoned. As long as Eugene gave them no reason to suspect anything other than an accident, he should be okay. He could come back a few months later and help himself. He could wait on a haul as good as this one.

Eugene put the doctor on his side next to the tub. He took several practice swings with the bat to be sure he would hit exactly the right spot on his skull, then followed through with plenty of force. He waited a few minutes and checked for a pulse—he found none.

Then, for good measure, Eugene scraped the impact area of the bat onto the most likely impact area on the edge of the tub. He knew that if the police checked closely they would find cells from the man's scalp right where his head would have made contact in his fall.

Eugene cleaned the bat thoroughly, as well as any surface he could remember touching. He was satisfied that he had done a convincing job, but after he left the house, he waited a while in the woods and watched the place. He wanted to give his mind time to think in case he remembered any detail that might incriminate him.

Before long, one of the Mercedes came back to the house, followed by a pickup truck with an auto service placard on the door. The Mercedes parked in the driveway. Its driver got out and hopped in the pickup. That explained it. The car had been driven away by a mechanic that morning for service. Eugene slipped through the woods to his van and drove back to Heritage.

Sure enough, the headlines two days later read: "Local surgeon victim of fall." Eugene felt so proud he bought two newspapers. He returned to his normal procedure, confident that someone as sharp as he was could survive in the difficult world of crime.

But the incident with the doctor made him think he needed to review his operation. He had established a pattern, and the cops had to be keeping track of the robberies. They would no doubt be trying to predict his next burglary locale. He decided to take a break from stealing and try to reduce his inventory of merchandise. He decided to diversify his fencing a little.

He began to sell the stuff to truck drivers. There were several truck stops within a 15-minute drive of Heritage. The drivers were nearly all from out of state, and they wouldn't ask him any questions. Most of them were happy to get a good buy on jewelry, power tools and guns. There were lots of guns available in country homes. He fenced the stuff in the evenings when many truckers were sitting in the parking lots with time on their hands.

He spent lots of spare time at the truck stops, too. By getting his meals at the restaurants and mixing with the truckers and waitresses, he could keep his ears open for any talk of his activities. He had been reading religiously the two major newspapers that covered his area of operation.

He could live off the income from the toilet job. He saved everything he got from burglary, careful not to put it all in the bank. He was afraid someone might get suspicious that a man with his modest income had so much cash in reserve. He got rid of nearly everything he wanted to sell and was about ready to start picking out places to rob again when he noticed a small headline on the second page of the *Heritage Globe*: "Police to reexamine death of surgeon."

It seemed that the doctor's wife was never satisfied that her husband, a safety- conscious person, could have allowed such a freak thing to take his life. She and her husband were well connected in the county, having operated on judges or their wives at one time or another. A few phone calls got the house dusted for fingerprints. They didn't turn up any strange ones, but they did find several items that strangely had no prints at all on them, especially a certain ball bat that the dead surgeon had been fond of and handled regularly. After a closer look at the photographs the coroner had taken of the head injury, they had a possible homicide on their hands.

The news story went on to say that state police believed the murder, if indeed it was a murder, might be related to a string of rural burglaries. By linking the two, the police had reason to mount an intense investigation, and they were going to do just that.

Eugene Wythe began to shake. Up until now he had been confident that no one suspected his covert enterprises. Probably the police were simply keeping quiet about the burglaries. But they could not keep quiet about a homicide. Eugene knew the police would start looking for fingerprints in the other places he had robbed. Chances were they would find his prints, since he hadn't been careful about it in most places. His fingerprints were not on file anywhere as far as he knew. But what if he got nabbed doing one of his burglaries? The police would link him to the dead doctor.

Eugene decided to stop the burglaries at once. He went

through his stock of stolen merchandise and sold off or discarded anything that might be traceable or identifiable. But he couldn't shake the fear that sat upon him now. He had murdered an important physician. The police would see capturing him as a great trophy. They would never stop looking for him.

He was more diligent on the job now. He thought that if he could develop a good relationship with his employer, he might be seen as a trustworthy person and not be suspected by anyone. But driving a toilet truck was still an undesirable job. It wouldn't do to act like he enjoyed it.

He spent more and more time worrying about the police. He could not sleep at night for fear that they would come knocking on his door. Any time he passed a trooper on the highway, he broke into a sweat and his hands shook so that he could hardly steer. He was afraid to look at the newspapers anymore, yet he wanted to know what was going on in the investigation. He tried listening to the local news, but he couldn't make it past the introduction and commercial before shutting off the radio.

Eugene spent months in a state of fear and paranoia. He would have gone to see a psychiatrist, but what could he tell them the trouble was? "I'm afraid I'm gonna be caught for this murder thing I committed?" He lost weight, and his skin got pale. His boss expressed concern about his health.

Eugene feared that he was beginning to lose touch with reality. He walked around in a fog of dread every waking minute. He tossed fitfully at night, dreaming of handcuffs and stale bread for dinner. One wintry afternoon he got home from work, and there was a squad car parked in front of the duplex he called home. That was all it took. Something snapped inside him. He wanted to run.

He would get as far away as he could. He drove right past the duplex and made a beeline for the storage locker place. He knew how he could get away. He had learned a lot about trucking. He would get a ride with a trucker to someplace no one would suspect him to go to, someplace where no one knew him. If he had to use a little coercion on some driver, he would. He had a nice Smith & Wesson revolver, one that had the serial numbers filed off so it couldn't be traced. He'd found it in a hunting cabin, one of his early jobs. It was the only thing worth taking from that shack. It even had a shoulder holster so he could keep it hidden under his winter coat.

He went to a truck stop about 60 miles east of Heritage and parked his car in the far corner of the lot. He figured that leaving his car east of his home might throw people off track about where he went. He bummed a ride back toward Heritage on an empty gasoline tanker. The driver was friendly and would have been easy to hijack. Eugene didn't want to hijack that truck, though. Since it only ran locally, it would be missed too soon. He got off the tanker at exit two, just east of Heritage. There was a large truck stop there. Hundreds of trucks, maybe thousands, passed through the place each day. The drivers bought fuel, took showers, ate good meals and moved on for points all over the continent.

Eugene knew that when the diesel tanks on an 18-wheeler are full, they could travel about a thousand miles before needing fuel again. He figured he would commandeer a truck just as the driver was ready to pull away from the pumps. That way he could be sure of getting lots of distance between him and Pennsylvania before having to make contact with people again. It would be easy to do.

CHAPTER TWENTY-SEVEN

Ross was ready. He left H.A. Murphy a good hour before he had to and drove to the truck stop at exit two. He parked in the back of the lot and got into the bunk, so he could give the whole thing one last going-over in his head. There really wasn't much to think about anymore. He had been thrashing it all out for weeks now.

His future as a husband and father was shattered. The only thing that could bring any good into the lives of Shelley and Randall was his death. Randall was young enough to learn to love another man. Shelley was good-looking and charming enough to find another husband. If the Port-Wine Stain was a problem, she could use some of the life insurance money to get cosmetic surgery. When Shelley was smaller, her parents had looked into that. The doctors said there was something called a pulse-die laser that could remove or at least lighten her stain. The problem then had been that her stain was too close to her eyes and using the laser was risky. But Ross knew that medical science got better every day. Perhaps the day was coming when Shelley's face could be fixed. Shelley liked family life enough that Ross figured it would not be long before some other guy took his place. It would be someone more competent who would not accidentally kill the people he loved. There would be more children to tie them all together. Shelley would have a chance for happiness at least, with him out of the way.

He knew some would call the thing he was doing "the coward's way out." But he didn't care. It was not as if he were trying to avoid something. He was trying to protect Shelley and Randall, he told himself. The path he had chosen was an honorable thing, an act of love. His family would be better off this way. The insurance would provide plenty of money for them.

And what of God? Ross was supposed to be a man who believed that God played an active role in his life. That is what Pastor Sawyer had been telling him, and that was what Chaplain Jim had told him, too, more or less. Ross wasn't sure what he believed, except that in the days since the accident, since he had fallen on his little son and broken the boy's neck, he had experienced nothing of the support or power or love that God was supposed to provide for people who were in trouble.

Was it like some said, that God was just an imaginary friend for simple-minded people, a product of wishful thinking maybe, a contrivance used by the clergy to manipulate people into acting more decent? If there were a God, Ross would find out soon enough, he supposed. He might ask him why he wasn't given some aid in avoiding the fall on his baby. If there were no God and no afterlife, then it didn't really matter anyway, did it? At least Ross would find release from the torture he had been stoically enduring. It was time to move on. Time to shake the damned monster that jumped on him every day and chewed his guts and tormented his thinking. If there was a hell and if he went there, could it be worse than living had become?

Ross got back in the driver's seat and tooled the heavy rig up to the fuel pumps. It was normal for him to buy fuel here. H.A. Murphy got a volume discount, and he was expected to top off his tanks before passing this point. If he didn't do that, someone might figure out that he knew he would not need the fuel and had skipped the stop intentionally.

After he paid for the fuel, he went to the sandwich shop, one of those franchise places that were springing up in truck stops all over. He loved a good sandwich, and since he could not get his favorite dish, Shelley's spaghetti, for his last meal he decided to have a steak-and-cheese sub.

He took the sandwich back to the truck and ate it right there, with the truck sitting at the fuel pump. It was considered bad manners to tie up a fuel island longer than necessary—

better to make room for the next driver—but Ross mused that a condemned man could allow himself an indulgence such as that. It wasn't busy anyway now; no truck was sitting waiting for a pump.

He ate slowly, trying to savor each bite. He couldn't really taste anything, hadn't tasted food for so long. He just chewed and swallowed it. He had been eating plenty, though, because it helped to settle the wrenching in his gut. He had put lots of mayonnaise on the sandwich, and it oozed out the sides, the tangy warmth pleasantly dripping down his fingers.

He took a napkin and wiped the remnants of the mayo from his fingers. He threw the napkin over against the passenger side window. He never just dropped his trash on the floor like that, but it didn't matter now. In a little while the interior of his truck would be crushed, and there would be mess everywhere.

Ross pulled in another breath of air and girded up his courage. This was it. He pushed the yellow button on the dash, then the red one. He had released the brakes on his truck for the last time. He took hold of the shifter and pushed it straight forward into second gear. He looked at the photographs of Shelley and Randall pasted on the dashboard. He began to release the clutch.

He was just feeling the friction point with his left foot when motion caught his eye. He looked to the left. There was a young man running up to him waving, as if he had some important message. Ross had never seen him before that he could recall.

Ross reached over and pushed down on the window switch reluctantly. He didn't need anything to distract him now. Chances are this fellow was looking to scam him somehow. The guy didn't strike Ross as being a truck driver. Ross figured he would either ask for a ride or for a handout. It wasn't unusual in truck stops. Either way the answer was going to be no.

The man hopped up onto the step on the fuel tank. He stuck his face almost in the window. "I need to talk to you about something."

"What?" Ross said with a tone of disgust and impatience. He wanted to get on with his plan.

"Well, it's just this." The man was reaching under his coat. He pulled out a large, shiny handgun. Ross's eyes almost bugged out as the guy put the muzzle of the gun just under his eye, where it was almost resting on his cheek.

"Set your brakes again," the man said.

Ross was holding the truck with the foot brake pedal. He didn't know quite how to react to this. Was he being hijacked? Is this how it went? He'd heard stories about it but never thought it might happen to him. He made no move to comply with the man's request.

"I said, 'put your brakes on.' You think I won't shoot?" the man said.

Ross reached over and pulled the yellow knob, resetting both the tractor and the trailer brakes at once. There was a familiar gush of air, a sound heard so often in this place that nobody would take notice.

"Now let me in. Just slide over onto the other seat."

Ross did what he was told. The man pulled the gun out of the window and opened the door calmly. Ross thought maybe he should bolt, jump out the passenger side during the brief time the door was between them, but he had no compulsion to flee. The man seated himself behind the wheel as if he belonged there. He swung the gun toward Ross and looked him squarely in the eye. Ross returned the gaze with the kind of intensity only a man without fear could muster.

The man looked back into the sleeper berth, making sure no other driver was back there. Silently, he slid out from under the wheel and seated himself on Ross's bunk. Then he looked into Ross's eyes again.

The man spoke with an exact and deliberate manner, as if his words were cut out with a razor. The tone was calculated to intimidate Ross. "You don't scare easy. I like that. But let's you and me get this straight right now. I will not hesitate to kill you. I've got no more to lose."

Ross dropped his eyes then. Not in fear, but because he sensed that showing submission to this guy was the better course, at least for now. Ross needed time to think about what he wanted to do. This was an event, and it held a potential, almost a promise of something good, though Ross didn't know quite what. A sense of awe fell on Ross, an almost pleasant mood of anticipation.

"Pull this thing around to the back row. You and I have to get to know each other."

CHAPTER TWENTY-EIGHT

Dorothy Smith had been a fuel cashier at the National Truck Stop for seven years. It was the first job she had really enjoyed since entering the work force after her children were all grown. The work was demanding and often frustrating, and the pay was nothing to brag about, but she got to mix with people, and that's what she liked.

Southerners, cowboys, Yankees, city people, farm people, rednecks, hippies, bikers, retired military, burned-out professionals seeking a different kind of stress—not to mention a wide variety of losers and malcontents—came and went in the trucking industry. Sooner or later, they came by her counter. There was rarely a dull moment.

Truck drivers came from all over North America, and she could make them all smile. Well, most of them. She enjoyed the good-natured teasing and banter that truckers seemed obliged to indulge in. Most of the drivers were far from home and craved the kind of homespun warmth she and her co-workers could provide.

The job allowed her to get to know a few regular drivers, too. People who ran the same route on a routine basis would gravitate to her truck stop in hopes of exchanging abuse with her.

One driver she had gotten familiar—but never really comfortable—with was this young, good-looking H.A.M. driver named Ross. He had a serious nature about him and wouldn't tease as easily as most. Still, she could tell he was a kind, well-mannered fellow. She saw him once or twice a week since all of the Murphy drivers bought fuel at her stop. Lately he seemed sullen and preoccupied, even depressed.

Today he had seemed even more morose. Today he'd bought a sandwich, something she hadn't seen him do before, but hey, maybe he was hungry. It was the slow part of the afternoon, and with her eyes she followed him to his rig, which was still parked at the fuel pump. She watched him get into the cab, and for a long time the truck didn't move. She supposed he was eating the sandwich. She wondered about his mood. She had a son in Arizona about his age. Ross reminded her of him.

There were other people around the truck stop who Dorothy was not particularly fond of. One of them was a beady-eyed loser who drove for a toilet service company. Dorothy didn't trust him. In fact, she thought he was some kind of thief. It was nothing she had any evidence of, just a feeling she got. There was nothing about the nature of his job that required him to patronize her truck stop. He didn't even buy fuel. He gave Dorothy the creeps. His name was Eugene; that's about all she knew. She kept her eyes on him when she could.

She was just finished wrapping up a transaction with another driver when she looked out and saw Eugene running out to Ross's truck. He was waving at the truck, as if trying to get Ross to wait for him. Ross stopped, and Eugene hung on the side of his truck for a minute. Something about it smelled bad to Dorothy. She took her binoculars out from under the counter and focused them on Ross's truck.

Eugene got into the cab, into the driver's seat. Then the door closed. But just before it did, Dorothy saw something shiny in Eugene's right hand. Was it a gun?

☙

Following the man's orders, Ross got back into the driver's seat and again released the brakes. He backed into the same spot he had been parked in before he fueled. He shut off the engine and turned out the lights. It seemed deathly quiet now. Neither man spoke for a few moments. They were sizing each other up.

Eugene had never held anyone at gunpoint before. He'd thought the driver would show fear, maybe tremble or stutter or something—but no, it was nothing like that.

Ross was still wondering what to make of it all. He realized his situation was incredibly ironic, almost poetically ironic. There he was, ready to end his life by driving this load of auto parts into a concrete bridge pier, and now there was this gunman, this outlaw, threatening to kill him unless Ross gave him his way.

"So what's it gonna be, Sport?" He emphasized the word "Sport," as if he were trying to ridicule Ross with the moniker somehow. The man's voice was cocky now, almost condescending. Ross supposed that by changing his attitude to one of submission he had given this guy a feeling of superiority and power over him. That was good, Ross thought. He wasn't sure just why it was good.

"Are you gonna cooperate with me or am I gonna blow a hole in your skull big enough to drive this truck through?"

"Well, I'm going to cooperate. Just what do you want me to do?" Ross said

"All you have to do is drive. Hey, that's what you were fixin' to do anyway, right?"

"That's what I do," Ross said.

"So what are you hauling anyway?" asked Eugene.

"Auto parts. We pick up, sort, consolidate and deliver auto parts, among other things. You need a fuel pump for a 1985 Buick maybe?"

"You trying to be funny? It isn't going to help," Eugene said.

"Sorry."

"What's your name, Sport?"

"Ross. Ross Martin."

"Okay, Ross Martin. I like 'Sport' better." Eugene looked around the interior of the truck. He saw the photos of Shelley and Randall. "Is that your family?"

Ross sighed deeply. "Yes."

"Well, don't worry, Sport. You treat me right, and you'll be back to see them again in a couple days. Okay?"

"Okay," Ross said.

"So let's get started. Take me west. Go west, young man, go west." Eugene was beginning to like giving orders to the trucker. It gave him a stronger feeling of superiority than he'd gotten from ripping off those comfortable homes in the country. He was back in control again. He wasn't scared anymore. His fear had all melted away when he had made up his mind to hijack this truck. His grip was steady and sure on the revolver.

Ross started the truck and eased out of the parking space. He drove to the westbound on-ramp like he'd been instructed and accelerated up the ramp, going through the gears. It dawned on him as he felt the speed growing, the rig responding to the throbbing, growling horsepower under his feet, that he was no longer bound for the bridge pier at the 28 mile-marker. Something had happened to change his course. He was going away from the bridge now. The change had happened at the last possible moment.

Ross remembered the thoughts—rather the doubts—he'd experienced earlier about the existence and goodness of God. How bizarre did a thing have to be before it pointed toward some higher power?

CHAPTER TWENTY-NINE

Dorothy Smith didn't know what to think now. She wasn't sure she had really seen a gun, and yet she didn't want to ignore the possibility. She knew guns; her husband and sons hunted one thing or another all year round. She had fired many of them. Good handguns were often shiny like that, either nickel-plated or stainless steel.

She had watched as Ross's rig had gone to the parking lot instead of the highway. H.A. Murphy drivers never spent any time sleeping in this lot. They were too close to home for that. But Ross had parked, and there was no sign of activity from the truck for a few minutes.

She was tempted to put on her coat and walk out to the truck. But she would feel stupid doing that, especially if she was mistaken. Maybe Ross and Eugene were old friends and had decided to catch up on things. She couldn't believe that. Ross and Eugene might know each other, but she was sure they were not friends. But why were they sitting out there in the lot like that? What could be going on?

Dorothy didn't wonder for long. The Murphy rig left the parking space now and headed toward the highway. She had been paying close attention, and Eugene never got out. She was torn now. It wasn't any of her business, was it? Yet in the instant she had beheld a weapon in Eugene's hands, things just seemed to fit together for some reason.

She was sure now that it was a gun. She reached for the phone. She would tell the police exactly what she saw, exactly what she feared. They might think her a trouble-making old fool, but she didn't care. If her fears and suspicion weren't enough for them to stop the truck, so be it. She wasn't going to let a decent young guy like Ross be victimized—maybe robbed or shot—as long as she could speak up

☙

Ross began to feel something he'd never felt before. It wasn't fear exactly. It was missing some element he could not define. He reflected back on his life. He was still very young, wasn't he? He had never been in any perilous situation before, unless you counted those heart-stopping moments when his truck nearly jackknifed on ice.

Ross knew that at his age many young men had been to war. Was this what it felt like to have your life threatened? His life had been threatened, and he was not scared, not as he would have imagined. He felt a surprised sadness as he realized that he had indeed been ready to take his own life; he would have driven his truck straight into the bridge pier.

Earlier in the day he had acknowledged in his mind the possibility that he would chicken out or rethink his decision just before the time to steer into the pier came upon him. Now, since it wasn't going to happen, he could see clearly that he had been capable of it. He also knew that he wasn't capable of it anymore. Something had happened to change his mind.

Yet, even though Ross now wanted to go on living, he wasn't sure he valued his life the way he had before. He supposed that being under this threat was clouding his thinking process and that he needed time to sort this all out the way he normally did with any unexpected turn of events. But he didn't have time to do that. He had to deal with the menace at hand.

Ross decided to try engaging the man in conversation. He might be able to get some clue about what was going on.

"Where are we going anyway?"

"I told you west."

"But where are we going. West is a big place."

"Don't worry, Sport, I won't let you take any wrong turns."

"What's your name, anyway?" Ross used a familiar tone now, deliberately, to measure the man's response. Before, he had opted for submission, now he wanted to feel the guy out some more.

"Just call me 'sir.' And do it with respect."

Ross felt the muzzle of the gun then. The thug brought it up and rested it lightly under his ear, against the hinge of his jaw. The steel was cold and hard. Ross's flesh was soft and yielding, and the contrast sent a wave of terror through him. He became submissive again.

After a while the gun was removed, and Ross kept his eyes dutifully on the road ahead. His mind went back to work. He began to wish he had a weapon of some kind. He knew some drivers carried guns, even though it was illegal in some places to have a gun on board a truck. Not that it would do him much good now that the man had control of everything. Even if he had one, he would be at a disadvantage while driving. He could only turn so far in his seat without losing control. He would have to wait till they stopped to use it. He decided not to waste time dreaming about what he didn't have. Better to assess what he did have and figure out what he could do, if anything.

Ross had one of those folding hunting knives. But it was in his toolbox, which was in the side compartment. It may as well be on Mars for all the good it would do him. He had a "tire billy," which was nothing more than a length of steel pipe with a handgrip on one end. Truckers used them to thump tires when they were mounted on dual wheels. It was an easy way to be sure they were full of air. Rapping a tire would produce a thump if it had air pressure, a disappointing thud if it were flat. It was a necessary precaution because when two tires were mounted together, one going flat would not deflate since the other would hold it up. Ross kept the tire billy on the floor, tucked into a space between his fire extinguisher and the base of his seat. He thought he could reach it by leaning, crouching low to one side. He decided to make sure of its position if he got the chance. It was no match for the revolver, but it was better than nothing.

Ross remembered with chagrin something he had read in a novel, probably by Louis L'amour. It went something like, "If a man with a gun wants you to go somewhere, you are safer if you don't go anywhere at all." The sense of the idea was clear as crystal to Ross. If he had only stayed there at the truck stop, with its lights and many people, this gunman would probably never take the chance of shooting him. He could have simply jumped out, or blown his air horn for attention. The man would not gain a thing by shooting him in that situation.

Ross also faced the fact that he would probably be murdered at the end of this trip. Wherever this guy was taking him, whatever he wanted, Ross would be a liability to him afterward.

Ross remembered the guy saying that he had "no more to lose." What did he mean by that? What if this guy wasn't after his cargo? All the stories about hijacking Ross had heard about involved someone actually taking the truck from the driver. Someone else drove it to wherever it went. Besides that, the man had asked what Ross was hauling, as if he didn't know or care. Hijackers targeted specific products. Ross decided to go fishing again.

"Are we taking the turnpike?" asked Ross.

"I told you, I won't let you take any wrong turns."

"I need to know if we're taking the Ohio turnpike," Ross said.

"Why."

"Because if we are, I have to get the card out of my permit book."

The Ohio Turnpike Commission issued charge cards to its regular customers, and Ross carried it in the pocket of the little binder where he kept the truck's registration and insurance certificates along with all the other necessary papers he had to have. The book was in the sleeper, at the head of the bunk. Ross knew that one of them would have to reach for it. If he could get the tire billy in hand, he might get a chance to swing it, if "Sir" was dumb enough to turn his back to get the book and if he could do so without losing control of the rig.

"Do you need it when we get on the turnpike?" asked the hijacker.

"No, not until we get off."

"That's what I figured. Let me take care of those details, all right?" The gunman's voice sounded annoyed now.

"So we are taking the turnpike?" asked Ross.

"Sure."

"What are you going to do with my load?" ventured Ross.

"What makes you think I have any plans for your load?"

"Why else would you do this?" asked Ross.

There was no answer, but Ross could tell his questions were frustrating the man. He decided to keep them up.

"Are we going far?" asked Ross.

"Look, Sport, I saw you put fuel in this thing. I saw you eat that sandwich. I figure you're good for 1,200 miles before you have to stop again. By the time we get that far, we will be where I want to go," Eugene said.

"I can't drive that far. I can't stay awake that long."

"Sure you can. I hear you guys braggin' all the time about how many miles you can cover on a run. That's just a day's work for you."

"You've been listening to Billy Big Rig too much," Ross said. Billy Big Rig was a sort of mythical self-proclaimed hero invented by truckers, a character of folklore that sprang up in CB radio conversation. He had a big, fast, shiny truck, and he could run forever on coffee and his ego. He spent most of his time bragging about his exploits on the big road—how he had outrun the police, made a fool of the scale master or amazed dispatchers with his incredible ability to move freight long distances overnight.

Every so often Ross would meet a driver who fit the image, one who not only told tall tales but actually seemed to think others believed them. Billy Big Rig described the driver who had become a legend in his own mind, Walter Mitty with an 18-wheeler. There were plenty of them in the trade.

"Give me a break. You know you guys don't pay any attention to your log book rules," Eugene said.

"Oh, I'll give you that much. Maybe I could even stay awake for that long. But after so long my eyes get buggy, and I don't see things I'm looking at. There ain't no way I'll keep it between the ditches for 1,200 miles," Ross said.

"No matter. Like I said, I'll tell you what to do," Eugene said.

Ross felt bolder now that he was engaging the man in conversation, albeit worthless. "What did you do anyway?" Ross said.

"Right, like I'm gonna tell you all about it."

"Why not, you're gonna kill me anyway," Ross said.

"No, Sport, you got me all wrong. I just need you for transportation."

"But I can describe you to the cops. What do you think is going to happen if you turn me loose?" Ross said.

The hijacker did not answer, but Ross could see he was taking some time to think it over, as if he hadn't thought that far ahead yet. He was beginning to show signs of instability, thought Ross. One minute he seemed annoyed with questions and the next he seemed to be enjoying the talk. Ross wondered if this fellow was sane. The silence continued from the other seat.

"So what are you gonna do about me, if you don't kill me?" Ross said.

"Shut up!" the hijacker's anger was palpable.

Ross was taken aback a little. But he was beginning to think he could push his passenger, maybe goad him into doing something stupid. He renewed his courage.

"Shut up nothing. I'm the one that's going to be shot, and you want me to shut up," Ross said with a calm voice. He knew that keeping his self-control would irritate the man further. "You said you had nothing to lose. Truth is, I'm the one with nothing to lose."

The man was trembling now—not much, but enough that Ross could see he was rattled. Ross was sure now that he could provoke his captor whenever he wanted. He didn't think it would serve any purpose to do it yet, though. He needed time to figure out what to do next. The question was how much time did he have?

CHAPTER THIRTY

Dorothy Smith dialed 9-1-1 and waited for the operator. Another trucker walked in then with a sense of urgency on his face. He strode up to her as if he couldn't wait for her to finish the call.

"Ma'am," he said.

"Just a minute, sir, I'm in the middle of something important," Dorothy said.

The driver got a disgusted look on his face and began looking around.

Finally the voice came on the line, "Mercer County Emergency operator."

"Yes, I'd like to report a kidnapping," Dorothy said.

"Did you say kidnapping?" the operator said.

"Yes, well I work at the National Truck Stop, here at exit two. A little while ago, this guy stopped one of the truckers out here by the fuel pumps. He had a gun. Pretty soon, they left. I don't know which way they went, but I'm sure there was a gun."

"So there's no injury or fire to report?" the calm voice at the other end of the line said.

"No," Dorothy said.

"Okay," the voice responded, with obvious skepticism about the reality of a gunman. "I'll connect you to the police."

When the policewoman answered, Dorothy repeated what she had told the operator.

"Give me your name, please," said the operator.

"Dorothy Smith. I work at the fuel desk. Can you have them hurry?"

The driver who had wanted Dorothy's attention overheard

what she was saying on the phone. He came back toward her, nodding his head. "I saw the gun, too!"

Dorothy made eye contact with the driver. "You saw it, too?"

"If you mean that Murphy truck that just rolled out, yes. I was coming in, and we passed each other. The streetlights were shining just right for me to see into the cab. The passenger had a pistol pointed at the driver. Looked like a big'un—Smith & Wesson model 29, I'd say, probably a .44 magnum." The man obviously knew firearms.

"I heard that," the policewoman on the other end said.

"They went west. I could see," the driver said. "I watched them get on, going westbound."

When Dorothy hung up the phone, she went directly to her stack of fuel receipts. She had copies of every sale on her shift, and it didn't take long for her to find Ross's. She made a photocopy of it and highlighted all the pertinent information about Ross's truck, mainly the license plate number. When the trooper showed up, he wouldn't have to waste time writing it all down.

Then she went to her files and got the phone number for H.A.Murphy Industrial Service Company. She dialed the number. John Murphy himself answered the phone.

"John Murphy here. May I help you?"

"Yes, Mr. Murphy. My name is Dorothy Smith. I'm the head fuel cashier out here at National. I'm afraid it looks like one of your drivers has run into some trouble."

"Okay. Which driver and what kind of trouble?" Murphy said.

"It's Ross Martin." Dorothy could read Ross's signature clearly on the receipt. She had never bothered to get to know his last name before now. "I'm afraid he's been hijacked or something. There is another driver and myself; we're both convinced we saw him being held at gunpoint. The guy with the gun was in his truck when they left here."

"What time was that?" asked Murphy.

"Not more than five or 10 minutes ago. Here, you talk to

this other truck driver. He saw even better than I did." She thrust the phone into the driver's face. He had been following her conversation and took over without any preliminaries.

"There was a man riding in the passenger seat of one of your trucks. He had a handgun pointed at your driver. I saw it plain as day. They went to the interstate and jumped on westbound. Like she said, maybe 10 minutes ago. That's everything I know." He handed the phone back to Dorothy without waiting for any questions.

"Did you get that?" Dorothy asked Murphy.

"Yeah, I got it. And you must be right about the trouble. He was supposed to be going to Harrisburg. West is the wrong way."

"I called 9-1-1. They said they were sending a trooper down here right away," Dorothy said.

"Thank you, ma'am. I'll be coming down there myself. Wait, hell's-fire, I might be able to catch them myself if I get out there quick enough. They would be coming this way." John Murphy realized he couldn't waste anymore time. He dropped the desk phone and picked up his cellular. He leaped out of his chair and headed for the door. He didn't bother to tell anyone what was going on; he couldn't lose a second. Ross Martin's rig could be going by the Heritage exit at that moment. He climbed into his Explorer and gunned it out of the lot. In a few minutes he was approaching the on ramps. He decided to position himself on the overpass and wait for the truck to come by. If more than five minutes went by without Ross coming in sight, he could assume that Ross and his passenger had already passed that point. He didn't want to go west right away because he might get ahead of them that way. Waiting meant they were getting farther ahead, but it couldn't be helped. He had no way of knowing whether or not they had gotten this far yet. If it appeared they had already gone past, he could maybe catch up, if they stayed on the interstate anyway.

He parked the Explorer tight against the curb of the overpass and turned on his flashers, then jumped out and ran to the edge to search the oncoming traffic for one of his trucks. It wouldn't be easy to pick them out until they got close because of the deep blue color. Thankfully this interchange had some lighting, enough for him to tell his trucks from others.

CHAPTER THIRTY-ONE

Ross and his hijacker kept going west, rolling along at the speed limit with Ross keeping silent now. He'd decided to bide his time, to see if they were really going to use the Ohio Turnpike. They would be there in another half hour, and there were usually more state troopers patrolling there than anywhere else. If he waited until they were near Cleveland, there should be even more available, since areas of heavy population generally had more cops than rural areas. Chances of getting ample force directed against them would be better. That would also give him more time to think.

They crossed the state line, and Ross kept his speed at the Pennsylvania limit, 65. The Ohio limit was 55 for big trucks. "Sir" was aware of the difference.

"Okay, Sport, you can slow it down now. We're not going to give the Buckeye Bears an excuse to pull us over. You'd just love that now, wouldn't you?"

Ross did not respond. He had been thinking that getting pulled over might be his best chance for survival. There was no way of knowing what "Sir" might do if the cops did want them to pull over. Would Ross become a hostage? Would this guy surrender? Would he take a shot at the cops? Troopers always approached with their guns holstered when they pulled someone over. Unless they had reason to believe they needed to be armed and ready, any cop would be an easy target if the hijacker were a killer. Ross had to assume he was. That meant Ross couldn't just let himself be pulled over. He would have to do something to prepare the cops for gunplay, but what?

They came to the state scales only a few miles into Ohio.

This chicken coop was open, true to its habits. Ross's truck rolled slowly across the scales like all the others. He wished he could somehow get the attention of the man inside. Not that he could have done anything to help Ross. The scale-master was not a policeman and was not armed. But he had a line to the troopers and could have one on-site quickly.

Just like "Sir" said, when they got to the entrance of the Ohio Turnpike, he instructed Ross to get on it. Ross decided that when they got near Cleveland, he would simply put his foot on the floor and keep it there. It wouldn't be long until a Trooper was behind the truck with his "disco lights" flashing. If the man were willing to pull the trigger, then he would have to gain control of the truck with Ross's dead weight in the driver's seat. Maybe he could accomplish that, but then what would the man do? Killing Ross would not eliminate the trooper.

♪

John Murphy had waited long enough. There could be little doubt that Ross's truck had already passed the Heritage exit. He got back in the Explorer and took a cloverleaf route off and on the ramps until he was headed west. He gunned the SUV until he was doing 80 mph, passing everything on the road. He would be in Ohio in a few minutes. But he knew he could only find the truck if it had stayed on I-80 West. Once it reached the Ohio line, the possibilities opened up. Many trucks got off the Interstate and ran the bypass route around the dreaded "Buckeye coops." Would the hijacker want to avoid exposing himself to law enforcement by taking that route?

If they got on the other side of the scales, he might choose to follow Route 11, either north or south—that was a freeway, too. Shortly beyond that, there was a choice of I-76 toward Akron or I-80, the Ohio Turnpike. Not only that, but there were smaller roads and streets at exits every few miles. John could only pick a route and hope to catch up. He knew the police would never allow him to take part in the chase, if they knew what he was up to, and he figured he had the obligation to at least try. He didn't even know if the police had initiated a search, or if they had even arrived at the National Truck Stop. If he could spot the rig, he could positively identify its location for the cops—if he didn't get stopped first.

He switched on his CB radio to listen for any reports the truckers might be giving of speed traps. He keyed the mike and called, "Break one-nine. Any Hamster truck out there tonight? How about it, any Hamster trucks copy this? Ross Martin, you read me?"

CHAPTER THIRTY-TWO

Kent Rogers was an Ohio State Trooper with a regular beat on the Turnpike. It was routine Highway Patrol work—maintain visibility, enforce the speed limit and keep the paperwork up. He was lucky; his beat had a doughnut shop in the service plaza. Not that he ate doughnuts. He liked them well enough, but he just couldn't stand the smiles people gave him since the stereotype about cops and doughnuts became popular. But doughnut shop coffee was always fresh and rich. He'd just stopped and grabbed a cup, and was planning to drink it while he finished his paperwork.

Kent pulled his cruiser into the median crossover and turned off his headlights but left the parking lights on. His cruiser became a presence as the dark winter night settled onto the highway, reassuring to the law-abiding, annoying to those who pushed the speed limit. Truckers with their CB radios would be informing other trucks of his location, and most of the traffic would come by his position at the speed limit.

He was just getting set to enjoy the coffee—it was always too hot to start with anyway—when the post supervisor advised all units to be on the lookout for an H.A. Murphy truck. There was a report of one being possibly hijacked. He was given a license and unit number and told to follow the truck and wait for backup if he should spot it. This was something out of the ordinary, one of those things that might take him far from his usual patrol range. It was one of those times when he was glad he took the time to keep himself physically fit, strong and ready to do battle if need be. Most nights he wrote tickets, helped broken-down motorists and arrested the occasional drunk. A guy could get soft if he let himself.

Kent was familiar with H.A. Murphy trucks. They had a consistent paint scheme, and the lettering was done with fluorescent paint, easy to read in dim light. He could spot the truck easily from where he sat. If one came by, he would be able to follow it at a distance, creeping slowly up behind to read the license number without the driver ever knowing he was there. That is, if the driver was not listening to the CB. He began mentally rehearsing the way he would handle it if he had to pull the truck over. He double-checked his pistol. You didn't hijack an 18-wheeler with a slingshot.

※

Ross knew he should act quickly now that he had decided to initiate some action to attract police attention. Soon he would be nearing the Cleveland area. The hijacker might have him exit there. The implication was that they were going a lot farther, but Ross couldn't trust this fellow to tell him anything straight. Ross believed that the longer he went along with "Sir's" demands, the worse off he would be.

Ross looked up ahead and spotted the familiar sight of an Ohio Highway Patrol car sitting in the median. It was routine for the troopers to park there and watch traffic, use their radar guns and so on, but there was no guarantee there would be another one soon. Ross decided to seize the opportunity. His courage seemed somewhat fragile, and he wasn't sure it would stick with him.

He realized that this cop sitting in the median was just what he needed. The nose of the cruiser was projecting out just enough that Ross could actually kiss it with his truck if he chose to. He made a quick check of his mirrors and determined that no other vehicles would be jeopardized with what he had in mind. He breathed a quiet prayer for Shelley and Randall, and then went into action.

Ross's truck was in the right lane, and there were two clear lanes between him and the trooper. Suddenly, he steered gently left as if he were changing lanes. But when he should have corrected to stay in the center lane, he did not. His truck was now pointed straight at the cruiser. He pulled up on the dimmer switch again and again, flashing the high beams directly in the trooper's face.

❧

Kent Rogers saw the Murphy truck coming on. He reached for the microphone, getting ready to report the sighting over the radio, to let the post know he would be following it for identification purposes, when suddenly it bore down on him. The sight of headlights coming straight toward him was so strange that he hesitated momentarily, not realizing what it meant.

He reacted then, grabbing the gear selector and pulling the cruiser into reverse. He was frantically hoping to get the car behind the concrete barriers. It looked as if he were going to be rammed. Even as he felt the transmission engage, Kent knew he was too late. But at the last instant before the two vehicles made contact, the nose of the truck swung away, back toward the center of the highway. The gap between the fender of the truck and the bumper of Kent's Crown Victoria Police Interceptor was scant inches.

The sense of being swallowed by a strong tide swept over Kent now as the massive sidewalls of the trailer bulldozed thousands of cubic feet of dense winter air over his cruiser and sent a rush of adrenalin into his body. The car bucked in the wash like a canoe wallowing in the wake of a speedboat.

Kent knew the idea of following undetected was history now. His foot pushed smoothly down on the throttle, the experienced chase car driver controlling the power to his rear wheels in an effort to gain maximum traction without spinning the tires. The soft rubber lugs bit into the pavement, and the gray-sided Ohio Highway Patrol car vaulted into the flow of traffic as if it were launched from a cannon, its siren and flashing lights telling every motorist within sight to make way.

❧

Ross trembled as he swung the rig back into the center lane of traffic. He feared that his life could end in the next second, his soul swept clean of his body in the wake of a bullet. But now he was ready for that, if it came. In the briefest span of time between initiating the rebellious maneuver and feeling the cold hard muzzle of the hijacker's gun against his scalp, Ross reached out to God and surrendered his fate into the hands of the gracious Savior, who up until now had been little better than a pleasant focal point during the emotional swell of Pastor Sawyer's preaching

⁂

Eugene Whythe was flabbergasted. He could not believe what had just happened. He felt betrayed. This truck driver had gone along with his demands, had allowed him to go this far without any resistance, only to defy his orders after he was convinced he had it made. Eugene felt the welling of sadness in his throat, the same way he felt when he was being fired from all those jobs. He was being picked on again. But this time he had some power.

Eugene stuck the muzzle of the gun against Ross's head and pushed and ground the unyielding steel as if he would burrow a hole through Ross's temple. Ross gave way to the pressure, and the rig responded to the shift of Ross's body by swinging gently back to the left side. The drift was unintentional, and Ross's conditioned reflexes corrected the course of the truck despite the pain he was enduring. As he did, the pushing of the gun eased some. It gave him an idea.

⁂

Eugene relaxed the force on Ross's head. Since the unit he used to service toilets was relatively small, he was unfamiliar with a truck this size. He did not know how much weaving sideways a truck like this would do before it upset, and he was unnerved by the sway. He'd seen rigs lying on their sides.

Eugene realized that Ross was calling his bluff. The man he had cowed by threatening to kill was actually defying his threat. It wasn't supposed to work this way. Eugene wanted to kill Ross. He knew he was capable of it, but it was too late now. If he pulled the trigger, it would probably mean a crash. Even if he did get control of the truck, what would he do then? There was no hope of escaping the law, especially not on a turnpike. The only way off was through the narrow tollgates, and the cops would probably block them.

The highway patrol car had come after them, and it was right behind now with its lights creating a wild show in the mirrors. There was no mistaking the wailing of the siren. Ross had drawn the attention he wanted.

❧

Ross brought the rig slowly over to the right shoulder, then moved it back across the three lanes of traffic. He did it again and again, as if he was following a winding road rather than a relatively straight piece of highway. He wanted to have control of the situation. By weaving he kept all other traffic behind him. If he did the same thing over and over the trooper would know there was a purpose to it. Ross would keep this up until it was to his advantage to stop.

The trooper would not be taking anything for granted when Ross finally stopped the truck. And, unless Ross missed his guess, there would soon be more troopers, probably a lot more. Ross's rig had become a rogue vehicle and a threat to everyone on the turnpike. The lawmen would never give up until they had him in custody—that meant they would get the gunman, too.

❧

After getting behind the H.A. Murphy rig, Kent Rogers related to the post what he had just experienced. He thought perhaps a madman had taken over the rig. He couldn't see why the driver would deliberately charge his car that way—unless the driver had a death wish. And now the truck was weaving from one side of the road to the other as if the driver wanted everyone to stay back and let him have the road to himself.

❧

Eugene realized what Ross intended to do. He decided he would be better off if he could just get away from him somehow. He decided to try conceding. It wouldn't be long before there would be more police cars.

"Okay, Ross, I guess I underestimated you. You've got nerve. Tell you what, you pull this thing over to the side, and I'll just get out and be on my way. No hard feelings."

"What happened to 'Sport'," Ross said. "And why would I do that?"

"Why not?" Eugene said.

"Because you think you can run away, maybe escape into the darkness while the cop is trying to get control of me. It won't work. You're going to meet some troopers tonight, one way or another," Ross said.

Eugene became frantic then. He stood up as far as the low ceiling of the truck's cab would allow and grabbed Ross in a headlock. "You pull this truck over now, you bastard!"

Ross could feel the vertebrae in his neck threatening to snap as Eugene squeezed his forearm together like a nutcracker under Ross's chin. Ross put some of his weight on his feet now and stretched up to ease the strain his captor was putting on his neck. He had to maintain control until more cops came on the scene.

"Okay, okay, you win. Let me go." He didn't mean what he was saying, but he had to do something to keep the man from twisting his neck off. "Just relax, will you? You don't want to get out here. Just another few miles, past this next exit, it gets into farm country. You can get into one of those big fields, and it will take the cops forever to figure out just where you are. The fields are full of cornstalks, and you can get away easy. They can't get their cars off the turnpike, you know. By the time they go to the next exit and find their way back to this point, you can be miles away."

Eugene settled down then as if he were thinking about what Ross had proposed. Ross stretched his neck and hoped there wasn't any permanent damage. It was sore. He looked in the mirror and saw a whole kaleidoscope of flashing lights.

He hadn't been watching, and now there was more than one car. Ross had no idea what was beyond the next exit. He'd been there enough times to know, but he couldn't take time to think about it now. He was sure there were no cornstalks anyway, not this time of year. But evidently he had given "Sir" something to think about.

Another highway patrol car went over a bridge just ahead of them with disco lights flashing, probably on his way to the nearest turnpike access road. Ross guessed he had enough police cars now. He was still weaving from side to side, but not as hard as before. Nearly getting his neck pulled off was a close call. This guy was strong, or maybe he was just scared. Ross slowed the rig down a little now, hoping he could do it in a way the hijacker wouldn't notice.

❧

Kent and the other troopers weren't about to try anything with their patrol cars. They would be no match for an 18-wheeler; they would only get knocked completely out of control. There were other cars moving to get in front of the truck by way of side roads, and only seven miles ahead of their present position was the Highway Patrol station. There were three more cars waiting there. The plan was to put those three in front of the rogue truck and try to ease it to a stop.

The entrance ramps to the westbound side of the turnpike had been closed as far west as Route 57. The relatively slow speed of the truck kept it from making problems with existing westbound traffic; it had all outpaced the truck right from the start. The following traffic was keeping well back of the police cars. No one had made the decision to make the remaining traffic exit, but that would probably be done soon. If this outlandish parade didn't come to an end soon, they would block the highway with snowplows. That would end it for sure.

❧

"Why don't you turn on the CB and see if they are trying to talk to us?" Ross said.

"No. No CB," Eugene said. He didn't want them to hear his voice or give Ross a chance to say anything to them.

CHAPTER THIRTY-THREE

John Murphy got onto the Turnpike just before they closed it. He was rolling west monitoring the CB when he heard the eastbound truckers talking.

"Those Buckeye bears are chasing a real desperado out there by the 200 mile-marker. One of those HAM trucks tried to ram a trooper sitting in the middle. Now he's just running along with a whole posse on his tail."

That had to be Ross. John figured all the cops were busy following his truck now, so he got in the left lane and pushed his Explorer up to 85. He would catch them before long—at best the rig could go 70, and he doubted Ross was doing that. Evidently Ross had done something to get the troopers after him even though he had a gunman beside him. He and Leeroy had been afraid Ross was on the verge of suicide. Maybe that was where his courage was coming from. Someone who was suicidal wouldn't fear death, would he? He was skeptical about the "ramming," though. Truckers often got things distorted on the CB.

He picked up his cell phone and punched the speed dial to the number of his office. Kim answered on the second ring.

"H.A. Murphy. This is Kim. How can I help you?"

"It's me, Kim. I left in a hurry, I know. Ross Martin was hijacked from the National Truck Stop just about an hour ago. He's running west on the Ohio Pike with some cops on his tail. That is, according to the CB anyway. I'm trying to catch up with them."

Kim's mind started a list of questions, the first of which

spilled out excitedly. "So the cops know about it—why don't they just pull him over?"

"I think they've been trying to, Kim. For some reason he hasn't stopped yet."

"How do we know he was hijacked anyway?" Kim said.

"Some people at the truck stop saw a guy with a gun get into his truck, and he's not going toward Harrisburg. What else could it be?" John said.

"So, what can I do?" Kim said.

"To start with, maybe we should call Mrs. Martin and tell her what's going on. Leeroy called earlier and said the Martins were having some kind of trouble. I think we should let her know what's going on. Unless you think it would be better not to tell her."

"What do you mean by trouble—a fight?" Kim asked.

"I guess so. It's probably something to do with what happened to their baby."

"I was wondering why he came back in and took the load to Harrisburg," said Kim, as if some profound mystery had just been explained. "If he had a fight with his wife, that explains it, I guess. If I were Shelley, I'd want to know about this. If I don't tell her, she'll be mad." Kim paused. "So Ross could be a hostage, sort of?"

"Yes, but don't use any words like that when you tell her," John said.

"No, no, I won't," Kim said.

"After that, you'd better let Harrisburg know what happened to their parts load. No way it will be there in the morning," John said.

"Anything else?"

"Not right now. I'll get back to you when I know more."

Kim shook her head. Even when one of the drivers was in grave danger, John Murphy still had his mind on the business.

❧

Shelley was sitting by the phone and answered it before

the first ring ended. "Shelley, this is Kim, down at the Murphy office."

"Kim, I'm glad you called. Do you know where Ross is?" Shelley said. "I need to talk to him."

"Shelley, you'd better brace yourself. Something really scary is happening," Kim said.

A sense of dread swept over Shelley. She hated herself even more for being so cruel to Ross. Part of her wanted to hang up the phone and cry, but the other part was too eager to make contact with Ross. She was afraid something dreadful had happened, and she knew she was the cause of it. But Kim had said something bad "is happening"—not "has happened."

"Okay...so what is it?" Shelley said.

"I don't have many details, and what I do have is hearsay. So don't jump to conclusions, okay?" Kim said.

"Just tell me what you know," Shelley said.

"Mr. Murphy just called here and said that Ross's truck was going the wrong way. That is, he was supposed to be headed for Harrisburg, but actually he's going west. They think someone might have hijacked him," Kim said.

"Oh, Kim, I said some terrible things to Ross earlier today. I'm afraid I might have pushed him into doing something rash." Shelley broke into sobs then, wishing even more that she could call back her selfish words.

"Well, things should be okay soon enough, Shelley." Kim was trying to sound more certain than she felt. "I understand the police are following them."

"Is that all you know?" Shelley said.

"For now it is. I'm sorry, Shelley," Kim said.

"Who was the last person to see him?" asked Shelley.

"I don't know for sure. All I know is what Mr. Murphy said. Some guy with a gun supposedly got in the truck at the National when he was buying fuel," Kim said.

"That's really all you know?"

"It really is, Shelley. I hesitated to call you. I know there's nothing you or I can do to help, but I thought you would want to know," Kim said.

"I can pray! I can pray, Kim!" Shelley said with determination.

Kim promised to call the minute she had more news.

Shelley had been praying almost constantly since Leeroy called her earlier. She had gone through the motions of caring for Randall but always with part of her soul reaching toward heaven, pleading for Ross to call her and give her the chance to set things right. Now the overwhelming sense that God had stepped in and was allowing something untoward to happen came over her. Now she had to keep her faith and trust God to do the right thing, whatever that was.

She remembered her earlier thoughts about how nothing had ever taken place in her life to test her faith until the death of her baby. Now that the possibility of losing her husband was present, she was determined not to fail this test of faith.

As she knelt on the floor to pray, she was surprised that her mind would not cooperate with her heart. As if another person's will directed her mind, she began to think. She tried to stop it and concentrate on prayer, asking God to keep Ross safe, but the thoughts marched into her consciousness like determined soldiers. She surrendered to them then, hoping that if she let her mind spend its reason, she would find some peace.

She knew faith was supposed to be more than just holding fast to convictions when things were going wrong—it should have power. Not always power to change circumstances but power to change her. And she'd been taught that the power of faith would outweigh even the worst that could happen to her. Not because it would solve her problems, but because it would enable her to recognize the presence of God in all that took place. And now for the first time in her life she truly knew what it all meant.

She could see now that everything she had been told about God was inadequate. It wasn't because the teachers were wrong, but because words lacked the power to express what it really meant to belong to almighty God. She could see that heartache and suffering were as important in the scope of God's purpose as happiness and joy. It was something one had to find for themselves, because it could not be captured on the pages of a book and could only be alluded to in song or poem. That was why Pastor Sawyer and other ministers she had heard always seemed like they were reaching for something they could never quite grasp, pointing to something only they could see.

Now she was ready. She knelt forward on the floor and gave herself up to a complete trust in God. Something drained from her or washed into her; she didn't know which, and she didn't care. She felt complete now.

Shelley knew the thoughts that had forced their way into her mind had come from God. All her life she had heard stories from other believers about such experiences. Not every Christian had such an experience, and they were varied in how they happened, but the ones who did were changed forever because of it. She no longer believed solely by faith—she knew. She knew with a quiet, peaceful, absolute certainty that what she had just felt was not of her own emotions or mind.

CHAPTER THIRTY-FOUR

Dorothy Smith gave the police all the information she had to give. There was little doubt they would know the identity of Ross's hijacker soon enough. The owners of the portable toilet company could be contacted with a description. But it was probably moot now, the trooper said. The Ohio Highway Patrol had already located the truck and may have stopped it by now. Thanks to the sharp eyes of Dorothy and the other trucker, this was one crime that would be solved in short order. When the trooper left, she picked up the phone again to make one more call.

"Newsroom," the answer came from Dorothy's son-in-law who worked the evening shift at the local newspaper.

"Hi, Benny, it's Dot. Have I got a story for you."

ॐ

Ross and his passenger were still rolling west, zigzagging gently from right to left. Ross could see up ahead the big sign that said "Service Plaza—Two miles." He knew there were a lot of people there. Usually dozens of cars and trucks stopped for food and to use the restrooms. Truckers slept there, row after row of them. He slept there from time to time.

Ross decided he should not let his hijacker get that far. If the man got out of the truck somehow, he could easily capture another hostage. Ross didn't know what the guy might be capable of, and he wasn't about to get other innocent people involved or put in harm's way. Not if he could help it.

Ross reached up and turned on the CB. He was reaching for the microphone when the glint of shiny steel flashed in his eyes, and the barrel of the gun came down on his hand. Ross heard a crack, as the smallest knuckle of his right hand was broken. He winced and cried out as the pain shot through his hand.

"I said no CB!" Eugene shouted in his ear.

Ross lost track of what he was doing for a moment, and the truck stopped weaving from side to side. He could see the gunman was uncontrollably angry now, and he could hear the man's heavy breath coming out like a winded animal and blowing directly into his ear. Again the gun came down as Eugene lashed a glancing blow across Ross's head. It was an effort to inflict enough pain on Ross to make him cooperate. The blunt steel tore through his hair and gouged into Ross's scalp with sharp, searing pain.

"No CB, ya hear me, no CB!"

Eugene knew he shouldn't knock Ross unconscious, but he drew back and brought yet another stroke across the driver's head, lost in his anger and fear, dancing on the threshold of insanity. He drew the pistol back until his fist was against his shoulder and thrust it forward, stabbing in an effort to drive the barrel of the gun through Ross's face.

Ross felt the soft rubbery skin of his cheek smash against his teeth. The impact made blood squirt over Ross's tongue in a warm gush and he could feel the teeth loose in his mouth. He reeled from the shock and nearly blacked out.

The truck was slowing now. A lower gear was required, but Ross was too distracted to concentrate on what was happening, and the RPM dropped well below the range where the engine could produce sufficient torque to propel the truck. The drive train began to shudder as the engine bucked and struggled against the force of burning and expanding diesel fuel.

Ross heard the smooth metallic series of clicks the mechanism of the handgun made as the hammer was pulled back. It was an unmistakable sound. He felt a rush of terror now, knowing that the gun could go off at any moment. He reached up to the dashboard with his broken right hand and pulled the yellow brake knob. As he did so, he let go of the wheel completely and used both hands in an effort to get a grip on the pistol.

Spewing a string of profanity, Eugene pulled the trigger of the magnum just as Ross's left hand deflected the barrel away. The explosion in the confined space filled the air with sound, and the sudden rise of pressure popped the ears of both men. Ross thought he'd been shot.

❧

Kent Rogers and his fellow troopers watched as the truck gradually stopped weaving and slowed some. They were sure something was about to happen, and they were ready. They heard a rush of air as the truck's brakes were released and eight sets of fibrous metallic lining pressed against smooth iron with the pressure of heavy steel springs. The truck's wheels slowed first, then locked, and the rig began to jackknife as it slid slowly to a stop on the pavement, nearly centered in the lanes.

The posse of cruisers encircled the truck, and the troopers jumped out and took cover behind their cars. With their weapons drawn, they trained powerful searchlights on the cab of the truck. Then they heard a shot.

❧

John Murphy caught sight of the flashing lights a few miles ahead. He made a few attempts to call Ross on the CB, but with no success. He slowed his speed and threaded his way to the front of the traffic, rudely cutting in and out between vehicles, changing lanes abruptly. The traffic was all keeping a safe distance back, largely because one of the troopers had stayed behind the main body of chase cars in order to create a sort of buffer zone. John could see that he was as close as he could get, for now.

❧

Ross could tell the truck was coming to a stop without hitting anything or turning over. He only had to keep this crazy man from putting a bullet in his head long enough for the police to close in and overpower him. Oblivious to the intense pain and continued rush of blood from the missing teeth in his mouth, Ross held on for dear life.

Ross thought of Shelley and sensed strength coming from somewhere. Now that he had been given a chance at survival, he hoped maybe her opinion of him might somehow change, too. Maybe, if he managed to pull this off, he might see himself—she might see him—as a worthwhile person again.

❧

Eugene pulled again on the revolver's trigger, hoping to force it against Ross's head, even though he knew it was hopeless now. The troopers had strong lights blazing in through the windshield. He couldn't see anything but the bright light. The gun fired the second time, and as it did he managed to twist it until it was pointed at Ross's head. He pulled the trigger again.

Ross only had a short length of the hot gun barrel in his left hand and little strength in his right hand. On top of that he could only move so far against the restraining seat belt. He felt the gun slip out of his grip and knew he could not stop Eugene from twisting the muzzle against his head. He thrust his thumb up, fear enabling him to ignore the incredible pain. He found the space between the drawn hammer of the gun and its frame. He felt the hammer fall against his thumb and concentrated all his effort on keeping that thumb in place.

A gush of cold air signaled the arrival of the cavalry, as the troopers jerked open the doors from both sides simultaneously. They could not risk firing with both men so close. Kent Rogers stepped up into the doorway and choked up on his baton so he could swing in the tight space. With his stout right arm he brought it down against the skull of the man with the gun, using all the force he could muster. Eugene Whythe fell still.

❧

John Murphy and all the following traffic came to a stop. John watched from a long way off as the cops closed in on the rig. He saw the assault on the cab but couldn't see what went on inside. He pulled his Explorer over to the side and walked slowly up to the Highway Patrol car. The trooper had his window down, and he could hear a voice on the police radio calling for an ambulance.

He approached, and the trooper caught sight of him. He stuck his hand out the window and said in a commanding voice, "Go back to your vehicle, sir."

John stepped closer so the cop could hear. "But I have an interest in this. I own that truck. That's my driver in there, Ross Martin."

The trooper nodded and waved him forward. John couldn't make out what the police were saying on the radio, but he could see a look of relief on the trooper's face. He could see the troopers at the truck gingerly stretching a limp form onto the pavement. Apparently all was secure.

The trooper got out and said, "Come along, sir. I guess your driver took a pretty good beating. He will be going out on one of the ambulances. You can see him before he goes."

The phalanx of troopers parted for John to climb up into the cab. Ross Martin was slumped over the steering wheel. A paramedic was applying a bandage to his head. There were splotches of blood on Ross's shirt, and his face made John cringe. It was swollen and discolored. He could hear Ross moaning and trying to talk. The paramedic was telling him to relax in a soothing voice.

"Ross, it's John Murphy. Are you able to speak? It's all right if you can't."

"Mr. Murphy." Ross sounded surprised, and his words were thick, like a drunken man. "Will you call my wife? Tell her what happened."

Ross was dizzy now, and as much as he knew the medic was trying to help him, he just wanted to be left alone. Simply knowing he was going to live and not be killed overwhelmed him with gratitude and relief.

Ross figured Shelley wouldn't care anyway. Still, he wanted her to know about the mishap. What had happened to him should at least evoke some pity for him from her. He now meant to go on living. He promised himself that no matter what else happened in his life, he would never consider suicide again. He owed it to both of the Donnies that he had loved, to all the people he loved, to make the most of his life.

As John Murphy scrolled through the numbers on his phone, the medics helped Ross out of the truck and onto a gurney. John dialed Ross's home. He looked down at Ross, grinning as he waited for the phone to connect. "She's been hoping you would call her."

The phone was answered before a full ring sounded. Ross was looking up at his boss now. Oblivious to the pain shrouding his consciousness, a look of hope spread across his face.

"Shelley, this is John Murphy. Yes, Shelley. Yes, Ross is right here." His voice cracked with emotion as he sensed Shelley's mood. A tearful smile lit up Murphy's face. "He's got some bruises, but I think he's gonna be all right. Of course you can talk to him."

He handed the phone to Ross.

The End

EPILOGUE

Steve Porter pulled his state-owned car into the parking lot of the National Truck Stop, right beside an unmarked police cruiser. Porter was district engineer for the Northwest Region of the Pennsylvania Department of Transportation. It was one of those paperwork-intense, behind-the-scenes jobs that were far more important than people realized. That's why he felt so gratified when Gerald Fox, a gray-headed state trooper, gave him a look of respect and admiration. On the other hand, it was obvious the trooper wanted something.

Porter was here because the trooper had called his office and requested he come and meet with him. Fox had something he wanted Porter to see firsthand. The men shook hands and went through all the usual pleasantries calculated by each to diminish the awkwardness of the situation.

Fox beckoned Porter into the front seat of the bland-looking Ford and headed the car onto I-80, eastbound from exit two.

"Did you catch the story about the trucker that was hijacked from here last week?" Fox asked.

"Didn't everybody?" replied Porter. "Hard to believe, a man having the nerve to do what that guy Martin did. That's not something you hear about every day," Porter said.

"You got that right. I guess he's gonna do some TV shows—after his face heals up some, that is."

"Hey, why not? The media loves to show off a real hero when they can find one, and the guy deserves the glory, I say."

"No doubt. The scumbags would think twice about crime

if they thought more citizens would stand up to them like that," Fox said.

"I suppose Martin had it figured the guy was gonna shoot him anyway. Don't you think?" Porter said.

"Maybe," Fox said. "But there are lots of cases where victims like him have gone along willingly, right up to the point of kneeling down for the killer to shoot them. I guess they hold onto hope until the very end. Or maybe they just resign to their fate. Who knows?"

"Is it true that the guy was trying to put a bullet in Martin when the Ohio trooper clubbed him down?" asked Porter.

"That's the way the report read. The guy even broke Martin's hand. He fought him off just long enough," Fox told him.

"Remarkable," Porter said.

When they reached the 28 mile-marker, Fox turned on the flashers and pulled the cruiser onto the shoulder in the shadow of one of the bridges that crossed the highway.

Porter looked out and beheld the massive structure. Three columns, each five feet square, reinforced with steel and absolutely solid. The column closest to the road was gouged and scratched from the repeated impacts it had taken over the years. There were hundreds of such bridges on I-80. Most of them were not situated on curves like this. It was simply impossible to move everything necessary to make some crossings straight.

Before Fox opened his mouth, Porter had a feeling about what the trooper wanted. This wasn't the first time someone had wanted something like this from him. People just didn't know how much was involved or how far the highway department went before they settled for a less-than-perfect design like this.

"Last year, just before Thanksgiving, we had a tractor-trailer run into this head-on," Fox said.

"Not the first one, I'm sure," Porter said, trying not to show that he was annoyed by the trooper's presumptions. "This is one of those places that shows up in our surveys once in a while. Not a good place to stray off the road."

"Right. The reason I brought you out here is to show you

the marks firsthand. Can't something be done to stop vehicles from hitting this?"

"I suppose you think this is the only place in the state where this happens?" Porter slowly shook his head. "I'm sorry if I sound a little sarcastic, but I can show you a dozen walls and bridge piers that have marks like that on them. We can't close a state road just because truckers are hitting the bridges over the interstate. I'm sure the designers saw this as a possible hazard 30 or 40 years ago when this was laid out. There were probably other factors that interfered with making this crossing perfectly safe. I can't say for sure, but it has probably been studied since then. Drivers aren't supposed to fall asleep at the wheel you know." He looked away from the gouges on the column.

"I understand that," Fox said. "I was thinking maybe you could re-grade it or something. Why don't you try putting a little more elevation on the outside of the curve? If the drivers who fall asleep would go off into the median, they would impact that bank of dirt there and gradually upset. They would turn over in the median instead of hitting the pier. A lot more of them would survive."

"You're thinking that a few more degrees of elevation is all it would take to keep them on track until they got far enough around the turn to miss the bridge? Is that it, a little steeper bank?" asked Porter.

"That's the idea. What's it going to hurt?" Fox said.

"Well, there are limits on how much elevation we put in a turn like this. Too steep can be hazardous also. But you've got a point here—no reason we can't review it. This stretch is due to be resurfaced next year. No better time to try it," Porter said.

"And maybe a couple hundred feet of guardrail too?" asked Fox. "Wouldn't that help?"

"No problem with the guardrail. I don't know why there aren't any here. I can have them in by May. The change of elevation is something I'll have to submit to Harrisburg. Can you get some more troopers to endorse the idea? Write a few letters maybe? I'll let you know where to send them when I'm ready to submit the proposal," Porter said.

"Count on it. I appreciate your listening to me like this. Every time I've brought this up in the past, I've heard, 'you know the drill, do the paperwork.' But guys like me don't have the clout you do," Fox said.

"No, you just get to pick up the pieces," bemoaned Porter.

Fox nodded and sighed through his nose.

"Okay, Fox, I'll see what I can do. No promises, mind you," Porter said.

The two men were silent on the return trip to the truck stop. Fox hoped the man wasn't just going along with him out of respect for his job. Bureaucrats were usually deferent to cops, but administrative protocol could stop an idea like this before it got started.

They shook hands once again. Porter climbed into his car and retraced the route the trooper had taken. It was the way home, after all. When he got close to the bridge, he moved into the left lane and relaxed his grip on the steering wheel. Sure enough, his car strayed over the line and rumbled across the warning track before he took control again and brought it back into the center of the lane. Porter had never driven an 18-wheeler, but he supposed they were even less inclined than his car to follow the curve of the road surface through the turn. Whoever designed this curve had gotten it wrong; he could see that. The guy was probably dead now, or retired anyway.

Porter made up his mind to see this one through. He knew enough of the right people, and he had never pushed many things like this. He was confident he could get the change approved. If he played it right, it might even look like the whole thing was his idea. It was time to find out how much clout he really had.

The engineer moved back into the right lane and set his cruise control for 65. Home was an hour away. His wife was making Yankee Pot Roast for dinner, and he didn't want to be late.